the Fantasy Reader

by

Murray Ewing

Published by Bookship, 2015.

ISBN 978-0-9934239-0-1

The Fantasy Reader

BOOKSHIP

Tuesday

This is a diary. Which means it's PERSONAL and PRIVATE. So, unless you're me (in which case hi!), STOP READING.

Good, now I can say it:

Something strange is going on.

And I don't mean slightly strange. I mean *strange* strange.

But this is me, Carol Tanner. Strange is my middle name.

(Actually, Selina is my middle name, but I try to keep quiet about it.)

So let's take a look at Carol Tanner. Four foot ten and fourteen years old. No friends. Spends her evenings shut away in her bedroom reading about people that don't exist and places that don't exist and never *have* existed and never *can* exist.

What's strange about that?

What *isn't*!

But this thing with the stairs is strange on top of that. Like whipped cream on top of an already cream-topped trifle. (Mm, trifle.)

The first question to ask (as I'm sure you're already asking, diary of mine) is this: is Carol Selina-but-keep-quiet-about-it Tanner going a bit loopy?

I wouldn't put it past me.

The trouble is, trying to work out how loopy you are is like trying to look at the back of your head by standing in front of a mirror and turning round quickly in the hope of getting a glimpse. I mean, (a) it doesn't work, and (b) it's loopy to even try.

Hmm.

I think the only thing to do is approach the subject carefully. Creep up on it inch by inch, like Tollers might creep up on a mouse, if only he weren't the laziest cat in the world. (Honestly, I once snuck up on him while he was asleep and made squeaking noises right in his ear. He didn't even look at me, just flicked his ear as if to say, 'Go away you silly human. You're no more a mouse than I'm Gandalf the Wizard.')

So I'll start with the day at school. It didn't happen, this strange thing with the stairs, till the evening, so it might seem a while to go back, but I need to search the whole day for clues. I have to know just how loopy I am.

School, then. Six minutes' walk from 49 Willow Drive, if you take the no-cycling path to Sanders Close, then over the London Road by the pedestrian crossing and into the main building. I've got it down to the exact second so I can be sat in my seat *just* before the bell, which means Miss Michalowski (who, despite her American-sounding name, is actually from Poland) will be there, ready to take the register. That way, things in class won't be too boisterous. (Or girlsterous, which can be just as bad on a school-day morning.)

I arrange things this way for one very important reason.

I'm scared of Candice Cooper.

I'm not proud! I can say it! I'm scared of Candice Cooper.

You see, the thing about Candy (as she likes to be called, though I think of her as Canned Ice) is she's bored by school. So she's always looking for ways to entertain herself. And it just so happens she's the sort of person who's most entertained by inflicting misery on other people.

She inflicted it on me once. She pushed me over in the corridor and laughed, then pushed me over again when I started to get up. And I knew it was going to go on like that, with me trying to stand up and Ms Ice finding it oh so funny pushing me back down again, on and on and on. But then she left because a teacher was coming.

Just a small thing, a tiny incident, but I've thought about it every day.

Why?

Because any day it could happen again, or worse, and then could keep happening-or-worse for the rest of my time at school.

Which, oddly enough, is not what I want. Because once you're a victim you're always a victim, aren't you? You leave school and some other bully, a work bully rather than a school one, picks up where the last left off. Like an unending run of your least favourite TV show. But I want to *enjoy* life. When I grow up. When I leave school. When I'm no longer as strange or loopy as I am now. Somewhere over the rainbow.

Which is why I go to such lengths to avoid being noticed by Candice Cooper: arriving at school the moment before the bell so Miss Michalowski will be there, dawdling to the next lesson so there's no hanging round waiting for the teacher, zipping out at the end of the lesson before the teacher leaves, spending my break times in the sort of place Candice Cooper wouldn't be seen dead (the school library), and always making sure the coast is clear before leaving through the school gates (sometimes hiding behind a crowd of taller kids, if I can manage it).

That's not too strange, is it?

But here's another fact in the case of Carol could-be-loopy Tanner that is.

In lessons (and this isn't part of my anti-Candice strategy, it's just the way I am) I don't say much. I don't say much to anyone outside of lessons either, but you really only notice it during lessons. (I do speak to the school librarian, Mrs Barker, but that's just to say thank you when she stamps a book out for me. I can't really think of anything else to say to her. Surrounded by so many books — all of which, I'm sure, she's read and memorised — she must know so much. What could I add to her vast store of knowledge?)

Why am I so silent? I don't know.

Or I do, but it's silly.

You see, when I started at this school last year (after Dad's promotion and our house-move), I didn't know anyone and kept to myself. I *still* don't know anyone and *still* keep to myself, so nothing's changed there, but back then I wasn't self-conscious about it. I thought it would get better soon enough, once I found myself a friend or two. (Two! Such ambition!) Then one History lesson early on Mr Isher said, 'You don't speak much, do you Carol?' And of course I blushed like a neon tomato and couldn't think of anything to say.

The whole class jeered, and from that moment my reputation, and with it my schoolside personality, was signed, sealed, and lost in the post. Sure, before it I hadn't talked much, but *until* that moment I wasn't self-conscious about it. Then suddenly I was, and not only me but the entire class. It was like I'd been standing on thin ice all this time, and Mr Isher had come along with a tiny hammer and chisel and given it a little tap, and this huge, ever-widening crack had opened up. From that moment, I was what he'd said I was and nothing more: someone who didn't speak much. Someone about to fall into a deep, dark hole, away from the reach of anyone. The deep, dark hole of my own strange loopiness.

Pathetic isn't it? I mean, right now, here in my bedroom, I can speak. 'Isn't that right, Wumpus?' I say, and my voice *works*, it actually reaches the other side of the room, to where Wumpus sits on my bed. (I suppose 'sits' is the wrong word for what Wumpus does. He flops or lolls, so maybe I should say 'to where Wumpus *flolls* on the bed'. That's it, Wumpus *flolls*. It's something only he can do. He may have the body of a pink fluffy oddity, but there's a wise and powerful mind somewhere in all that stuffing.)

But in class, if ever I feel I have something to say, I remember that moment with Mr Isher and have to really think hard about whether I want to risk the jeers that'll come if I try to say it in my small, rather feeble squeaky voice, and by the time I've gathered up my courage (which shouldn't take long, there's so little of it), it's too late, the moment's gone and the time to say the thing I wanted to say is gone. Or if I just dive in and put my hand up, the teacher always says something like, 'Why yes, Carol, this is a pleasant surprise,' and I'm instantly reminded of Mr Isher's comment and all the jeers, and I either put my hand down, mumble an apology and blush the rest of the lesson away like a slow-burning fizzed-out squib, or manage something like a tiny squeak, which the teacher has to ask me to repeat until she (or he) works out what I'm trying to say, while all the while there are mutters and comments from the rest of the class and my blush is quickly heading towards melt-down.

So that's school.

On the day in question (yesterday) I had double English, then Science, then Music. I like English (though double anything is asking too much most days), if only because Miss Michalowski, who takes us for English as well as being our class tutor, knows what I'm like and doesn't make things difficult for me. (She'd *never* have said 'You don't speak much, do you Carol?') Sometimes she starts talking to me as everyone leaves the classroom, and she does it like I'm a normal person, not the incommunicative lump of lead that I am. Sometimes she even manages to get a response out of me. Mostly, it's about school stuff. Like, this time she said, 'I have a question, Carol, about a word you used in your essay.'

It's odd to think she's teaching us English even though she's from Poland, where they probably speak something harsh and beautiful with lots of strange curls, dots, and dings on the letters. (I wish we had curls, dots, and dings in English, bût wé dön't.) She told me once she came to this country to study English Literature when she was eighteen and hasn't been back to her homeland since. (I've no idea how long ago that is, because Miss Michalowski seems quite young to me, even though she can hold her own in a class of rowdies. Perhaps you get used to that sort of thing, coming from a land full of Bolsheviks. (If Poland *is* full of Bolsheviks. It might not be. I've no idea what Bolsheviks are, anyway. Something like orcs or goblins, I think.)) She told me she fell in love with English — with the language, with the literature, and with one particular young man.

That last detail broke my heart. Because she's *Miss* Michalowski. Which means she didn't marry this 'particular young man'. Maybe he was just *too* particular. He rejected her, or ran away with another girl, or sniggered at her with his friends when she asked him out. Or maybe he was killed in a car crash or electrocuted by a toaster or something tragic like that.

I think of this whenever I think of Miss Michalowski.

Anyway, back to this thing she said.

'I have a question, Carol, about a word you used in your essay.'

It wasn't really an essay as such. We're doing Shakespeare in English at the moment — you know, 'To be or not to be', 'Shall I compare thee to a summer's day' and so on. (That man wrote so many quotes it's a wonder he got any real writing done. Perhaps quotes pay more. You can use them on birthday cards and things.) The play we're doing is called *A Winter's Tale*, and to start things off Miss Michalowski got everyone to do their own bit of writing under that title. It could be anything we liked, an essay, a story, a poem, or just the usual string of words some of the boys cobble together in the hope they'll make up for all the time they haven't been paying attention in class. Perhaps Miss Michalowski was hoping one of us would come up with the same idea as old Shakeybones himself! Unlikely, but you never know.

Anyway, it didn't have to be long, and I rather like mine. Here it is:

A Winter's Tale
by Carol S Tanner

One morning I woke to find the world had been transformed almost magically. Snow and frost sparkled everywhere and my breath came out in little puffs. A man was standing outside my window, so I opened it and said good morning.

'Good morn to you,' he said, speaking rather old-fashionedly, but he *was* dressed rather old-fashionedly, with tights and those funny-looking puffball shorts on top of them, as well as a ruff round his neck. He had a beard as pointy as a quill pen, and a bald head.

Not wanting to let the conversation flag after such a good start, I said, 'Would I be correct in thinking you are Mr William Shakespeare, the famous playwright?'

Mr Shakespeare (for 'twas he) bowed.

I then decided to be rather forward, this being a unique opportunity and one I shouldn't waste. 'Can I ask a question of you, Mr Shakespeare?'

'Pray do,' he said.

'We're about to start studying your play, *A Winter's Tale*, in English, and I wondered if you could tell me what it's about?'

'Why milady,' he said (very politely), 'it is about this very thing, is it not?'

'What do you mean?' I asked.

'It is about you, Miss Carol Tanner, and me, Mr William Shakespeare, conversing across the centuries, in a world magically transformed by the glamour of winter.'

At this point I was so confused I couldn't think of anything to say. Mr William Shakespeare bowed once more and walked off across the snow. I believe he was muttering sonnets as he went.

Evening came, the snow sparkled frostily, and a voor fell across the land.

THE END

Miss Michalowski produced my story from the wad of papers she had in her bag. (By this time, the classroom had cleared and it was lunch break next so I was in no hurry to go anywhere.)

'This word you used,' she said. 'This word "voor". I looked it up in my best dictionary but couldn't find it. Did you make it up?'

Now, the thing is, I read a lot, and a lot of what I read is fantasy. Fantasy is full of invented words, and perhaps inventing words is catching, so, yes, I might have. All I could remember, though, was coming to that point in my essay and having the word 'voor' pop into my head, and thinking, 'Yep, that's the word for me.' Which is pretty much how I do all my writing. I don't stop each word to ask for passports, baggage checks, and birth certificates, I just let them through. (Which may be why my head is such a mess.)

Unfortunately, as both Miss Michalowski and I were finding out, my mouth had other ideas on border control. Sometimes it doesn't let *any* words through, or only those that have been thoroughly checked, re-checked, and stamped with an official stamp, till they're all tired and useless, and about an hour or so late.

What I come out with was, 'Um, I must have, um, read it somewhere.'

(Even that was an effort.)

Then I blushed, because I really wanted to say more, but couldn't, and I felt ashamed of myself for being such an uncommunicative lump. (Not a major blush on the Carol Tanner scale. I'd say about 2.5, with 0.0 being my normal complexion, 7.5 being cherry-coloured, and 10.0 being the mythical 'purple as a beetroot' blush, which I've yet to achieve.)

Miss Michalowski, however, carried on for all the world as though I was a normal person. 'What do you like to read, Carol?'

Now, I know the answer to *that* one.

'Fantasy. Great big wodges of fantasy. Books like door-stops. Books in trilogies and quadrilogies and more. My real, absolute, utter favourite is S T Faye. She writes this series called *The Wizard of Eldara*, which you must have heard about, because it's so good. I'm sure it's taught in all sorts of English Literature courses at universities. It's five books long but the fifth hasn't come out yet. I've read all the others countless times. In fact I've read the second book, which is called *A Maid of Dian*, and the third, which is called *Nor Stone, Nor Earth, Nor Boundless Sea*, about six times each, but that's because I bought the second book first, thinking it was the first, and only realised my mistake once I'd bought it. But by then I was so caught up in the story I couldn't go back to the first book but had to keep reading them in order, because I so needed to find out what happened next, and it was only when I got to the fourth, which is called *Gates of Steel*, that I went back and bought the first, called *Winter's Ragged Hand*, which is where the evil sorcerer makes his first appearance, and then I re-read them all in order. Then I had to re-read them again because the last book hasn't come out yet and I can't bear *not* to be reading them while I'm waiting. But it's coming out soon. It's going to be called *In Sleep A King*, and it's the last book. But even when I've read that I'm going to read all five books again. And then again, probably. Because I like them so much. Mum says I seem to be doing nothing else, but I don't mind, because really it's the only thing I *do* like.'

But of course I didn't say all that. I wanted to. All those words, though... They rushed at my mouth like a bunch of slapstick comedians and got stuck there, all trying to get through at once. I did manage to mumble, 'Um, fantasy, miss,' though it came out more like a question than a statement, which is annoying because this is *the one thing in my life there's no doubt about*: I read fantasy. Why couldn't I say it? Well, I know the answer to that one. I was mouth-locked, word-jammed, throat-stopped and tongue-hobbled. In a word: I was Carol. I was me.

'Well, you certainly have an imagination,' Miss Michalowski said, as she put my essay away. Then, as she was looping her bag over her shoulder (such a lovely loopy bag, though not half as loopy as me), she said, with a little point at my forehead and a conspiratorial smile, 'And you can go places with an imagination.'

Then I grinned and she grinned, and she went off to the staffroom and I stood there thinking how wonderful Miss

Michalowski is. I could still feel that finger pointing at my forehead, like it had been a magic wand casting a spell. Then I thought how useless I am, not being able to say all that about what I like to read. And to Miss Michalowski, too! I'd so like to say all that to her...

Who'd be Carol, eh? She can't speak! Or when she does, what comes out is so poor she might as well not have.

Well, I *have* to be Carol.

Anyway, that's school.

What's after school? Home!

When I first get home, the whole house is mine, mine, all MINE HA HA HA! But seriously, Mum is still out at her 'part-time thing' as she calls it, Dad is of course never back till eight or nine, and usually even Tollers is out, doing that thing cats do all day, though sometimes he's waiting for me on the front step, all folded up like a furry loaf, blinking lazily like the Zen master he most certainly isn't.

There's something exciting about having the house to yourself. Maybe it's because that's what it must feel like to be properly grown up. (I say *properly* grown up because I'm always overhearing the girls in class talking about how they're 'grown up now', and so ought to be treated 'like adults'. What a load of rubbish! If being fourteen is what it feels like to be grown up, I'll skip it, thanks! But if being in a house on your own *is*, then take me there right now.)

The best thing about having the house to yourself is you can do whatever you want and not feel guilty about it. I rush upstairs, fling my schoolbag in the corner, and read.

I read. I read. I read and I read and I read. Why? Because it's what I do. I am a fantasy reader, a reader of fantasies. It's why I was put on this Earth, which is why I've always felt so out of place doing anything else. It's because doing anything else is not what I was made to do. Reading fantasy is.

Is that explanation enough? Then how about this: getting home after school and opening up *A Maid of Dian* or *Winter's Ragged Hand* is like realising you've been holding your breath all day and now you can breathe. It's like realising you've been wearing your left shoe on your right foot and your right shoe on your left foot and then *taking them off* and wiggling your toes. It's like being told you're adopted, because suddenly it all makes sense why you don't get on with your parents, and then your real parents show up and they're wonderful. It's like God appearing in a puff of cloud and saying, 'Sorry, Carol, you've been given the wrong life. This is the one you're supposed to have. Here you go.'

Hmm. Now you see why I think I may be a bit loopy. Little Carol only feels she's really herself when she's reading about other people who don't exist, in other lands that don't exist, doing things nobody has ever done or can do.

But it's great all the same. It's the one thing that *is*.

Mum usually gets home about forty minutes after me.

Clunk (as she drops her shoulder-bag on the floor). Clunk-thunk (as she kicks her shoes off). Really big *sigh*. Then, 'Carol!' And I always have to go to her wherever I am in the house and whatever I'm doing. Even if I'm at a really good bit in a book, I have to go straight down to the front door, else she gets in a huff. Well, she's in a huff anyway (if not a huff and half), because she's been at work 'all day' (which means all afternoon).

She always has a list of things for me to do. I have to take her bag upstairs. I have to make her a cup of tea. If she's in a really bad mood, she'll say something like, 'And would it really hurt you to do a bit of housework every now and then? Don't you think it would be nice for me to come home every so often and find you've vacuumed the stairs or something? Or do you think it should all be left up to me?'

'No, Mum,' I say. 'Sorry, Mum.' Even though I *do* do

housework every now and then. I just didn't do any today because I *so* needed to be reading.

And if she's in a *really* bad mood, she'll go into one of her routines, as I call them. She'll start by saying, 'I mean, what have you been doing all day?' (And this time 'all day' means the forty minutes since I got back from school.)

And I'll say, 'Reading.'

And she'll roll her eyes and give one of those disgusted groans people give when you say absolutely the wrong thing. Then she'll say, '*Reading*, Carol? Don't you get enough of that at school? Honestly, when I was your age I was more concerned with boys than I ever was with books, and I wasn't exactly a dunce, let me tell you. Or if not with boys, then with girlfriends. I could understand it if you said, even once in a while, you'd been on the phone to one of your girlfriends for half an hour. Or even if, God *forbid*, you brought one of them back here.'

And I have to say, 'I don't have any friends, so I can't bring them back here.'

But by this point she's well into her stride and I could announce I'm running away with Mr Morris the hairy games teacher to care for orphaned orang-utans in the Congo and she wouldn't bat an eyelid.

'And what were you reading, Carol? Something for school?'

She knows the answer, but she always asks.

'A fantasy book,' I say grudgingly, because I know what's coming next.

An even BIGGER disgusted sigh. 'Oh, Carol, are you still reading that rubbish? I would have thought you'd have outgrown it years ago blah blah blah.'

She doesn't actually say 'blah blah blah' but at that point I give up listening because I've heard it so many times and all it does is make me feel bad. I mean, even if I don't listen to her, I still have to stand there knowing what she's going on about, and that makes me feel bad enough. So I'm not going to actually write it down, am I?

This is the thing with my mother, you see. She doesn't like me reading fantasy. She doesn't like me reading. Perhaps she doesn't like *me*. I'm such a disappointment to her. She so wanted me to be a *normal* girl, whatever that means. Something to do with having a mobile phone constantly clamped to my ear and a crush on my favourite boy band, probably. Something to do with having a boyfriend.

A boyfriend. Me? Little miss silent? Little miss nobody? It's too silly to even think about. So please forget I even mentioned it.

Anyway, I make her some tea and listen to her blow off steam (two kettles going at once), and when she's calmed down I slip away, back up to my room, hoping against hope she won't add some parting comment. But she always does. This time it was, 'There she goes again, locking herself up in her bedroom with her books. I might as well be talking to a brick wall.'

Blah blah blah. I wish she *would* talk to a brick wall. Then it might fall on her.

Evil thought. Sorry.

Anyway, the next major thing that happens is Dad comes home. This is never exactly a happy event. Usually by this time I've come down from my bedroom to watch TV with Mum, in the hope she'll realise I'm not reading *all* the time (even though I want to) and stop nagging me. (It hasn't worked yet, but I live in hope.) At about eight o'clock or so Mum starts getting restless and keeps looking at her watch. Sometime after eight we hear Dad's car pull up outside. Mum will suddenly sit absolutely still. Dad will ratch on his hand-brake (he always does that, and Mum always used to get on at him for doing it, and the only reason she doesn't now is they haven't been in the car at the same time for ages), then a couple of seconds later we'll hear the car door slam, then a few seconds after that, the car boot. Then there'll be the sound of keys jangling, sometimes for ages because Dad has so many keys he never seems to be able to find the right one. (Or, more likely, he's putting off the moment when he finally opens the door and comes home.) During all this, Mum keeps letting out these angry little tuts and sighs, all the while muttering to herself. Then the front door opens. Pause. Slam. Dad takes his briefcase into his study (which is a tiny room not much bigger than a cupboard, but he somehow squeezed a table and chair in there, so we call it his study), then comes into the living room. Mum says, 'Your dinner's in the microwave. Two minutes on full.' Then she goes upstairs for the rest of the evening.

Dad goes into the kitchen and starts up the microwave. Sometimes he'll eat in the kitchen and spread out papers on the breakfast table to read while he eats, but sometimes he'll bring it into the living room and eat while watching TV. I just sit there saying nothing. Dad says nothing. I hardly ever speak to Dad and he hardly ever speaks to me. I'm not sure why. When he's finished eating he takes his plate into the kitchen, washes it, then goes into his study and does some work. At that point I turn off the TV and slip up to my room, where I read again. But the reading is never the same as when I've got the house to myself. I can hear Mum in her room, and Dad in his study, one on the ground floor, one on the first, both pretending to exist in entirely different worlds.

At about eleven, Dad switches the lights off downstairs, locks the front door, and goes up to his room (which used to be the spare room). I usually hear Mum turn off her light a few minutes later.

It's like that every night. Mum told me a while back that as soon as I grow up and leave home they're getting a divorce. Until then, they're staying together. For my sake.

I wish they wouldn't bother. Whenever it's like this I can

almost feel them wishing me older, wishing me grown up, wishing me gone so they can be rid of me so they can be rid of each other. Sometimes I find myself thinking about that more than the book I'm reading.

Now, you're probably wondering (*do* diaries wonder, I wonder?) about when I'm finally going to get to this strange thing that happened. (As if me being me isn't strange enough!) Well — ta-da! — it's now.

It happened after I'd gone to bed. I usually go to bed about ten-thirty. This time, though, I lay awake and at about midnight realised I had to go to the loo. (These things happen.) So I got up and padded onto the landing in my PJ's. The bathroom is the room next to mine. I did all that was necessary (you don't need the details), then, just as I was about to pad back to my room and snuggle under the duvet all warm and relieved, I paused.

I don't know why I paused. I just did.

The landing has four rooms coming off it. Going round from where the stairs reach the landing, there's my room, then the bathroom, then (opposite side) Mum's room, then Dad's room. Just outside Dad's room there's a hatch in the ceiling that leads to the attic.

But not last night. Something had changed. It took me a while to realise, and when I did, I stood there staring, not frightened, not even surprised, just wondering why I hadn't noticed it before.

There was another flight of stairs leading up from the landing. Stairs where there hadn't been any before.

I walked over to stand at the bottom and looked up. It was dark, but there was enough light for me to see the banister spiralling up to the next landing (which didn't exist), and another landing after that (which most *certainly* didn't exist), and then another, and another, and another... Forever and ever, upwards and upwards, into the realms of sheer, utter impossibility.

I wasn't dreaming. I was really seeing it.

I put one foot on the first step. It was solid.

And then I knew if I put my other foot next to it, I'd be on my way to leaving this world. That step looked just the same as the real landing, but it was an impossible step, and wherever it was going, somewhere up there, was impossible too. Impossible, and away from here. Away from all the faff and bother that's my life.

I could do it. I could go. Forever.

Do I want to?

I don't know.

I stood there trying to decide.

Then I went back to my bedroom and got into bed.

Thursday

Meanwhile, back on Planet Earth!

First of all, apologies. I've only just started this diary and I've already missed a day. But I missed it for a very important reason.

Do you need to ask?

I've been too busy reeeeading! And reading what? Don't say you have to be told! *In Sleep a King*, the fifth book, the final book, of *The Wizard of Eldara*!

It's out at *last*!

Every Wednesday after school for what seems a lifetime I've traipsed into town to check my fave local bookshop (our only local bookshop, actually — it's called The Book-ship, which is a silly sort of joke, but who cares, as long as it's got books in it) to see if it's come out. And every Wednesday I've been disappointed. Till yesterday.

Because it was there! For a moment I could only stare in utter disbelief. *In Sleep a King* by S T Faye, book five of *The Wizard of Eldara*, 'A Tolkien for our generation',

'George R R Martin meets J K Rowling', and all that gubbins, malarky and folderol.

First catch: it was in hardback. Which meant it was more expensive than I was ready for.

You see, because I didn't get into the series till it had been out for a while, I bought the first four books in paperback and never thought about the fifth being in hardback. But there it was, a good kilo and a half of wrist-aching, page-turning, gimme-moreish literary gold, and there was no question, hardback or not, I had to have it, and I had to have it now. Life is simply not liveable knowing *In Sleep a King* is out but I don't have it, indeed am not already nose-deep between its covers. I'd been dreaming of this day for months, and I *do* mean dreaming of it, and things are pretty serious once they get so far into your dank and murky lizard brain they occupy your night-time hours as much as your daytime ones. But what it came down to, of course, was the ageless question of greens, readies, cash, moolah — in short, money. I didn't have enough on me. I'd never carry that much to school, not with predators like Ms Ice roaming the Earth.

Thinking about it, though, I realised I might be able to, if pushed (and believe me, I was being pushed) obtain — no, I should say, *rustle together* — enough of the old royal family portraits to serve my requirements. In fact I was sure I could. However...

Second catch: I'd have to go home to get them. Now, I *did* have enough time to go home, fetch the money and get back to the shop before it closed, but...

Third catch: They only had *two copies*! I couldn't believe it. I mean, these people call themselves professionals, but here they were, stocking the hottest literary property since, I don't know, God's memoirs, on the first day of its eagerly-awaited release, and they had only *two copies*. What if I went to all the trouble of going home, getting the money and coming back, only to find it had been SOLD OUT!? Bought by OTHER PEOPLE?!? I mean, I'd have to WAIT for the bookshop to get another copy in, wait a whole DAY at least, maybe MORE. And I SO WANTED IT!

(I must apologise for all these capitals.)

I went home. Or, I floated, till I came to the school and saw some kids from my year hanging round the gates. I couldn't see if Candice Cooper was among them, but I took a detour anyway, so as not to have to walk past them, and ended up having to get to Willow Drive from the far end, down Old School Road, which meant more walking time, and once I'd started down Willow Drive I suddenly thought, 'What if Mum's home early? That would throw the whole plan!' I mean, she'd get me to make tea for her and take her bag upstairs and probably redecorate the bathroom or something, and then I'd never get back to town in time, so I started walking ridiculously fast like some overwound robot, and by the time I got home I was all hot and breathless.

But bliss — no Mum!

I rushed upstairs, got the money, rushed downstairs, rushed *back* upstairs, threw the money on my bed and counted it to make sure I really did have enough, put it all in my yellow daisy purse with a satisfying snap, checked it again to make sure I hadn't lost any in the rush, tweaked Wumpus on the floppier of his pink floppy ears (the left) for luck, rushed downstairs *again*, opened the front door and—

Mum!

Walking up the drive. And from the look on her face I could tell she was in a mood several shades redder than purple. (I hope you know what that means, because I don't.)

I had to think fast. I blurted, 'Hi Mum! I've got to go. I'm, uh, meeting some friends.' And she was so astonished, I was up the road and out of earshot before she had time to reply.

I don't like lying, and I try not to do it. But you've got to admit this was one of those situations where it was necessary.

Anyway, back in town. By now my legs were aching from all this super-fast walking. Even my shins ached — how is *that* possible?

To get back to the bookshop I had to cross the High Street, which all of a sudden had decided to get really busy. Honestly, I'd just breezed across it beforehand, but now every car in the world was taking a detour via The Bookship. (Slight exaggeration? NO.)

I could, though, see from across the road that the bookshop was at least still open. It hadn't been closed by a police raid, destroyed by fire, undermined by earthquakes or converted into a trendy coffee bar in the last twenty minutes.

I started edging along the road, trying to get the angle right so I could see through the door to where the fantasy books were, just *knowing* there'd be a horrible gap on the top shelf where *In Sleep a King* had been — and my heart fell into my stomach like a steel doughnut. Someone was picking a hardback off the top shelf, and yes, it was *In Sleep a King*! Someone was buying my book! *My* book! That book was for me, not him!

That did it. The road was clear (I checked and double-checked — I wasn't about to be run over before the pinnacle of my reading life). I crossed it with as much composure as I could muster, then did my best not to dash into the bookshop elbowing pensioners and toddlers out of the way.

There was still one copy left. Ten paces separated me from that copy, ten paces I'd have to endure before I could clasp it in my graspy hands and not let go till I was home in my room, ready to read.

Nine paces, eight, seven—

Disaster! I couldn't believe it! From out of nowhere, this

person comes and stands right where I had to stand in order to reach the top shelf.

But I didn't care. I'd go up to him and, breaking the habit of lifetime, *politely ask him to move.*

Six paces, five, four...

I came to a halt. It was Simon Lawne. From my class at school.

I couldn't talk to him. I just couldn't.

He stood with his back to me, unconscious of the distress he was causing, idly scanning the shelves as if this was some public art gallery, not a place of business. *Oh go away, Simon Lawne, please go away.* He swayed slightly to one side — *yes, go!* — then came back to the middle. *Go, go, go!* He bent forward, flipping through some paperbacks on one of the lower shelves. *Buy one and go, buy anything and go!* And then, horror of horrors, his head slowly angled back till he was looking at the top shelf. He saw my book. *No, no, no! It's my book, it's mine!* He picked it up. *Mine!* He opened it and looked at the price. *Too expensive, please let it be too expensive.* He reached for his wallet and started counting his money. *Please have to go and get cash from the cash machine, please let your mobile phone go off, meaning you have to go outside to answer it because the signal's too bad in here, please be carried off right now by policemen or firemen or aliens or aardvarks or anything!*

But no, he took the book, my book, to the counter, and bought it. Then he walked out of the shop.

I sagged. I actually felt dizzy. I stared forlornly at the empty space where the last copy of *In Sleep a King* had been moments before. If only I'd been faster. If only I hadn't paused to count my money that second time, if only I'd dashed across the High Street ignoring the screeches and hoots of cars, if only I'd run home not walked, if only I'd ignored the kids at the school gate and taken the quickest route home, if only... Oh, what did it matter? All was lost, lost.

Then a young woman came along with a box. She snipped its plastic straps, opened it up and started putting more copies of *In Sleep a King* on the shelf. I was so relieved, I could have exploded (quietly). Instead, demure and collected once more, I took one off the shelf and went and paid for it.

'Ooh, these are selling well,' the lady behind the counter said.

'Well they *are* the greatest work of literature devised by man, woman, or child,' I *might* have said, if only I hadn't just stood there hugging my freshly-bagged book and grinning like a gibbon. (Do gibbons grin? Perhaps it was more like a chimpanzee. Either way, I was walking proof of Einstein's Theory of Evolution at that particular moment.)

As I left the shop I felt numb. So much excitement in so short a time. I'm not used to it. I started telling myself how wonderful it was, how great that I'd *finally* got it, the book I'd been waiting for all my life. It was mine, mine, mine, and nothing short of a worldwide disaster on the scale of the moon crashing into the Earth could prevent me from reading it. (And even then, as long as I could find myself a cave with a fire to keep the wild animals at bay, I'd be able to read it.)

But, oddly, another thought was loping around the edges of my mind as I made my way home, a thought that really had no business being there when I should have been brimming with nothing but excitement at the book I'd bought.

'Simon Lawne,' the thought was saying. 'Simon Lawne bought the same book as you.'

When I got home, Mum was nowhere to be seen. There was a note on the kitchen table: she had one of her headaches and was going to be in her room for the rest of the evening. There was a microwave meal for me and one for Dad. I popped mine into the old X-ray barbecue, then took my book into the living room and released it from its plastic prison.

In Sleep a King by S T Faye.

I basked in its presence. I ran my hand over its matt-and-shiny dust-jacket with its raised gilt lettering. (So classy!) I savoured the creak of its as-yet uncracked spine as I lifted the cover and allowed myself a glimpse of a sentence here and a sentence there, and breathed in the tangy smell of newly-printed ink wafting from its pristine pages. It gave me a little shiver of anticipation. I checked the last page (being *very* careful not to let my eyes stray to any of the words, particularly that vital last sentence). It was numbered seven hundred and thirty-three. That was forty-four more pages than the previous book, *Gates of Steel*, making it the longest in the series. I then read everything on the cover, on the inside flaps of the dust-jacket, and all the publication twaddle they put between the title page and the start of the story. I don't know why. Perhaps it was to build up to the moment when I'd start reading the book itself. Perhaps it was just to make sure I got my money's worth. On *my* pocket money, I wasn't going to be able to buy another hardback for a while yet!

Then the microwave pinged. I went into the kitchen, stirred the contents of the plastic meal tray (as directed) and put it in for another minute.

I lingered, watching my dinner rotate like the last lonely case at an airport baggage terminal, and thought that thought once more: 'Simon Lawne bought the same book as me. A fantasy book. My favourite fantasy book. And he bought it in hardback, too.'

What did this mean?

My dinner went ping. I took it into the living room and turned on the TV. (I might have been dying to read, but I didn't want to get food all over my nice new book, and anyway, there was something weirdly wonderful about making myself wait for the moment I could actually start.) I ate while watching the news. Every so often I'd look at the book on the settee beside me and grin. Also, every so often I'd think, 'Simon Lawne.' Just that. That particular mystery had compressed itself into those two words.

So what did I know about Simon Lawne?

Next to nothing. I knew nothing about any of the kids in my class, except Ms Ice of course. What little I did know: Everyone calls him 'Si' rather than 'Simon'. He isn't one of the more rowdy boys in the class. He quite often knows the answers to questions teachers ask, particularly in Science and History. He often gets good marks in English too, and once offered an explanation for a line in a poem we'd been studying which made some of the boys in class snigger, but which Miss Michalowski said showed 'a very mature insight'. I wished I could remember what it was. Suddenly I felt the need to know very much more about this mysterious Simon Lawne.

Then I realised I was sitting there with my mouth half-open and a forkful of unidentifiable microwaved mash in front of it, like some gormless idiot, and all because I was thinking about this boy from school.

Hello, Carol, hello? There's reading to be done!

I binned the remains of my so-called dinner, washed the dishes (one plate, one fork), made myself a cuppa, then took it and my book upstairs (sneaking past Mum's room in case she called out and asked me to wallpaper the shed or something — she always gets tetchy when she's ill and doesn't like anyone else being able to enjoy themselves).

And then I read and read and read. What more needs to be said?

Oh, one thing. Just before turning in for the night, I checked the landing.

No phantom stairs. All back to normal. You're not loopy

at all, are you Carol?

So that was my Wednesday. And how was my Thursday, my today, you ask? Why thank you for your interest! But who are *you*, anyway, when no one's supposed to be reading my diary but me, hmm?

Well, I'll answer anyway.

Let's break today into its main ingredients. Ignoring all the dull bits like getting up, getting dressed, eating meals, walking to school, walking home afterwards, and the lessons in between (Maths, Maths, French, and that lame beast of boredom known as Social Studies, which today was about how to say no if someone offers you drugs — hardly a problem for me, as I've never been offered so much as a mint in all my time here) the events of the day divide into two main areas, if you don't mind my being scientific about it.

First of all, there was the reading. The reading has been good, excellent, and generally top-ho. I actually woke up at about five this morning, and after rolling around under my duvet for fifteen minutes, telling myself I ought to try and get another hour's kip, I sat up and read till my usual breakfast time. Then I read for another half hour till Mum came looking for me and said, 'Do you intend to go to school today, young lady, or are you going to spend your life swaddled between the covers of a book?'

I was tempted to take this question at face value and say, 'Why thank you, I'll take the day off, as you're so kind to offer.' But I didn't, because I wanted to live.

I put my book down and started getting out of bed, but Mum lingered in the doorway.

'Is that a new book?' she asked, and I could tell from her tone this wasn't a mother trying to show interest in her daughter's interests, but a mother with another motive.

'Sort of,' I said. After all, I'd been reading it a good few hours, so it couldn't strictly be called new.

'When did you get it?'

'Yesterday. It only just came out.'

And that was that. Mum went downstairs. I followed. We barely said another word to each other till breakfast was over and I was ready to go to school, and I couldn't tell if the silence meant she was still thinking about our brief but un-illuminating conversation, or whether she was just being her usual dour morning self.

Anyway, I was supposed to be talking about the reading part of my day. I didn't take *In Sleep a King* with me to school — it's just too heavy! And I was disappointed to find they hadn't yet invested in a reference copy for the school library, so I couldn't continue my reading there, though I *had* memorised my page number, in case. Instead I had to wait till home-time and, you guessed it, I've spent every spare moment reading since I got back. (I did, however, vacuum the hallway, the living room and the stairs as soon as I got back, so She-Who-Must-Be-Obeyed wouldn't decide to take her inevitable post-work grouchiness out on me and get me to re-tarmac Willow Drive or anything like that.)

You know, it's been such a long time since I've read anything but the first four books of *The Wizard of Eldara*, it's strange to find myself reading something else, something new, even though it's part of the same series. At first I was a bit anxious, till I realised I was just afraid it wouldn't be as good as the others.

But it is, in buckets! In absolute buckets of buckets! A *Sorcerer's Apprentice*-load of buckets.

The only trouble is, *In Sleep a King* is the last in the series. After this one, it's the end.

What am I going to do?

I'll just have to do what I've been doing. Once I finish, I'll start the whole series over again, and read it and read it and read it.

Sometimes I worry this makes me a bit strange. Well, we've already established that, haven't we? But what I mean is, I worry it pushes me that fatal inch closer to the Cliff-Edge of Oddity till I'm teetering over the Pit of Utter Peculiarity, which is the sort of place you find bag-ladies and car park attendants and one-man-bands and all sorts of other social outcasts.

But who cares, if the reading's good?

Anyway, onto the other part of the day — the non-reading part, the part I might tentatively call the Simon Lawne part of the day.

You see, I decided (while I was rolling about in bed searching out those delicious cool spots under the duvet) that I most definitely had to put paid to the mystery of Simon Lawne. As in: who he was, why he bought a copy of *In Sleep a King*, and why it should matter to little old reading-machine me. So, as I couldn't spend my time at school reading, I decided I'd spend it studying Simon Lawne. (We go to school to learn, don't we?) I wanted to know what made him tick, and if he didn't tick, what made him tock, and if he didn't tock, then, well, I'd just have to find out what noise he did make, and what made him do it.

Now before you get any ideas, that's *all* I wanted to know. It was curiosity, nothing more. Right? I mean, Simon Lawne has friends, Simon Lawne has interests, Simon Lawne is good-looking. (Eek! Did I just write that?) What I mean is we have absolutely nothing in common, and no chance of ever having anything in common. (Apart from, maybe, the fact that both of us bought *In Sleep a King*.) So no getting any ideas, right? What follows is purely detached and scientific. You have to imagine me as a hard-boiled detective wrapped in a trench coat, chewing a matchstick and lurking in dark alleyways. (Not what I really am, a soft-centre in a duffel coat, chewing my lip and hiding in the school library.) I have no personal interest in the matter at all. Now, I'll get on with it before I doth protest too much.

Simon Lawne. Everyone calls him Si. (As in *dreamy sigh*... Eek! I can't believe I wrote that!) At registration he sits one desk forward and two desks to the left of me. I studied the back of his head for the three minutes it takes Miss Michalowski to read out everyone's name. (I *do* manage a mumbly 'yes' when she reads mine, though I always get nervous when the moment's approaching, and sometimes my 'yes' comes out as nothing but a throat-constricted squeak. But that's me to a T: a throat-constricted squeak.)

From this study of the back of Simon Lawne's head I learned: nothing. I mean, how much can you learn from the back of someone's head? Sherlock Holmes would no doubt have been able to deduce his shoe size, what he'd had for breakfast, the middle name of his maiden aunt, and precisely what he was doing at the time of the Cleopatra's Tear Diamond Robbery but, as I've already said, I'm more of the hard-boiled detective type — not so much logical deduction as hanging around waiting for a lucky break while socking villains in the jaw with my iron right hook. (Luckily there were no villains around, otherwise I might have found out how far short I fall of even the hard-boiled detective type. But the hanging around waiting for a lucky break is definitely me.)

First lesson of the day, as already noted, was Maths.

Maths. We learn all sorts of useful things in Maths, don't we? No, we do not. In Maths Simon Lawne sits on the other side of the classroom and one row back from me (I'm right by the door, alone at a two-person table), so I didn't have a chance to watch him. I did, however, get the chance to listen to him answer the teacher at one point. I can't remember the question, but the answer, according to Simon, was 'four point two'. I analysed that 'four point two' for all it was worth. And learned: very little. Only that Simon Lawne, unlike me, is confident enough to put his hand up in class and answer questions without finding his throat clenched to the diameter of a straw. And he seems not to suffer the inevitable after-effect (with me anyway) of blushing ferociously — I *did* risk a glance in his direction after he'd answered the question to check on this. (And then, of course, I blushed.)

I'm sure Simon Lawne never blushes. He's just one of those people who seem to be able to handle such things as talking without getting in a flap about it.

Some folk are *born* lucky.

After Maths was more Maths, so no possibility of learning more till lunch break. By this time I was beginning to feel my hard-boiled detective lucky break wasn't going to come, and that I'd have to step up my efforts. So, I decided to follow Simon Lawne through lunch.

You have to realise this was a big decision for me. Usually my lunch breaks are a time of retreat into the school library, where (a) I'm safe from the perils of Candice Cooper and her ilk (if she *has* an ilk, and if she does, I certainly want to be safe from it), and (b) I have the quiet and calm I need to recover from the events of the day so far, including that stressful 'yes' at registration.

Pathetic aren't I? And I hope that makes you realise what a major decision it was to change my routine and actually go out into the world during my lunch break. Not that this Simon Lawne investigation was important to me at all. Nope, not in anyway, not one bit, not one iota... (Oh, shut up Carol.)

A brief digression to change the subject. If you're wondering how I eat my lunch if I'm in the library, I have to admit I sneak down one of the aisles and take a few bites of a sandwich every so often. They don't allow eating in the library, but I've never been caught, and the risk is worth it compared to the degrading experience of having to find somewhere to sit in the dining hall. There, you walk past the tables with your food tray, like Oliver Twist going up to ask for more, and everywhere people are shoving bags and lunch trays onto the empty chairs beside them to make sure you don't sit there, and you have to sit at the end of an empty table, as far from anyone else as can be, and not only feel wretched and dejected, but look it, too.

As lunchtime started, Simon Lawne headed back to the main school building. He stopped by the double doors for a brief chat with Liam Bodiwell and Ali Saeed. (I pretended to be hunting for something in my schoolbag so I could observe.) Ali was bouncing a football, though somewhat ineptly, as he twice in two minutes had to go jogging after it when it bounced wrongly. Si was cool with this, and once even stopped the ball from rolling too far with a timely hook of the left foot. They were obviously asking him if he wanted a game, and I was thinking, with a sinking feeling, that I was going to have to watch a whole lunchtime of football, when Si gave them a wave and moved on.

Into the main school building. Si paused to take a small notebook out of his pocket, make a couple of ticks, then put it away. (Which made me wonder if he planned his lunch breaks in meticulous detail. 'Brief chat with Liam and Ali.' Check. 'Head into main school building.' Check.)

Next, he headed for the boy's toilets. Well, nature calls to the best of us, I suppose. Not that I'm saying Si is among the best of us, but... Oh, you know what I mean! Don't get me in a fluster!

I couldn't hang around outside the boy's toilets, but the cloakroom was close by, so I was about to hide in there, till I spotted Candice Cooper and a couple of her buddies, like school-uniformed tigers crouching in a coat-and-scarf jungle. I froze (as all the best prey animals do when faced with their key predator — there must be a good evolutionary reason for it, but I'm damned if I can think of it), and was about to scarper double-speed to the library when Miss Michalowski appeared.

'Carol, I found your word!'

For a moment, I just stared at her. Did she mean she'd found a word to describe me? One simple, single-word explanation, something I could wear on a badge or have tattooed to my forehead, as a warning to others and an all-purpose excuse? I often wonder what it would be like to open a dictionary and find, laid out in black and white, a word that exactly describes me. As in:

carolous *adj* withdrawn and uncommunicative with a marked tendency to blushing; obsessively reading one particular fantasy series over and over again, while occasionally hallucinating phantom staircases. — *vi* **carolising** sitting in a school library during lunch hour wishing the day would hurry up and be over so you can get home and read. — *n* **carolisationalism** a long word with no particular meaning, for occasions where a long word with no particular meaning is called for.

It would make life so much easier. (It would certainly make this diary shorter.)

But Miss Michalowski didn't mean that. Instead she produced, much to my surprise, a shiny new paperback copy of *Winter's Ragged Hand,* opened it where she'd left a scrap of paper for a bookmark, and pointed at a word. 'Voor.'

'Oh,' I said (just one more example of my remarkable conversational abilities). I should have known it would be in *The Wizard of Eldara* somewhere. I wondered how Miss Michalowski had found it. (Any normal person would have asked. I am not a normal person.)

She regarded the page for a short while, frowning and

smiling at the same time, then closed the book with a snap. She smiled at me, said 'voor' once more with an eye-widening relish, then carried on down the corridor quite jauntily.

I wondered how she could be so jaunty, having lost her particular young man. Perhaps hunting for obscure words is how she takes her mind off it. Then I saw Si emerging from the boy's toilets. My own hunt was still on.

Si (I mean Simon Lawne, I really mustn't allow myself to slip into familiarity, this is supposed to be detached and scientific!) next headed along the main corridor (bypassing, I was glad to see, the dining hall). He stopped for two brief chats, one with Charlie Storridge (who was picking loose staples out of the sports noticeboard — well, we all have our little hobbies), and one with a boy from another class whose name I didn't know, but who I recognised because he's the tallest person in our year. After each, out came the notebook for a quick tick. ('Chat to Charlie.' Check. 'Chat to tallest person in year.' Check.)

Perhaps it was a Guinness Book of Records thing? Chat to as many people in one lunchtime as possible. If so, I wonder if I should go for the opposite record? (Though my chances had been spoiled by Miss Michalowski. She'd hoisted my lunchtime chats-with-people average way above its usual zilch.)

Simon pocketed his notebook and carried on down the corridor. As I followed him, I went over what I'd learned so far. Which was: not very much. In fact, nothing. I felt so silly, following this boy I didn't know. I mean, what was I trying to do? All I wanted to know was why he'd bought *In Sleep a King* — was it for him, was it a birthday present for his kid sister, was it so he could set fire to it and dance around it laughing? Any normal person would have gone up to him, tapped him on the shoulder and said, 'Hi Simon, you don't really know me and I don't really know you, even though we're in the same class, but I happened to notice you bought *In Sleep a King* by S T Faye the other day, and I just wanted to say that I bought it too, and I think it's the most wonderful fantasy series ever written. What do you think?' But, as I've already said, I'm not a normal person. I don't have their advantages.

We passed through the main school building, then into the sixth form block, where he headed for the school library.

Irony of ironies. I'd given up my usual lunchtime in the library to follow Simon Lawne, and where does he lead me?

He stopped at the librarian's desk, so I walked past and found myself a table, ready to observe which aisle he went down after he'd returned whatever book it was he was returning. But he wasn't returning a book. He was having a talk with the librarian. And, this being the library, both were talking too quietly for me to hear.

I decided to go for a quick sandwich-nibble down the aisle marked Fiction (A-L).

When I came back, Simon Lawne was gone, and the librarian was stacking books on a trolley.

So, that was my lunchtime of following Simon Lawne. What had I learned?

Nothing. Other than Simon Lawne has far more interesting lunch breaks than I do.

(I'd take a rough guess that *everyone* has far more interesting lunch breaks than I do.)

I felt deflated for the rest of the day. Simon Lawne was there at afternoon registration. He chatted with Gary Rhybie and Debbie Wood (or, really, just with Gary while Debbie stood with her arm draped round Gary like he was some sort of fashion accessory) then sat down when Miss Michalowski came in. French followed registration, as it inevitably does on Thursdays, and I could barely rouse myself to tell my *avoir* from my *être*. Then it was, as I've already (yawn) said, Social Studies and (yawn) the less said about (yawn) that lame mule, the better.

By the time the final bell went I'd given up studying Simon Lawne and given up thinking about him. All I wanted was to go home and get lost in my book. I wanted to read and read and read till I disappeared, or at least forgot I existed.

I shouldered my bag and filed out of the classroom with everyone else, counting the seconds till I could be back in my bedroom reading, meanwhile avoiding the elbows and bags of the taller members of the class (I'm short and have a tendency to get elbowed or bag-thumped in crowd situations, usually without an apology or even being noticed). I was right behind Simon Lawne. He was chatting to Todd Wale. (So many friends, so many chats. Sigh...) His school bag was level with my face, and I stared at it blankly till I realised his pencil case was poking out from under the flap. (It was one of those rugged, straps-and-flaps schoolbags that make you think of the backpacks of soldiers in that World War, whichever one it was, before they'd invented zips.) And then, as if it had a will of its own, the pencil case jumped out of his bag and, because I was being pressed so close in the crush to get out of the classroom, it dropped into my hands.

Simon Lawne's pencil case.

I tried to say his name, but even I couldn't hear myself in the post-school roar. I was about to tug at his bag to get his attention when we burst out of the classroom and I got swept away by one current of pupils while he went with another.

I didn't know what to do. I felt like a thief. I tried to turn round and go against the tide of pupils, but I'd have had more chance against a herd of elephants.

So here I am, at home in my bedroom, with Simon Lawne's pencil case on the table in front of me.

I've examined it thoroughly. It contains a mechanical pencil with a 0.5mm lead, a black biro, a blue biro, a red biro with an elastic band wrapped around it, a green felt-tip, a day-glo yellow highlighter pen, a short shatterproof ruler, a nearly new eraser and several small balls of fluff. I have, in the course of my examination, held each of the pens as I imagine Simon must hold them, have emptied, counted and replaced the spare leads in the mechanical pencil, and have even put my face right into the pencil case and breathed in (though I immediately felt stupid for doing so, because it was hardly the sort of thing a great scientist like Einstein would do, and I'm not sure what I expected to learn by doing it).

Isn't this all just too silly?

And I still haven't learned anything about him!

Tomorrow, I'm going to have to find a way of giving it back.

Friday

Politicians said it would never happen, scientists *proved* it would never happen, but today it happened: this morning, I left early for school.

You mean you didn't hear about it on the news? Such a rare event, surely they'd put it on the news?

Huh. These 'they' people, what a dead loss they are.

Anyway, what I wanted, of course, was to give Simon Lawne his pencil case back, and to do it when nobody else was around. Why I thought turning up for school ten minutes early would mean there'd be no one around *except* Simon Lawne, I don't know, but it seemed totally logical while I was planning it in bed.

Beds are good places to plan things. You lie there drifting in and out of dreams, occasionally turning over to nuzzle your face into a fresh bit of pillow, and everything you think of seems possible. 'I know, this morning I'll find a beautiful multi-coloured parrot on my way to school and train it to say "Simon Lawne, this is your pencil case", so it can fly through the window in History and return it without me having to.' And this seems like a good, even possible, idea.

It's when you get out of bed that things start going wrong. Reality has ideas of its own. Usually not involving parrots.

For instance, I was dismayed to find, on turning up at school ten minutes early, that there were just as many people about as when I turn up with my usual on-the-dot timing — if not more, because instead of being gathered together in their proper classrooms, they were scattered through the playgrounds and corridors and doorways in little groups like cliquey penguins.

My first thought was, 'Plan gone awry! Panic!'

My second thought was, 'Penguins? Carol, you're strange. Take the day off.'

Luckily, I don't usually act on my first or second thoughts. My third was, 'Maybe he's in the classroom looking for his pencil case.'

So I headed for the classroom.

Reality had more surprises lined up. (It's been a day of reality-surprises. It saved the worst for last, though.) Simon Lawne *was* in the classroom, but so were about a dozen other people, perched on desks and chairs, not like penguins this time, but like hungry pterodactyls, with me as the optimistic minnow who's decided today's the day to swim on dry land for a change.

Simon Lawne (who, I should point out, doesn't remind me of a pterodactyl, or any other psort of pdinosaur) was chatting to John Stocker (who's maybe a trifle on the triceratops side) and was about the only person who didn't turn and stare at me with a 'Carol Tanner? At *this* time of the morning?' look when I opened the door.

I almost bolted. Fortunately, my innate cowardice kept me rooted to the spot long enough to realise that bolting would make me look twice as stupid as staying, then Simon Lawne's chat with John Stocker came to an end and I decided, if I was going to do this at all, now was the time, before this pencil case became as difficult to get rid of as Sauron's Ring.

So I went up to Simon Lawne and said, 'Um,' which, I feel, is always a great conversation opener. I tried to add his name but it stuck in my throat after the first letter, and the whole thing came out as 'umsss—' so it's no wonder he looked at me in a mildly quizzical manner.

I froze. Suddenly I had the full attention of another human being of my own age, and for perhaps the first time in my *life* I had the full attention of a *boy* of my own age, along with the sudden awareness that that was what he was. So is this normal? My heart was pounding so hard it must have looked like I had an overexcited frog in my top pocket. My knees went weak. My eyes went blurry. I have no idea if I was blushing, but it's odds on I was. The whole effect was something like a clapped-out boiler about to blow, all steam, heat, and wobbliness.

And what did Simon Lawne do? He smiled. And, if I remember right (and the trouble is I've been thinking about it so much all day I can no longer be sure if what I remember is what really happened or some alternate version I made up through thinking about it too much), it was a kindly smile.

I giggled. It was only a little giggle, but it released enough nervous energy for me to squeeze out a few words. Opting for the get-the-message-across-as-quickly-as-possible approach, I thrust his pencil case toward him and managed something like, 'I found this. Sorry.' Which is totally illogical if you think about it, because why should I be sorry for finding his pencil case? Of course, the truth, as you know, was a bit more complicated, but I wasn't going to go into all that then, what with the risk of total verbal collapse at any moment.

Then I sat in my usual seat and concentrated so hard on *not* thinking what an utter idiot I'd just made of myself, I hardly noticed when Miss Michalowski came in and started taking the register. When she called my name, I came back to the real world so suddenly I blurted out a full-voiced 'Yes Miss Michalowski', and immediately made up for it by blushing a good 6.2.

But I'd just spoken to Simon Lawne.

I think it was at some point halfway through the next lesson I came back to Earth.

Lunchtime, as usual, I headed for the school library, thinking I could do the Social Studies homework we'd been given, and so gain a bit more reading time this evening. But I couldn't concentrate. My mind kept drifting back to that conversation I'd had with Simon.

Alright, so 'conversation' is dignifying it a bit. Perhaps I should call it an 'exchange', though even that makes it sound more two-sided than it was. Still, I thought about it endlessly, spinning out imaginative alternatives in which I'd actually said something witty or interesting or just intelligible.

I wondered what Simon Lawne thought of the whole thing.

Probably nothing.

Or maybe, 'What was what's-her-name doing with my pencil case?'

I tried to put it out of my mind. The weekend was almost upon me, and I was halfway through *In Sleep a King*. I'd finish it on Saturday if I did what I intended to do, which was spend the entire day doing nothing but reading. And Sunday? Begin the whole series again, and read and read and read.

But reality still had its final, big surprise. Passing the cloakroom on my way from Craft to the final lesson of the day (Religious Education) I realised Simon was standing in the corridor right in front of me. He was chatting with someone I couldn't see because they were sitting on one of the cloakroom benches. But he saw me, and he did that thing again, that thing he'd done before: he smiled.

I immediately felt the return of all those symptoms — heart thudding like a flat tyre, head light and airy like a hot-air balloon, knees weak and springy like defective pogo-sticks. I was like a walking reject from the Transport Museum's 'Mad Inventors' department.

But there was more to come. As I got closer, he said my name. He actually said my name. And not just that. He said, 'Carol, I wanted to say thanks for finding my pencil case.'

Now, the fact he even knew my name would have been enough to make me sprout little wings and hover several inches off the floor like a Disneyfied cherub. His actually *saying it*, and *to me*, might well have resulted in me zinging around the ceiling like Tinkerbell on a knicker-elastic bungee dive.

But instead, something even more surprising happened. It happened, I suppose, because I'd been thinking about our sort-of conversation all day, and the things I might have said, and imagining myself actually saying them, and going over it again and again so much that I'd somehow slipped into this weird zone of actually *being able to talk*, and I said (with not a blush nor a stammer), 'That's okay. Actually, there was something I wanted to ask you. I was in town the other day, in The Bookship, and I saw you buying *In Sleep a King...*'

It was like being carried along on a magic carpet, finding

myself saying this thing I'd been wanting to say for days. It might have been a wonderful moment — it *was* — but then the awful thing happened, and it was the worst thing that could.

The person Simon Lawne had been chatting to stood up and stepped out of the cloakroom.

It was Candice Cooper.

Simon Lawne had been *chatting* with Candice Cooper.

I stared at her. I couldn't do anything to stop the sheer terror from showing on my face. And I know she saw it, because she smiled the smile only the truly evil can smile when they've learned something they can use to further their wicked plans.

Oblivious to all this, Simon Lawne was waiting for me to ask my question.

I dried up like a jellyfish in a Saharan summer.

'Sorry,' I mumble-choked, then hurried, head down, to the next lesson as fast as my little legs would carry me.

But it was too late. The damage was done. I was a marked girl. Several times in Religious Education I glanced up and saw Candice Cooper looking at me and smiling that lizard smile of hers. That I-know-something-about-you smile. That smile that said it had found your most vulnerable, painful point and was going to needle it till you begged for mercy.

She came up to me as soon as the lesson ended.

'Why don't we walk home together?' she said. 'You live on Willow Drive, don't you?'

'Yes,' was all I could say, not looking at her.

'I can go that way. Come on.'

We walked through the school building together. I tried going slowly, hoping to get lost in the crush, but Candice kept her eye on me. I felt like begging her to leave me alone. I felt like offering her money. I felt like bursting into tears right now, so she could be satisfied with the pain she'd caused without having to go through the whole fear, hurt and bullying thing.

But I couldn't. I was under her spell.

She said nothing as we left the school grounds. We walked to the crossing and waited for the green man to show. We crossed the road, and still she said nothing.

It was only when we started down the no-cycling path at the end of Sanders Close that she turned to me and said, 'So, you fancy Simon Lawne.'

'No!' I said, and however honest I meant it to sound I blushed so hard my eyes brimmed. I stared at her shoes. I was shaking. There was no one else about.

She folded her arms. 'There's no need to be shy. You can tell me. I'm your friend.' (Said the Balrog to the hobbit.) She leant closer. 'And let's face it, Carol Tanner, you don't have many friends, do you? Oh, did I say "many"? I meant to say "any". You don't have *any* friends, do you?'

This was my every fear come true. And there was no escape, nowhere to hide.

'*Do* you?'

'No.'

'Come on, then. Empty your pockets.'

I did, showing her my keys and paper hanky.

'And your bag.'

There was nothing in there but school stuff and the remains of my lunch.

'What a boring girl you are. Boring and pathetic. And you fancy Simon Lawne.'

'I don't,' I said, but she ignored me.

'How boring and pathetic. Well, I'm bored with you now. We'll have to continue this conversation later. And we *will*. I'll see you Monday.'

And with that she walked off.

Tollers seemed to know something was wrong when I got home. He meowed at me in a sympathetic way. But he can't *do* anything. No one *can*. It's begun, what I've always been afraid of, and in the worst possible way.

It's the weekend now. I'm going to read. That's all I'm going to do.

Later

The stairs were back tonight. The phantom stairs. I went to the bottom of them and looked up. I can't see the next landing (the impossible landing) too well in the gloom, but it looks real enough.

I could go up there. I could actually go up.

What would happen if I did?

Saturday (morning)

So Mum starts off the day by saying *we're* going shopping. Which means me and her, whether I like it or not. She said this to Dad, who was making a rare weekend appearance at the breakfast table. He just grunted, then acted as if Mum wasn't there anymore, which is exactly what annoys her the most. So she started off in a foul mood.

'Go and get properly dressed, Carol,' she said.

'Do I have t—'

'*Go and get properly dressed, Carol.* Why do I have to say everything twice?'

When I came downstairs again, Dad had moved to the living room and closed the door. He was watching kids' cartoons. Mum was upstairs taking ages, so I stood in the hall, telling myself shopping couldn't take more than a couple of hours, so I'd have plenty of time left for reading.

She came down five minutes later, all dolled up. And

even though she'd just spent all that time in front of the mirror in her room, she still had to look at herself in the hallway mirror to check her face (yes, it's still hanging on, Mum), patting and puffing her hair as if the exact angle of a single strand made all the difference between acceptable and disastrous.

Then she looked at me. 'Is that what passes for fashion these days?'

I shrugged. The day what I throw on passes for fashion, you'll see machine-gun-toting pandas patrolling Willow Drive on jet-powered roller-skates. Or something equally unlikely, like Mum smiling.

'What if one of your friends sees you?' she said. 'Do you really want to go around the town dressed like that?'

I shrugged. Hardly my biggest worry, as I'm sure you can guess.

She sighed the sigh of the eternally afflicted, then said the thing that set off the worst day of my life. (Really. You thought yesterday, with Candice Cooper, was bad? Just wait for today.) She said, 'Go get your book.'

I looked at her blankly.

'You know the one I mean. The one you were reading the other day. That hardback, that—' (impatient wave of the hand as if even saying it brought a bad taste to her mouth) '—fantasy book. You *know* the one I mean, Carol. Go upstairs and get it.'

I went upstairs, picked *In Sleep a King* off my bedside locker, and brought it down, puzzled.

'Right,' she said, with one last check in the mirror. 'Off we go.'

I stopped in the doorway. 'Am I bringing this?' I said, still holding my book.

'Well I didn't ask you to fetch it all the way downstairs so I could look at it. Come on.'

I got into the passenger seat, still puzzled. I mean, the

only reason I could think for Mum wanting me to bring my book was if she expected me to wait in the car. So why didn't she say so? Why did she have to be so mysterious? And anyway, usually she'd do anything but encourage me to read 'that fantasy rubbish'. Perhaps she'd had a change of heart? But no, there was something odd about this whole thing, like the way she'd asked me to bring this book *specifically*. (And didn't I know, deep down, what this was about? But I had to pretend I didn't — had to, had to, had to — so it couldn't happen.) I sat there with *In Sleep a King* on my lap and a little jitterbug of worry in my tummy as we reversed out of the drive and started towards town.

At first, Mum was silent.

I risked a glance at her. She seemed almost happy. That was a bad sign. Mum's never happy. She's either in a bad mood or a *very* bad mood. The only thing that even makes her *look* happy is when she's about to spread her ill-feeling to others (i.e. me). I played with the cover of *In Sleep a King*, wondering if I should risk a quick read.

Finally, she said, 'So, Carol, did anything happen this week I should know about? Any emergencies?'

'No,' I said.

'Are you quite sure?'

'Yes.'

'Only, you know the emergency money I told you I keep in my dresser? The money I said you could use if ever there was an emergency? Some of it has gone.' She looked at me. 'Ten pounds of it.'

I looked at the book on my lap.

'Would you know anything about that, Carol?'

Of course I do.

'Did you take that ten pounds, Carol?'

But it *was* an emergency. It had *seemed* an emergency.

'Did you buy that book with it, Carol?'

But it had been so *important*. And I was going to pay it

back as soon as I could...

Why wasn't I saying any of this? Because I was so ashamed. She was right and I was wrong. It had seemed the right thing to do at the time, it had been so important. To spend even a single day without *In Sleep a King*, knowing it was out there waiting to be read but not being able to read it, was a real emergency — not flashing lights and police cars and ambulances, but... an emotional emergency. But hadn't I also known, even while I was doing it, it was wrong?

'*Did* you?'

'I'm sorry Mum. I was going to pay it back.'

Which opened the floodgates. What happened if there was a *real* emergency, girl who cried wolf and so on. And all about how hard she worked for that money and I didn't appreciate it, didn't appreciate anything she did for me. All about how I locked myself away in my bedroom and didn't know anything about the real world, didn't even make an effort. All about what a selfish child I was.

And it was true. Everything she said. All of it. I was wrong, and she was right. I knew it as I sat there, just as I'd known it when I took the money in the first place. She was right and I was wrong.

'Are you listening to me?'

'Yes Mum. I'm sorry.'

By the time we reached the car-park she'd finished and we parked in silence.

Mum got out, then I got out and put my book on the seat.

'No you don't,' Mum said. 'We're going to need that. Bring it with you.'

And that's when I realised just how bad today was going to be.

We walked through town to the High Street, heading for The Bookship.

'Mum,' I said as we got near it, but she took hold of my

shoulder and steered me into the shop.

We joined the queue where happy Saturday people were buying books and walking away with happy Saturday smiles on their faces. The woman at the counter was the one I'd bought *In Sleep a King* from, and she was smiling too. Everyone was smiling. Everyone except me and Mum.

We came to the front of the queue.

Mum said, 'I'm afraid I have to return this book. Put it on the counter, Carol. Only, you see, my daughter bought it with money that was not hers to use. I doubt we have the receipt — do we, Carol?'

'No,' I mumbled.

'Oh. I see,' the woman said.

The rest happened in slow-motion silence. The Saturday happiness was gone, bleached away from the shop and everyone in it, and I could only stand there knowing that, however much the people around me were trying not to look, the sheer weight of my self-consciousness and embarrassment was sucking their attention towards me. Everyone had fallen silent, and would stay that way till I was dealt with. I stared at the edge of the sales counter while the woman went through the motions of refunding the book. As she handed the money to my mother, she — the woman who'd sold me the book — actually apologised. That was how shameful the whole thing was. Everyone felt it.

I tried to say sorry but couldn't even lift my eyes.

'Come on, Carol,' Mum said, and started to herd me from the shop — a shop, I know, I'll never be able to go back to. Not now.

But there was more. The frosty icing on the poison cake.

'Excuse me,' the woman at the counter called. 'You forgot this.' And she held up my Winnie-the-Pooh bookmark with the red tassel. I'd left it inside *In Sleep a King*.

'Go and get it, Carol,' Mum said.

I walked back to the counter and took my bookmark.

Again, I tried to apologise, but the woman looked away and started serving the next customer. They all wanted me gone as soon as possible, so the shame I'd brought to their happy Saturday could be forgotten and happy-Saturdayness could resume.

I rejoined Mum. Neither of us said anything. Mum got on with her shopping as if nothing unusual had happened, and all I could do was traipse after her, glumstruck. I couldn't believe what had just happened. I was numb. Mum, on the other hand, was doing her best to make sure I noticed how cheerful she was, as if to say I was my own worst enemy and if I only pulled myself together and became a *normal* girl, I'd be cheerful too.

It didn't last. She started sighing and tutting to herself, and getting annoyed at little things, until soon she was back to her usual self. But she didn't stop there. By the time we got home she was in a foul mood and I knew what was coming. The same old thing. I've seen it a hundred times and I'll see it a hundred more. Mum was getting ready to have a row with Dad. (It *was* Saturday, after all.)

As soon as we got home she stormed through the front door and into the kitchen, where Dad was fixing himself a midmorning snack. The breakfast things were still on the table and there were toast crumbs and a jammy knife on the counter. The sight of this mess made Mum even angrier. She dumped her bags on the floor and folded her arms. There were still kids' cartoons on the TV, turned up too loud. Tollers exited at high speed through the cat flap, proving he is the wisest of us all.

'Well I hope you're happy,' Mum said.

Dad, chewing a mouthful of toast, refused to take the bait. 'Quite happy,' he said.

'You're turning our daughter into a thief,' Mum said, which I thought was hugely unfair, but of course she was only saying it to provoke him. Still, I blushed red as a radish.

Dad scratched his unshaven chin, then rinsed the jammy knife under the tap before dropping it in the washing-up bowl. 'Are you a thief, honey?' he said over his shoulder. 'That's nice.'

Mum snapped. 'Don't you dare treat this lightly, David. Tell him what happened, Carol.'

I looked at my shoes. 'I wanted to—'

'She took the emergency money I leave in my dresser upstairs,' Mum said. 'And what did you spend it on?'

'A—'

'A book,' Mum said. 'A book! One of these stupid fantasy things she reads. And I've just had to take it back and explain to the woman in the shop, in front of everyone, what our daughter has done, what she's *become*. It was so humiliating.'

Dad leant his back against the sink and looked unimpressed. 'What do you want, Joy, a round of applause?' (And yes, Mum's name is Joy, however ironic that might sound.) He started clapping his hands slowly. 'Come on, Carol, join in.'

I stood there wishing I was elsewhere (or, even better, nowhere).

'This is exactly what I mean,' Mum said. 'Here I am trying to teach our daughter some sort of decency, some sort of — WILL YOU STOP THAT?' (Dad stopped clapping, but tried to make it look like he only did it because he was bored.) 'Carol, do you want to end up like this?' Mum asked, waving her arm at Dad. 'Because it's where you're headed.'

'Don't believe a word of it, Carol,' Dad said. 'Would you rather end up like your mother?'

And so on.

I felt like a tennis ball. None of this was about me. They were just using me to aim at each other. I did my best to stop listening and waited for the argument to take its usual course so I could sneak off to my room. Pretty soon they were shouting at each other and I made my escape. They're still shouting now.

I wish I could read. But *In Sleep a King* is gone. I could do my usual thing and go back to the beginning of the series and start again. But I can't. I just can't. All I'll be able to think is that I should be reading *In Sleep a King*. It just won't be the same. Anyway, with all that shouting I can't concentrate.

I've just been out on the landing.

They're there, the phantom stairs. In full daylight. Real as real and strange as strange. The carpet continues seamlessly from the carpet on the real landing and looks no older and no newer, as if it's always been there. It looks so normal, so everyday. So peaceful and homelike and hidden away.

Where do they go, those stairs?

It doesn't matter. Anywhere but here. That's where they go.

I know what I'm going to do. I'm going to go up those stairs. I don't care what happens to me. What could be worse than what's going on now?

Saturday (night)

Well I'm back! Did you miss me?

Of course you didn't, you're just a diary.

But Wumpus missed me, I can tell by the way he's flolloping there on the bed. (Flolloping is a more intensely floppy version of flolling, which I've already discussed. Wumpus is just one of those rare individuals who needs a whole new vocabulary to express his pink tatty fluffiness in all its many facets.)

Tollers missed me, or at least he knew I'd been somewhere I shouldn't, because he gave me the look only a wily mog can give, then slunk into the garden to think things through.

What about Mum and Dad, did they miss me?

They didn't even know I was gone! Honestly, as soon as I got back I went straight downstairs thinking that, as I'd been away for hours, they'd be mad with worry. Mum was in front of the hall mirror trying to symmetrise her eyebrows. (I just checked the dictionary to make sure I didn't invent 'symmetrise', and I didn't. I wouldn't want to put her in the same league as Wumpus.) She said, 'You'll have to get your own dinner tonight. I'm off out.' Then, as if to prove her point, she went.

Dad, meanwhile, was slouched dead-eyed in front of the telly and didn't even look up when I poked my head into the living room. So I grabbed an apple and came back upstairs, slightly deflated by this underwhelming response.

Well, I suppose I wasn't going to tell either of *them* about it anyway. But I'm going to write it down, then I'm going to read it to Wumpus, because he at least has an opinion worth listening to.

So here goes. I went up the stairs. The stairs that shouldn't exist. And what did I find?

The short answer is: more stairs.

The long answer is: well, I went up those stairs-that-shouldn't-exist, and came to a landing-that-shouldn't-exist. It was exactly the same shape and size as the first floor landing, the real landing, below. It had the same type of carpet, just as worn in the middle where everyone walks and just as dusty on the outside where everyone doesn't. The walls were painted the same lemon yellow. Unlike the real landing, though, there weren't any doors. I walked past where my bedroom door was, below, and where the bathroom door was, below, running my hand over the smooth, unbroken wall, and even gave a little knock where those doors should have been, but everything felt solid.

It did have a window, though, this unreal landing. The window on the landing below (the real landing) looks onto Willow Drive. What about this window? What would it look out at? Some magical realm? Acres of rolling, unspoilt greenery, with a distant dragon snoozing in the sun? An enchanted forest, chock-full of fairy-types, from little flitty dragonfly-winged pixies to gnarly, rooty, tree-like trolls? A vast, dark chasm, dropping down from craggy heights to mysterious, infinite depths?

No, it was just filled with a golden, fuzzy light, like you get if you run a hot shower for too long and it fills up the bathroom with steam. (Which I used to do, till Mum had a go at me for making the toilet paper all crinkly.) I couldn't see anything out the window no matter how hard I peered. Was it mist? Was it fog? Is there a difference? I tried opening the window so I could poke my head out and see what this magically extended house looked like from the outside, but the window was locked and (conveniently like the one on the real landing below) the key was nowhere to be found. (And if it's anything like the nowhere-to-be-found key for the window on the real landing, Mum will blame Dad for losing it, and Dad will blame Mum.)

On the other side of the landing, there was no Mum's door, and no Dad's door, then... more stairs. More unreal stairs.

I went up them.

And?

The same. Landing, carpet, no doors, and a window looking out onto nothing.

Sort of disappointing. And more superfluous than supernatural, don't you think?

More stairs, though, so I went up.

Ditto.

And again.

Stairs, and stairs again.

I looked down the gap between the landings, and could just make out the real landing far below, so I wasn't simply going round and round the same landing, I really was climbing higher. Only, I wasn't getting anywhere.

I sat down to think about things.

Looking up, all I could see was an endless, tight spiral of banisters as the stairs went up and up.

It had to go somewhere. Did I have to go really, really high to get to that somewhere (wherever that somewhere was)?

Something told me yes, that was the thing to do, but thinking it made me dizzy with the height of it. What if I went up and up and up, till I was so far from the real world I couldn't get back? Scary. (But also, wasn't that what I wanted? To escape, totally escape?)

I glanced at my watch. It was late. And I'd just thought, 'Shouldn't it be getting dark?' when, almost instantly, like it had heard, the golden light coming through the window began to fade. I didn't like the idea of being on one of those impossible landings in the utter darkness, so I ran downstairs, down and down and down again, to my own familiar landing, where I could see dim and gloomy Willow Drive out the window and, downstairs from that, the hallway with its telephone table and living room door and the mirror with Mum in front of it.

So that was it. That was my little adventure into strangeness.

What did it mean? Perhaps it didn't mean anything. But, it's almost like — well, it's almost like they're saying, those stairs, that if I'm going to go up them, really go up, I have to go really, really far to get to where they're going. Like, far enough to leave this world totally behind. I have to cut myself off, with no going back. Leave the familiar far behind.

Or is that just me being loopy?

Anyway, I've popped out onto the landing again and the phantom stairs aren't there. Have they gone forever? I don't think so. I think they're biding their time.

Will I go up them if they appear again? And go really far this time?

I'm not sure. I'm not sure.

I'll sleep on it.

Sunday

It's 10 p.m. Mum is in her room, and has been since eight. Dad is downstairs in front of the telly. It's all he's done all weekend. I was just down there with him and I realised he wasn't watching the TV. He was staring at the wall. I don't know what's going on with him. It took all my nerve to sneak out of the living room and get back up here. It was scary.

But everything scares you, doesn't it, Carol?

Dad scares me. Mum scares me. She sat me down and had 'a talk' with me (actually, a talk *at* me, because I didn't have the chance to say anything) about 'what we're going to do' about my taking that money. I mean, I thought what she'd done was enough, but now she's going to stop my pocket money for at least a month to make me realise the value of what I took, and then we're going to 'see how things go', so even that might not be the end of it. I mean, I *know* I was wrong, and isn't it enough I feel really bad? It's not like I'm ever going to do it again. Does doing this one wrong thing mean I'm going to be at her absolute mercy for the rest of my life?

If nothing else, it means I won't be able to get *In Sleep a King* for ages.

And here's the next thing that scares me (next in a very long list): I haven't been able to read anything all weekend. All the other books in the series — all books, in fact — have lost their flavour. I try reading, but after a while I realise my eyes are just going over the words and nothing's getting through. I tell myself to concentrate, then a few seconds later my mind's on other things, reliving that horrible moment in the bookshop, or thinking about Mum, or Dad, or Candice Cooper.

Yes, Candice Cooper. She, of course, is the BIG thing I'm scared of. She said she'd see me on Monday, and that's tomorrow. I've tried not to think about it (and I've had plenty of other things to think about, as well you know), but every so often she wanders into my brain and gives a little wave to let me know it's still going to happen.

And what else? What else scares me? Come on, let's get the whole lot out of the way.

Can I say that Simon Lawne scares me? Not in the way Candice Cooper does or Mum does or Dad does or my inability to read does. It's a whole different thing. Simon Lawne is another of those things I've found myself thinking about all weekend. I just keep thinking of him, I can't help it. But I don't *want* to. I know what it means if you can't help thinking about someone in that way, and it's supposed to be wonderful, but it's *not*, not if you know there's no possibility of ever, of even — oh, I can't be bothered to write it. It's just impossible, that's all. Impossible and horrible.

It's just another thing on top of everything else.

So, my decision.

I'm going to go up those stairs again. I've checked, they're out there, solid as ever. But this time I'm not going to just go for a little explore, a little there-and-back-again. I'm going to go up and up and up and up. Forever. There-but-NO-back-again. In fact, I hope that as soon as I go up them they disappear, so no one will ever find me and I can never come back.

I'm *sure* there's something up there, if I go far enough. There *has* to be.

I don't know what's going to happen to me. I don't really care. I'm fed up with this world. I'm fed up of being me, and I'm fed up of being scared. I want NONE OF IT anymore. So I'm going where nobody will ever find me ever again.

I'm taking this diary with me. I don't want anyone reading it and finding out where I am. Also, I've got used to writing in it and might need the company. I'm also going to sneak downstairs and get a few supplies and put them in my school bag, as well as the torch we keep in the kitchen, and anything else I might need.

(My duffel coat. Definitely my duffel coat. Might be cold up all those steps. Plus, I like it.)

Anyway, that's it for now. Next time I write in this diary I'm going to be in another world.

(Oh, and I'd better take a supply of pens in case this one runs out. I doubt they'll have W H Smiths where I'm going!)

Monday (I think)

...But it could still be Sunday. Or it could be Tuesday. It could be morning, it could be afternoon, it could be midnight. It could be half-past Christmas and quarter-to-nowhen, for all I know. I forgot to bring my watch, fool of a Took that I am. But I'm not going back for it. I'm not going back for anything. I now live in a world without time. (Ooh, spooky.)

Anyway, here I am. My first diary entry in this unreal world.

I'm sitting on the stairs between the I-don't-know-which floor and the I-don't-know-which floor plus one. I've no idea how many sets of stairs I've climbed, or how many landings I've come to. Countless stairs, countless landings. (My poor legs! I'll have Conan thighs by the end of this.)

How much further does it go? Surely it can't go on like this forever?

Only one way to find out!

Later

What I meant to write about earlier was how I came over all miserable a little while back, but I didn't want the first diary entry of my new fantastic life to be about being my gloomy old un-fantastic self.

I'm going to write about it now, though, to get it out of my system.

So, about ten unreal floors up, I sat down and had a cry. My plan had been to get as far from Mum and Dad and the rest of the world as quickly as possible, but pretty soon I found myself slowing down. It wasn't gravity, it wasn't tiredness, it was *down there*. I wasn't escaping from it, I was still carrying it with me. Like someone had tied a big lead weight round my neck. A numb, glum plumb-line.

So I sat down and miserated.

Miserate is a word I made up, but it's a useful word, so maybe they should put it in the dictionary. What happens is, sometimes you feel sad but can shake it off by thinking of other things — good things or funny things — or by doing something that takes your mind off it, like maths homework (which completely nullifies my brain, so it's good for taking my mind off anything — even, bizarrely, maths homework). But sometimes you feel sad and know nothing's going to work but a really good sob. You don't feel quite miserable enough for that, though, so what do you do? You miserate. You think glum thoughts, trying to push yourself that little bit further into mopish melancholy so you can have a cry and feel better.

So that's what I did. I thought miserable things like, 'I'm never going home again. I've got no home now. I'm homeless and friendless and familyless. I'm never going to see Tollers again. I'm never again going to tell Wumpus my deepest darkest secrets (not that they were ever very deep or dark). I'm never going to see Mum or Dad again. Oh who cares. They never really liked me anyway.' Thoughts like that. I can get quite inventive at that sort of thing, and pretty soon I was totally glumstruck, so I slumped over sideways and nuzzled my face into the crook of my elbow.

Nothing happened.

I sat up again and did some more miserating. 'I'm never going to read the end of *In Sleep a King*. It'll torment me till I die, not knowing if they finally defeat the evil sorcerer, or if Princess Iyala gets to marry the handsome warrior Hendris. I'll never be able to wear my comfy purple slippers on those frosty winter mornings when you don't have to go to school and you get up late and make yourself some breakfast and loll about in your PJs reading. I'll never be able to do any of that ever again.' Loads of thoughts like that. Anyway, it finally did the trick and I had a sob. Then I fell asleep. That's why I have no idea what time, or even what day it is, because I don't know how long I slept. It could have been a full eight-hour cruise on the Seas of Nod, or a mere toe-dip in the shallows of Snoreswater. All I know is I woke up feeling better, determined to put that old stuff behind me and get on with my new life as an explorer in the unknown.

It worked for a while. But now I feel miserable again.

It's stupid. It's *silly*.

I tried miserating again but it didn't work. I don't have

the energy for two big sobs in such a short time. I just feel...
dull. Like a tin-foil gong being hit with a foam-rubber
hammer.

Why can't I just be happy? I've got rid of everything
that was making me unhappy, haven't I?

Oh, I don't care. The stairs are going up and up, so that's
what I'm going to do, whatever this sulky little girl who
lives inside me decides to feel. *I'm* going to get on with it
and enjoy myself.

So there!

Later still

I wonder what everyone's thinking?

If I knew what time it was I might be able to guess.

For instance, if it's still Sunday (and I don't see how it
can be, what with my sob-sleep and all those stairs and
landings, but you never know, time does strange things in
the Faerie Realm) nobody will have noticed I'm gone.
Sunday evenings, Mum and Dad retreat to their separate
lairs. They avoid each other in our small house with such
skill, they ought to get an award for it. A Dafta, perhaps.

Surely, though, it's at least Monday morning, if not later.
In which case Mum will know I'm gone. Or she'll be standing at the bottom of the stairs shouting at me to get a move
on as it's nearly time for school. Or she'll be tramping
upstairs grumbling about how the last thing she needs is a
daughter trying to get the day off school when she's got so
many things to do today. Or she'll be standing in the doorway of my room staring at my unslept-in bed.

I wonder if I should have left a note?

If it's later than that, Miss Michalowski will have
marked a red O in the register next to my name where she
usually puts a blue tick. No one else will have noticed I'm

gone, except maybe Candice Cooper, who will no doubt feel a glow of satisfaction at how she scared me so much on Friday I couldn't come in today. And she, of everyone, will be closest to the truth, but still a million miles off. (Or a million stairs, because I'm sure that's how many I've been up by now. Don't you need breathing apparatus this high?)

I wonder what they'll do when they realise I'm gone for good?

I don't care. I wish I'd decided to write about something else. It's making me glum. I shouldn't be thinking about *down there*, I should be thinking about *up here*.

The trouble is, up here has come to an end.

There are no more stairs.

What happened is, things started getting bare-looking. For some time now I've been walking on floorboards because the carpet has come to an end. (Strangely, I can't remember when there stopped being a carpet. I can't remember seeing some ragged carpet edge giving way to wooden floor, or hearing my footsteps change from pad-pad-pad to clonk-clonk-clonk. I just noticed there wasn't a carpet anymore, and realised there hadn't been for some time.) The walls went through a patch of being wallpapered rather than painted, but the wallpaper was old and peeling, and pretty soon that gave way to bare, cracked plaster.

Then I came to a landing without any more stairs.

I wasn't so much shocked or surprised as, sort of, blank.

I've been up here for hours, now, trying to decide what to do. I could go back down. But I'm not going to. I'm *not* going back to my old life. It'll be the same as it always was, with me afraid of everything and miserable about everything, and I don't want that, no matter what.

So what options *do* I have?

I don't like it, but there is one.

The attic.

You see, just like the real landing all the way back down

in 49 Willow Drive as-it's-supposed-to-be, this landing has a hatch in the ceiling, outside where Dad's room would be. A little while ago I put a foot on the banister and a hand on the wall and hauled myself up so I could lift the hatch with my head and have a peek.

The attic was completely dark. So, I got down again and fetched the torch from my schoolbag and did the whole thing over, but this time shone the torch into the darkness.

Now, if this was the real attic, back down there on the first-floor landing, I'd see roof-beams and boxes and probably lots of spiders (I don't go into the attic for that reason). But I saw nothing. The light from the torch went up into darkness and faded, and when I listened, there was just this big empty sound...

I clambered down, turned off the torch and thought about what to do.

I'm not going back down all those stairs. And there's no point staying here. I decided to see this thing through, didn't I? The attic's the only way to go, so the attic it has to be. But, to go up there, into all that *nothing*...

I'll have a meal first (my supplies are quite low already), then it's, well, onwards and upwards!

Some time later

(I've really lost track of what day it is, so don't expect any meaningful diary headings for a bit.)

Okay. Things are strange. Very strange.

And good?

Maybe good. I can't be sure. But definitely strange.

Let's begin with the attic.

First off, I had trouble getting through the hatch. I hoisted myself up as before, with one foot on the banister and one hand on the wall, and got the hatch open and my elbows on the ledge. But this time I had my schoolbag on my back, and when I tried pulling myself up, it wouldn't fit through with the rest of me.

No go.

'Great!' I said, meaning the exact opposite, and clattered back down in as controlled a manner as I could. (I dropped like a sack of spanners.)

Then — bright idea — I took off my schoolbag, gave it a whirl, and chucked it through the hatch.

I'd meant to throw it just a little way, but it sailed up in an arc and disappeared.

Goodbye bag.

'Oh,' I said, this time meaning exactly that.

I hauled myself up after it.

The air in the attic was dead still. It smelled dusty and woody. The light coming through the hatch only let me see a short way, and that didn't include wherever my bag had landed.

This was when I realised that, if only I'd thought my bright idea through (ha ha), I'd have taken the torch out before launching my bag into the void. That way, (a) I'd have it in my hand now so I could use it to find my bag, and (b) there'd be no chance of it having been broken when it landed.

Oh what a twit I am.

I stared into the darkness. The floor was nothing but girders or rafters or whatever you call those wooden beams that make up attic floors, with fluffy yellow insulation between them. (And the one time I went up into the attic — the real attic, I mean — Dad told me not to touch the insulation, making me wonder if it's poisonous or something.)

I knew, roughly, the direction my bag had flown off in, so I decided to follow a pair of rafter/girders, crawling along them like a train on tracks, so at least I'd keep my sense of direction and could get back to the hatch if I had to.

I paused every so often to feel around, and after what seemed a very long time (probably only a minute or two), found my bag.

Whew.

But — no torch.

I tried not to panic. It must have come out when I threw the bag. (It had not, not, not been nicked by attic-dwelling goblins. No, no, no.)

I glanced behind me. I could still see the squashed square of light that was the hatch. Good.

I patted the insulation around where I'd found my bag, but no torch.

Where next?

Best to check further on, in case it had come out when the bag landed, and had bounced or rolled.

I shouldered my bag and moved on, checking around me all the while. Then I turned round, shifted a pair of rafters to my right, and searched again, moving back towards the hatch. Then I turned, shifted right twice, and searched again.

Nothing.

I glanced at the hatch. Still visible. Good.

I ventured a bit further, doing the same thing — turn, shift and search, turn, shift-shift and search — and, whew, there it was, nestled in the insulation.

Oh, torch, I love you!

And what was more, it still worked!

Double-whew. My twit-ness had been forgiven, and I lived to twit another day.

I shone the beam around.

Girder-rafter things stretched before me, and behind me, and in endless rows off to my right and left. No sign of any walls. No sign of any ceiling, either. The real attic (from what I remember) is pretty small, and you can see the inside of the roof slanting down on both sides by the light coming through the hatch. But here, when I shone the torch straight up, I could see... nothing. Absolutely nothing. Just darkness, with the occasional dust mote. This was the Gormenghast of attics.

'Wow,' I said.

No echoes. No dull closed-in sound either.

Big space.

The thought of it made me dizzy.

I glanced over at where the hatch should be, but couldn't see it.

Okay, no need to panic. It's the torch, blinding you to what must be a very slim sliver of light, I told myself.

I turned the torch off.

No hatch.

Still no need to panic, I told myself. Let your eyes adjust to the darkness, *then* look.

I closed my eyes, counted to ten, and opened them again.

No hatch.

Okay, I said to myself, *now* you can panic.

Luckily, I had no idea how to panic in a dark attic.

Instead, I reasoned that, as I'd followed these two beams (or was it the next two beams, or two the other way?) out from the hatch to get my bag, I only had to follow them back to find the hatch again.

So I did that.

And, no hatch.

I had a horrible thought: the hatch was gone. It had been waiting for me to get far enough into the attic before disappearing. And now I was stuck in the dark with no way out.

I decided to try and be sensible about this.

Now, I asked myself, how do you be sensible?

Well, the thing was (I answered), if you're going to be sensible, you're in the wrong place to start with. Sensible people don't go up phantom staircases. They don't get into the sort of mess that makes them *want* to go up phantom staircases. They most certainly don't climb into enormous dark attics and get lost. Face it, Carol, being sensible is not one of your options right now.

Okay, so what *are* my options?

Tum te tum.

Any options? Any tiny little optionettes?

'No. No options.'

I think I must have said that aloud, because I heard it and opened my eyes and turned on my torch and shone it around, but there was nothing there but darkness. I *had* heard something, though. So it must have been me, talking to me.

I sighed.

Wasn't this the point, though? To go so far I couldn't go back?

Yes, but, like *this*? In darkness? What if this was *it*? What if I'd been tricked into a dead end, and I'd be here forever?

No. That couldn't be it. It couldn't, it couldn't, it couldn't.

Without thinking why, I started to walk.

What else was there to do? Stay in one place forever, or try to go somewhere? So I tried to go somewhere. After a while I stopped and shone the torch around. Nothing but girders below me and darkness above, so I turned the torch off and carried on. It wasn't like I was afraid of bumping into anything. I'd've quite *liked* to have bumped into something, there just weren't any somethings about.

I stared into the darkness.

It stared back.

(In a staring competition, darkness wins every time.)

'What am I doing?' I said.

If I'd been hoping for an answer, I was disappointed.

'Why am I here? And where is here?'

No answer.

'What shall I do?' This seemed a better question. I pondered it.

But, no answer. I mean, what *could* I do up here, in the dark, surrounded by so much nothing?

Maybe there was a better question.

I stopped walking and tried to think.

'What do I want?'

Yes.

I said it again. 'What do I want?'

Then a few variations. '*What* do I want? What do I *want*? What do *I* want?'

That last one sounded the best. I mean, here I was, alone in a sort of nowhere nothingness. I didn't have to worry what Mum would say I *should* want, or what the likes of Candice Cooper would laugh at me for wanting. If I could just say it, free of all the usual world-and-people stuff that gets in the way. If I could just say it...

'What I want is... Well, I don't want to be here. I don't want to be in the dark. I don't want to be on my own... What I want is... What I want is...'

I sighed. This was far more difficult than I'd thought. It sounds silly, but I was finding it difficult to say what I wanted, even though there was nobody about, nobody to laugh at me or make fun of me, and it didn't matter if what I wanted was possible or not. I just wanted to *say* it, so I could hear myself say it, and know what it was. Why was that so difficult? Because everything is, for me. Everything's on a scale of difficult to impossible, with most of it at the impossible end. Like finding your way out of an enormous, dark attic. Impossible. Like being anything other than the me I am, the disappointing, cowardly, no-good me. Impossible.

'Because, what I want,' I said to the darkness, 'is a little bit of magic. Like they have all the time in fantasy books.

But that's stupid isn't it? And impossible, too...'

I gave up. I sagged and gave up. I almost threw the torch into the darkness, because what good was it? *I* wasn't any good. So, nothing could ever be any good to me. Maybe a dark attic was the best place for me. Maybe this was it, what I wanted...

Then something glimmered.

It's the best word I can use to describe it. It glimmered. Off there in the darkness. It glimmered briefly, then was gone.

I lifted the torch, but didn't turn it on. If something was glimmering, the best way to see it was to let it glimmer in the darkness, not in the light.

I stared.

It glimmered again. A shape. A little way off.

'Hello?' I said, before I had time to think whether I wanted to meet anything that spent its time glimmering in enormous dark attics.

The thing glimmered again, and this time it stepped briefly into view. It was, I thought, a human shape, maybe a child. Then it was gone.

I started walking forward.

Immediately, I tripped. I put my hands out to catch myself, thinking I was going to land face-down in the dreaded insulation, but instead I hit something completely different.

Grass. And cold, firm mud.

I still had a grip on the torch, so I switched it on and shone it at my foot to see what I'd tripped over.

A loop of tree-root, all knobbly and gnarly, and tufted with a little crest of moss. A patch of mushrooms was growing nearby, delicate and pale like fairy umbrellas.

I picked myself up and shone the torch around. Trees. Real trees. Tall, thick, ancient trees. Silent, too. There must be no breeze at all. I looked up but couldn't see any leaves. The bare branches twisted into the dark, as if the trees were as rooted in the darkness above as they were in the soil below. And they were all around me. Even behind me. Which meant I must have been walking past them for a while. Or they had just appeared. Neither possibility was even remotely possible, but had happened anyway, because here I was, in the midst of a forest.

I started forward, picking my way over roots, but also keeping an eye on the spot where I'd seen that glimmerling (my word for it) glimmering.

'Hello?' I said, timidly, Brave Explorer into the Unknown that I am. 'Is — is someone there?'

And suddenly someone was. It — he, she, whatever — stepped from between two trees to stand in front of me.

For a moment I just stared. It was short (shorter than me, anyway, which *is* short, unless you're an atom or something), and human-shaped, but not very detailed. I mean, it had a head and a face, but its head was as shapeless as a ball of clay, and its face was two dots for eyes and an O for a mouth. The mouth had no lips or teeth or tongue, and didn't seem to go anywhere, it was just a hollow someone had poked into the soft clay of the head with the tip of their finger. And it was glowing, this pale yellow thing, like a weird woodland fungus.

'H-hello,' I said, once I'd recovered, and realised it wasn't about to do anything frightening.

It said nothing, but mimicked the movements of my mouth.

I felt sorry for it. 'Are you a child?' I couldn't help reaching out to touch it, though whether I was thinking of comforting it, or just making sure it was solid, not a ghost, I can't say.

Copying me, it reached out too. And the moment we touched (I think I felt something, very light, like the wing of a butterfly) *it changed*. It shimmered and changed. Suddenly, standing in front of me was a child, a human child, with proper eyes and a proper mouth and real hair and so on. (It was still glowing, but you can't expect perfection, can you?)

It stared at me as gormlessly as any human child can.

'Don't be afraid,' I said, illogically. But, as if I'd just reminded it of the very thing it was supposed to do, it ran into the woods.

'Don't—' I said, but it was too late.

Alone again.

I continued walking. After a few steps I turned my torch off. Another glow was coming from behind a tree up ahead.

'Is that you again?' I said, picking my way over the roots towards the glow. 'Or is it someone else?' (Great question, Carol!)

I rounded the tree where the glow was coming from, and there in front of me was the little glowing guy I'd just met, still in the shape of a child. But now he was holding the hand of another, taller glimmerling, slim and willowy, and just as simple-featured as the child had been before I'd touched him. I said, 'Is this your mother?'

The child-glimmerling made a babbling noise, which the mother evidently understood, because she, blank-eyed, reached towards me. I reached out my hand, too, and as we touched fingers I said, 'Mother.' I don't know why I said it, but when I did, just like before, the creature changed and this time looked like a woman. She smiled shyly, then retreated with her child into the darkness.

'Don't go,' I said. 'I want to ask you something.'

But she was gone.

I thought, maybe they're off to find Dad so he can have a make-over, too. There might be a whole family of them waiting to be changed. And then it struck me: had *I* done that? Had *I* turned them from shapeless dough-people into humans (or human-shaped glimmerlings)?

Anyway, I was alone again, so I carried on walking.

After a few steps I realised I hadn't turned the torch back on, but could still see well enough to avoid the tree roots and tangles of grass. There was a glow coming from all around me, not sunlight or moonlight, but glimmerling-light. There were dozens of them, half-hidden behind trees, dot-eyed and O-mouthed, staring at me with a hungry blankness that was, I must admit, a wee bit frightening.

I told myself they meant no harm, and said, 'Hello everyone.'

A glimmery ripple passed through them, like anticipation.

'Um, how are you all?'

No reply, of course. But one detached itself from the tree it was hiding behind and came towards me. Actually, it floated towards me, light as a dandelion puff, taking only the occasional bouncy astronaut step on the ground as it came. It lifted its arms. They didn't end in hands, but tapered away like brush-strokes of luminous paint.

I told myself not to be afraid, even though it looked a bit spooky floating towards me like that. 'Now what does this one look like?' I asked myself, knowing what was coming next. It didn't really look like anything special, but the instant it touched me with its light-as-a-breeze touch I said, 'Father', because of course I'd already made a child and a mother, so that seemed the logical thing to say. The glim-merling shimmered and a moment later had the shape of a man. Then, without a thank you (*'just* like a man,' as Mum would say) it turned around and walked away. (Not floating now. It had gained some solidity, so had to walk.) Maybe it went and joined the mother and child. That's what I hoped, anyway. (But most probably it went to work and stayed there far too late, then brought some more work home and didn't talk to anyone all evening.)

Two more were now floating towards me.

I felt a bit drained after that last encounter. Maybe, I

thought, it was all the excitement and unknownness of the situation. Plus I was a bit nervous in case I did something wrong — after all, here I was making things into other things and it could cause all sorts of trouble if I slipped up. I wanted to ask these next two to hold on for a moment and let me rest, but they were already too close, so instead I tried to work out what they looked like so I could name them appropriately. The nearest one was quite small, much smaller than the one I'd made into a child, and as it reached me I said 'Dog', and though I immediately felt bad for making this one into an animal when I'd made the others into people, it seemed happy enough and went into the woods just like the others. To the second one I said 'Cat', though more because it followed on from 'dog' than because this fellow (who was actually quite large) looked anything like a cat. Instantly, he was a cat — about ten stone of glowing yellow mog, what a sight! — and he slunk into the woods as only a ten-stone glowing yellow mog can.

Already, others were coming towards me.

I have to admit at this point I felt a trifle nervous (as in, cowardy custard!). Those last few had left me even more drained, and I was beginning to realise I wasn't just suggesting names and shapes to these creatures, but they were *sucking* them out of me, like mosquitoes or leeches. I was getting tireder and tireder. But I didn't have a choice. Maybe I'd had a choice with that first one, which I'd done by accident, and maybe with the second, which had been a kindness, but now I didn't have any. Each time one of the glimmerlings put its hands (or the ends of its handless arms) on me I was forced to say something, name a name, picture a shape, and it would take that shape and go away. But then there'd be another, and another, and another. They were crowding round me, not dozens now but a hundred or more, barely waiting their turn. Where they'd come from, when the wood had been so dark a moment ago, I don't know, but they were there and there was no way out. I was surrounded, swamped.

My mouth took on a life of its own as it said things like 'Monkey... hamster... giraffe...' (small one, fortunately) 'mouse — oh, don't get eaten by the cat! — horse... pony... aardvark...' (And as I don't know what an aardvark looks like, that glimmerling ended up resembling something like a spiny hamster that waddled into the woods lopsidedly.)

My limited knowledge of real-world animals was running thin, so I switched to an area I know slightly more about. 'Fairy — satyr — elf — unicorn—' And it was wonderful, because the fairy looked just like a tiny Tinkerbell, and she flew off into the woods trailing moondust. And the satyr was a funny little half-man half-goat with buds of horns growing from his curly-haired forehead. The elf, meanwhile, was your Tolkien-style variant, very tall and regal, looking like he could spout a tragic tale of long-lost-love at a moment's notice. And the unicorn, well, the unicorn was magnificent, beautiful, not just white but *glowing* white, so it looked really magical.

It was great to see these fantastic creatures so real, in front of me (if only briefly, because they all flew or skipped or strode or trotted into the woods as soon as they were formed). The trouble was, there's a limited supply of nice fantasy creatures. Most fantasy creatures are monsters, and inevitably my tired mind shifted gear again and started coming out with, 'Goblin, imp, troll, ogre — eek!' And I had to jump back from that last one, because suddenly in front of me was this great big shaggy oaf with jagged tooth-stumps in its mouth and a hungry look in its eye, like it could eat a human girl in one chomp. It shambled off into the forest, growling, and I told myself to change tack quickly or risk the appearance of a fire-breathing dragon or a balrog and *really* mess things up. But the glimmerlings were crowding round me, and the only thing I could think of was people, people I knew. So I started saying, 'Mum... Dad... Miss Michalowski... Mr Hodges...' And each one turned into a perfect (though glowing yellow) copy of the person I named, and really it was creepy seeing Mum appear in front of me with a totally blank expression on her face, like some zombified version of her, and then Dad, and poor Miss Michalowski. (If only I knew the name of her 'particular' young man, I could have made one of him for her, but alas, her glimmerling version was fated to be as lonely as the real world one.) The glimmerlings were pressing closer and closer, all eager to be named and shaped, and I was totally knackered by now, but I couldn't back off or make any room for myself. I could barely lift my hands. And as I got tireder my guard dropped and I found myself saying what I should never in a million years have said: 'Candice Cooper!'

And there she was in front of me.

Even then, it *should* have been alright, if I hadn't been tired and harassed, if I hadn't been crowded by hundreds of glimmerlings, if I hadn't been so scared by the sudden appearance of my arch-enemy right in front of me.

But it wasn't alright. I *was* tired and I *was* harassed and I *was* scared. I said, 'Don't hurt me!' And of course it was like when I said 'Don't be afraid!' to the child glimmerling, because what you're doing when you say 'Don't hurt me!' is you're thinking of someone hurting you, and these glimmerlings respond to what you're thinking, not what you say. (As with the invented aardvark earlier.)

So the Candice Cooper glimmerling grinned evilly, and I knew she was going to hurt me.

I struggled to get away. I flailed like a little girl drowning in a sea of glimmerlings. And though I was too tired and scared to say the names they wanted me to say, they still sucked them out of me each time they touched me. Only, my imagination had gone wild now, and was just coming out with anything, totally at random. And there in front of me was Brad Pitt, a giant ant, a policeman, Paddington Bear, an enormous walking banana — it went on and on and on, and all the time I was fighting to retreat from the slowly advancing Candice Cooper.

I needed (one small-voiced sensible part of me realised) to make one of the glimmerlings into something that would save me from her, and I needed to do it quickly. The first idea that came to me, rather embarrassingly, was Simon Lawne. But it was no time for qualms, so I said, 'Simon Lawne!' and did my best to picture him, and there he was, glowing slightly, but nevertheless looking like the real Simon Lawne.

The trouble was, as soon as I saw him standing next to Candice Cooper I remembered that the last time I'd seen him in the real world he'd been doing exactly that: standing next to Candice Cooper. Chatting to her. Which meant they were friends. They were *in league*. For all I knew they were secretly engaged to be married as soon as they were old enough, tied together by vows of them-against-the-world. And of course as soon as I thought that, the Simon Lawne in front of me took on the same evil look as Candice Cooper. And now they were both advancing on me.

There was nothing left for it but to shout, 'Help!'

But that was pointless. I was beyond help. Candice Cooper's evil grin widened and she raised her fist—

Then she stopped. Her eyes went wide and for a moment she looked like she'd just remembered putting a pair of new red socks in the wash with her favourite white top. I stared back, wondering what was going to happen next. Nothing good, I was sure. Then her expression turned more to the 'I can't believe I've been grounded for *three weeks*' sort, and a sword point burst through her chest and she was flung, with a flick of the sword, into the darkness of the woods. (Thankfully these glimmerlings don't seem to have any blood, otherwise I'd be in a real state right now.)

And who had done this? Who had rescued me from a pummelling worse than death? Would you believe me if I said it was a tall knight in full armour, spurs and spikes glistening from every shiny plated joint, a great plume of scarlet ostrich-feather rising from his bucket-shaped helmet like it was a cloud of steam puffing out of some magical inner boiler-room? Because it was. It really was. He was standing in front of me. He was tall and broad and heavy-looking, more solid than any of the other glimmerlings, and not glowing at all. And that made me realise he wasn't a glimmerling, he was a real knight (as far as I could tell at the time, that is, but we'll come to how real a knight he is in a little while).

Anyway, before my thoughts could catch up he turned on Simon Lawne, who'd lost his evil grin now Candice Cooper had been slain. (I just wanted to write that — 'Candice Cooper had been slain' — even though it wasn't the *real* Candice Cooper but some fantasticated creature summoned from the depths of my murky imagination. Still, there's a certain satisfaction in writing it. Candice Cooper had been slain.) But the knight was in full-swing Carol-saving mode, and he raised his sword for the blow that would put an end to Simon Lawne too.

'No!' I shouted.

He froze.

'You're not really evil, Simon,' I said (rather pathetically). 'Are you?'

Simon Lawne looked at me blankly, because of course this wasn't Simon Lawne at all, but a glimmerling. Glimmerling or not, though, I didn't want to see him beheaded right in front of me, so I quickly said, 'Shoo!' and he — it — ran into the woods.

I wish I'd told him to look like someone else before shooing him off. I don't like the idea of a Simon Lawne copy wandering about in the woods. But that's just me being silly, isn't it?

Anyway, the knight was now standing stock-still in mid sword-swing. The glimmerlings had gone, frightened off. The woods were silent and calm (and not totally dark, because I could see a little light coming through the tangle of branches above us, not glimmerling-light now, but moonlight).

'Um, I think you can relax now,' I said.

With a flourish the knight sheathed his sword then fell with a crash to one knee and bowed.

'You don't need to bow!' I said. 'I should be bowing to *you*. You saved me. And thank you. For saving me, I mean.' I gave a quick bow, then another, in case he'd missed the first.

The knight remained bowed for a moment longer, then rose to his full height (which is really quite tall), and said, 'I am but a messenger. Let me take you to my lord.'

'Um, okay,' I said. 'But can you answer a few questions, first? Like where I am and what those things were?'

The knight spent a moment thinking about this. Then he said, 'I am but a messenger. Let me take you to my lord.'

'Okay. I guess you've got your orders. But what's your name? Mine's Carol.'

But again all he said (and in exactly the same tone) was, 'I am but a messenger. Let me take you to my lord.'

So I said, 'Right you are then.'

I followed him as he clanked through the woods till we came to a white horse with its reins tied to a low branch. It was, now I think about it, standing suspiciously still and rather stiff-jointed, but I thought nothing of this at the time, being too wowed at having been saved by a knight in shining armour in true fairy-tale style.

The knight mounted his horse (without any help, which must mean he's really strong, because I always thought knights in full armour had to be hauled onto their horses with winches and cranes). Then he turned and offered me a hand. I grasped it and was whisked onto the saddle behind him.

'Are you comfortable,' he asked. Then, after a pause (and, rather oddly, a click), 'My lady?'

'Um, yes, thank you,' I said. And I started to say, 'But I'm not a lady, just a girl,' but before I could, he spurred his mount forward and we were hurtling through the forest.

I've never been on a horse before. I'm not really sure I can say I've been on one now, because this, it turned out, wasn't a real horse, as I'll soon explain. But either way, it was a truly frightening experience. We galloped at an insane speed through thick, thick forest, swerving round trees and leaping roots and streams and fallen trunks — always at the last second — and all I could think was that any moment we were going to crash and I was going to have my precious few brains bashed out in a head-on collision with a tree, because the knight, who I assumed (*hoped*) was steering this thing, had a bucket over his head with only a slit you could barely post a letter through for seeing out of, and the horse of course had eyes on the sides of its head so probably couldn't see in front of it at all, and anyway it was *dark*, so I clung to the knight's metal waist and shut my eyes.

It seemed to go on forever, one long nightmare of being bounced and jolted and swerved. But eventually the gallop slowed to a canter, then a trot (or is it a trot then a canter?), then a walk, then my favourite, a stop. I had the sudden urge to say, 'Wow, that was *fun*, let's do it again!' But thankfully I was a bit more sensible than I usually am and kept shtum. I unclenched my eyes, which I'd been holding so tight shut that for a while all I could see was purple splotches swimming in front of me.

'Please dismount,' the knight said, then that pause again,

followed by, '(click) my lady.'

'Yes,' I said, dizzy and exhausted, and more fell to the ground than dismounted. I got up quickly, in case Sir Bucket-Head decided to get down without checking I was out of the way.

I moved a few paces off and took stock of my situation.

We were in a clearing. Above us was a truly huge moon, full and bright as a brand new coin (worth, I'd say, about twenty pounds, by the size of it). The ground was grassy and bumpy, and a little way away there were some pale white stones, which I realised were bits of ruin, hidden among the weeds and trees.

My saviour had started to dismount, but seemed to be having trouble, because although he was half-turned in the saddle and leaning groundwards, he'd come to a halt.

'Are you alright?' I said. 'Do you need help?' Not that I'd have been able to give him any, because in that armour he probably weighed about three tons. 'You're not hurt are you?'

No reply.

I was just about to go over when he lurched into motion again. He dismounted, then paused again, slightly bent. And I was just about to ask again if he was alright when he straightened.

Then he did nothing for a long while.

'Um, where are we?' I asked, thinking maybe he'd pulled a muscle in some tender part of his knightly anatomy and was trying to hide the fact, so might appreciate a change of subject.

He turned to face me. There was a series of clicks. Then he said, 'I am but a — mess — sen — jur...'

Then he stopped.

'Um,' I said. 'Yes.' Then, when that didn't work, 'Are you sure you're alright?'

No reply.

I walked up to him and tried to peer into the slit in his bucket helmet, but it was dark as a demon's conscience in there, and way over my head. So I bit my lip and knocked lightly. I couldn't think of anything else to do. His helmet sounded more empty than I'd expected. He didn't say anything. He didn't even move.

'Um,' I said, 'shall I... Shall I take your helmet off?'

No reply.

I reached up and grasped it with both hands. But he was so tall that just grasping it meant my arms were at full stretch, leaving me no height for lifting.

I had an idea. I got up on the horse (which was as stock still as its rider, and didn't budge an inch as I clambered onto it in a very undignified way). Once up there I grasped the knight's helmet, and this time had enough spare arm-length to pull upwards.

His helmet was heavy. As soon as it came off I had to drop it, and it donged on the ground like a bell.

'Sorry!' I said, or squealed, because the effort of lifting the helmet had put me off balance and once again I fell off the horse.

I picked myself up and looked at the face of my rescuer.

He had no face.

Instead he had a big brass plate.

I peered closer. The brass plate was about the size of the sort of plates you have a sandwich or a slice of cake on, only it was completely flat, apart from some tiny irregularly-placed pins or bumps on its surface. And there was a thing like a comb resting vertically against it. I had no idea what it was, until suddenly it moved. The plate rotated a bit, and as it did some of the pins hit the teeth of the comb and made little sounds. And I heard, 'Let me tay...'

I jumped back. The knight was silent once more.

I came closer and tapped the plate.

This freed it up and it moved again. '...ake you to my... lor...rd.'

After that he was silent.

'Are you a mechanical knight, then?' I said.

No reply, of course, but I guessed he was. And he'd just wound down.

I walked all around him looking for a key and a place to wind him up, but couldn't find one, and there was nothing on the horse, either.

How inconvenient.

Anyway, I summed up my courage and, putting my finger on the plate, moved it clockwise. He said, 'Are you comfortable... My lord?.. My lady?.. Please dismount... My lord... My lady...' Most of which I'd heard before. Then he repeated the 'I am but a messenger' thing, which I'd heard enough times already. That seemed to be his entire repertoire. (I resisted the temptation to spin the plate fast then slow then backwards. Mechanical or not, he *did* save me, and I at least owed him his dignity by way of thanks.)

So, here I am. Sitting on a hummock of grass in a moonlit clearing, in the company of a wound-down mechanical knight and a wound-down mechanical horse. No glimmerlings have come from the woods in the time it's taken me to write this, so that's a good thing. (I did try to draw Sir Bucket-Head's sword in case I needed it to defend myself, but it took ages to get out of its scabbard, and once I'd done that I could barely lift it, let alone swing it, so I then spent ages putting it back again.)

I don't know what to do next.

I'm quite tired, but I don't think this is the place to have a kip. Just in case the glimmerlings *do* come back and I'm dreaming and it makes the glimmerings into whatever I'm dreaming of.

Besides, it's cold.

I wonder if the knight — who was, as he so often pointed out, but a messenger — was supposed to take me somewhere else after this, or whether this is where I'm supposed to meet his lord?

And also I wonder, do I *want* to meet his lord?

Well, I want to meet *someone*. Preferably not someone you have to wind up to get a conversation out of. And preferably not someone dangerous.

I think I'll wait here for a bit. Then think of something to do.

Yes, that's a good plan. Good plans always involve putting off the inevitable for a while.

The next day

You'll have to read this quietly because I've woken up with a headache. (I'm writing really small to muffle the sound.) My brains, meanwhile, have turned to ball bearings. It's okay if I stay still, but I tried getting out of bed a moment ago and everything rolled around, so I got back in.

Ick.

Anyway, rather than lying here feeling sorry for myself, I'm going to write up yesterday's events. A *lot* has happened.

(Hang on... There, just lit another candle. The room I'm in is underground, so no windows, and these candles are no replacement for a good bedside lamp!)

First I'll tell you where I am. I'm sitting propped up by pillows in a genuine four-poster bed, like they had in Victwardian times or whenever it was. It's really ornate. The corner-posts are carved into the four types of elemental: the flamey curl of a salamander by my left foot, a whirlwind whoosh of sylph by my right, a gem-dotted gnome behind my left shoulder, a whirlpool of undine behind my right. Above me, there's a canopy tapestry showing the four elements coming together. There's all sorts of storms and flashes of lightning (done in silver thread) and jets of steam and mighty waves and cracking rocks and so on. In the centre, a world is being created.

Hardly the sort of thing to send you to sleep!

But I guess I didn't have any trouble. I slept like a log last night.

The odd thing is, I can't remember coming to bed. Well, I have a hazy recollection of being *carried* here, but that can't be right, can it? I mean, why would I be carried? So embarrassing. And silly. And worrying, because then you have to ask who did the carrying, and it can only be either my host (which I doubt) or his rather incredible servant — but now I'm getting ahead of myself, because I've mentioned my host and not told you who he is, and I've mentioned his rather incredible servant without telling you what makes her so incredible. I must get into the habit of writing things down in the proper order. This is a diary, not a game of hopscotch!

So, back to the end of yesterday's entry.

You last saw me (quick flip back to see when you last saw me) sitting in that moonlit clearing with the wound-down mechanical knight and his mechanical horse, wondering what to do next. What I did next was I sat there and wondered a bit more. Quite a bit more, because it was only when the sky got pale and I realised it was almost morning that I shifted my lazy bones and decided I really ought to do something. I was hungry, cold, and more than a bit tired, and I was only going to get tireder, colder, and hungrier. I was already yawning fit to slip a jaw-hinge.

What to do, though? Stay put, or go for an explore?

Luckily, I had this brief burst of being able, for about a microsecond, to think clearly, and came to a conclusion. It went like this:

1. The mechanical knight had been sent by someone to

rescue me. Which was nice.

2. The mechanical knight had wound down. Which meant that...

3. ...at some point he'd been wound up. Now, if he had to be wound up every so often, you'd have thought that...

4. ...he wouldn't have been sent too far, because there'd be no point sending him somewhere he couldn't get back from. So, my...

5. ...conclusion (hooray!) was that whoever sent him shouldn't be too far away. I ought to be able to find them.

Whew!

So, explore it was. The next question was, which direction?

Well, I'm no Sherlock Holmes (you can tell can't you? it must be my lack of a pipe), but I reckoned if the mechanical knight was headed in *that* direction (the direction his horse was pointed in), then if I pointed myself in the same direction and went in a dead straight line, I had a fair chance of getting where he'd been taking me.

So that's what I did.

I came to a stop about six paces later because there was a ruined wall in the way.

From here the forest pretty much gave way to ruins, apart from the odd leafless tree looming out of the mist like a mournful survivor from the old days when all these crumbled walls and cracked flagstones and tumbled pillars had been a castle or a city or whatever. Tufts of tough grass were pushing up between the flagstones, and every so often there'd be a clump of thistles or brambles or dotty-coloured spiky-looking wildflowers. Everything was swamped in thick white mist, turning the furthest chunks of ruin to ghostly silhouettes.

I clambered over the wall and pressed on.

There isn't much you can say about wandering round a ruin in the early morning. I stepped in about four puddles (three with my right foot, one with my left), got squirted up the leg by a seesawing flagstone with a puddle beneath it, stumbled or slipped about five times, and for three of those stopped myself from falling by grabbing the nearest fragment of wall, which always had a great squidgy splodge of moss on it, so my hands got all slimy. The other two times I just fell over. (Not that I was keeping score or anything.)

After a while of this, I got thoroughly fed up. I sat down. On a squidgy splodge of moss. So now my jeans were wet, too. (They're hanging on a clothes horse by the fire at the moment. Meanwhile, I'm wearing a thick and rather comfy (though way too big) nightdress. Which I don't remember getting into. Which means my host's rather incredible servant must have put me in it. Another embarrassment to add to my list.)

I started to have this horrible feeling that my reasoning was wrong, that the mechanical knight was actually a leftover from the days when this ruin was a thriving city or castle, and he'd only just wound down after maybe two hundred years, so there'd be no lord waiting for me, there'd be no one anywhere.

Then I heard, 'And so it is with us all.'

I couldn't see anyone. It wasn't anywhere near fully light yet, though, and the voice hadn't sounded too far away.

I listened, and this time heard, 'You, my friend, are a great lesson. And, in many ways, a great consolation.'

It was a man's voice, slightly rough and world-weary, as if every word he spoke was a familiar yet tiresome burden. I couldn't see him, so I guessed he wasn't speaking to me, but I couldn't be sure.

Ahead, through the remains of a ruined arch, a dozen steps led down to what must have been a cellar or something in the old days, only now it had no roof so it was just a lower bit of ruin than all the other bits. Peering into the gloom, I saw a man with long, straight, dark hair sitting on a block of stone. He was wrapped in a black cloak, and was staring intently at the ground in front of him.

'And so,' he said, without looking up, 'in the smallest of things, we find the most profound of lessons.'

There was nobody around but him and me. And I don't think he was talking to me. (I may be small, but calling me 'the smallest of things' would be taking it a bit far.) So who was he talking to?

I decided to make myself known. After all, this might be the lord the mechanical knight had been taking me to. (It was. I hope that didn't spoil the surprise?) I gave a little cough.

He looked up. He was, I guess, somewhere in his twenties. It was difficult to tell because he had such an air of the weight of the world about him. He had a long, pale, quietly sad face with grey, distant-looking eyes, and he didn't seem surprised to find me standing there.

'Um, hello,' I said.

'Hello,' he said, as if he were making a very grave and solemn pronouncement, like 'Thy doom is upon thee,' or something.

There was a pause. Already the conversation was floundering! I tried something desperate.

'My name's Carol.'

The man in the cloak inclined his head by way of a bow. 'I am Lord Philosophus Soltharian Diamaxis Dolorous.' He smiled ever so slightly, an expression which somehow made his face even sadder. 'Dolorous is the family name, and the family nature.'

'Oh,' I said, thinking, 'Poor man. Surely if there's one advantage to having so many names, it's that you ought to have at least one you can use, but all those sound pretty awful.' Anyway, the conversation looked like flagging again, so I said, 'You wouldn't be the owner of a mechanical knight, would you?'

'I would,' he said, and might have added 'alas', for that was how he sounded about the matter.

'Only, I think it's wound down. In a clearing not far from here.'

He nodded lugubriously (great word, Carol — must remember to look it up sometime) then returned to studying the ground. 'As it must be with us all,' he said. 'We will all wind down, we will all come to a halt. Only this poor fellow seems capable of going on forever, and that is his curse.' He smiled at me that peculiarly saddening smile. 'I have been observing this insect for some time now, as it tries to pick its way across the cracked and uneven floor. When it comes to a crack too large for its tiny step, it is forced to turn around and go back the way it came. But it is surrounded by cracks. It has been doing nothing but crawl in circles all the time I've been here. With a little leap it might escape the trap it finds itself in. But it can't leap.' He looked at me. 'We are all insects trapped on a ruined floor going round and around, incapable of jumping the chasm-like cracks that hem us in, incapable of escaping our fate.'

Cheery soul. So I said, coming down the steps to join him, 'Why don't you give it a hand? Lift it over a crack and help it on its way?'

The Dolorous Lord (as I've come to think of him) shook his head sadly. 'But can I help every insect? Can I be there to lift each one over each crack? Or should I wait only in this place to help whichever insects need helping over these cracks? Or should I, perhaps, follow this insect and help it over whichever cracks it comes to? There is no answer.'

'Well, you could help this one now, and see how things go.'

He smiled that doleful smile, as if to say I was young and had a lot to learn. Then he stood up. He was quite tall. 'You are an idealist, young lady. Would you care to dine with me? But you mentioned my mechanical knight. We should see to that first. Do you remember where he is?'

I nodded.

'Then, pray, lead on.'

(At this point I cast a quick look at the ground to see the insect that had so depressed him. Disturbed by the breeze from the Dolorous Lord's cloak, it unfolded a pair of wings and flew off. I was about to point this out, but my host was already halfway up the steps, so I hurried after him.)

'You know,' I said, as we picked our way over the rubble towards the clearing, 'your knight rescued me from a pretty sticky situation. It was very kind of you to send him.'

'As much as I would like to deserve your gratitude, I did not send him,' the Dolorous Lord said, in an isn't-the-world-hopeless tone of voice. 'The mechanical knight has grown erratic of late and I rarely wind him up. This time, as soon as I did, he leapt upon his horse and galloped away as if in the grip of an urgent task. I even thought at first — well, it does not matter what I thought.' He shook his head. 'I was out looking for him when I noticed the insect, and became lost in a philosophical reverie.'

'Well, thanks all the same,' I said.

We came to the clearing.

The Dolorous Lord stood in front of his knight and regarded it for a moment. 'Thoroughly wound down. One day, my friend, there will be no one around to wind you up again. You will remain in your final fated posture for perhaps a hundred years. Your clockwork mechanics will rust, and you will become hollow, empty. And then you will disappear completely. Need I tell you how much I envy you?'

I, meanwhile, managed to pick the knight's helmet off the ground and stagger round with it. The Dolorous Lord set it back in its proper place, then, releasing some hidden catch, opened the knight's breastplate to reveal his inner workings. There were all sorts of gears and cogs and cables packed in there, brassy and shining, and right in the centre was this huge hypnotising swirl of a spiral spring. Taking a key from a little compartment where the knight's appendix would have been (I know where that is because Dad had his appendix out a few years back and the nurse spent some time explaining to me where it was), the Dolorous Lord plugged it into the centre of the spring and started winding it up.

At first I stood there kicking my heels, but then, when I realised it didn't exactly take much concentration to wind up a spring, I decided to ask a few long-overdue questions.

'What were those things that live in the woods? You know, the glowy people?'

'Liminal beings,' he said, which meant nothing to me. 'We are quite close to the Edge of the World here, the fraying edge where things cease to have proper form. Those are the sort of creatures you find at the Edge of the World. Formless, yet craving form with a terrible hunger. They have no name.'

'I called them glimmerlings,' I said.

The Dolorous Lord regarded me for a moment, then said, solemnly, 'And so they have a name,' as if this were a sad day for us all.

I kicked my heels a bit more. 'Do they always do that *thing*, though?'

'What thing?'

'Where they change shape when you touch them?'

The Dolorous Lord stopped his winding and looked at me.

I bit my lip, thinking I'd done something wrong. 'I didn't do it deliberately or anything. I mean, they were crowding round me and I couldn't move, and... and it got me into real trouble, so if I'd've known it was going to happen I'd've steered clear of them all...'

I bit my lip again and fell silent.

The Dolorous Lord looked at his knight briefly, then turned back to me. He seemed puzzled, which was the first non-sad expression I've seen on his face, and it actually made him look younger, or more his proper age, anyway.

'*They* changed shape?' he said. 'Surely you mean you touched *one* and *it* changed shape?'

'Um, no. Um... More than one.'

He raised an eyebrow.

'I'm sorry,' I said. 'I didn't mean to.'

'How many did you change?'

'I don't know. A few dozen? Maybe more. But I had no choice. They were all crowding round me. There were hundreds. If it wasn't for Sir Bucket-Head — I mean, your mechanical knight — I'd still be there now.'

But the Dolorous Lord hardly seemed to hear. He stared into space for a moment, looking blank. Then he shook his head. 'It cannot be.'

'I'm sorry,' I said, again.

'You misunderstand. You've done nothing wrong. But, dozens? Are you sure?'

'I wasn't exactly keeping count. Even if I had been, I'd have run out of fingers and toes by the time I got to the aardvark anyway.' (I do say some stupid things sometimes.)

He removed the key from the mechanical knight's winding mechanism and stored it away. Then he closed the breastplate and turned to face me again, a solemn look on his already solemn face. 'Usually, when touched by one of those creatures, those glimmerlings as you call them, a man has his own shape sucked out of him. The glimmerling takes on his form, briefly, for they keep such stolen shapes a few days at most. But the man is left a shell. If he is lucky he will survive until he staggers from the woods to be found, blank-eyed and speechless, after which he may last a few weeks at most before the life fades from him. But that is as a result of being touched by *one* of those creatures.'

'Oh,' I said, not at all sure what this meant. 'Um, maybe that's just for men, not girls?'

'I don't know,' the Dolorous Lord said quietly. He rapped his knuckles twice on the mechanical knight's chest and it came to life.

'(Click)' it said. Then, 'My lord.'

'We will return,' the Dolorous Lord said.

The knight mounted and rode quietly behind us as we picked our way back through the ruin. (Apparently the horse hadn't wound down, but only came to life when the knight was sitting on it, so as to conserve spring-power.) We passed the cellar where I'd met my new host, and followed various winding paths deeper into the ruin. My host said nothing, but frowned to himself, no doubt lost in another of those philosophical reverie things of his. Finally we came to another set of steps leading down, this time ending in a dark opening.

'All this used to be my ancestral home,' my host said as we descended the steps. 'In my youth I went to the Palace and spent my time building mechanical devices, such as this knight, for the service of Lord Paladin and the...' He hesitated for a moment, narrowing his eyes as if completing that sentence in thought alone. 'When I returned I found my old home like this. Crumbled and ruined as if nine hundred years had passed, not a mere nine.' He turned to face me, half-shadowed by the opening we were about to enter. 'But that is the way it is now. The world is fraying, declining, wasting away. The sun—' (and here he raised his eyes to indicate the pale disc just visible through the mist) '—never gets any brighter than this. Soon the night will be indistinguishable from the day.'

'Really?' I said, not liking the sound of this at all.

'It is what my studies reveal. It is partly why I came back here. To study the Edge of the World, to confirm my suspicions. Also, to write a philosophical tract on the point-lessness of all action. Then I realised that to write such a tract was itself an action, refuting the very argument it sought to maintain. It was a paradox that confounded me for many weeks. Now, I spend my days in the quiet contem-plation of futility and fate.'

'Oh,' I said. I didn't know what else to say to that.

'Contemplation is, of course, an action,' he continued, 'and therefore pointless. But I must do something to while away the hours until the end of all things.'

He produced an old-fashioned lantern from a recess in the wall and lit it, revealing a short corridor that took a turn near the top of another downward flight of stairs.

'This,' he said, 'is the only part of my ancestral home still habitable. Fate, that has had its way with the rest of this once-grand structure, saw fit to save one small part of it, the wine cellar. Fortunately, my family's wine cellar was ex-tensive, and there are more than enough rooms here for my needs. I have furnished it as best I can with what I found in other parts of the ruin.'

He led the way.

After descending the stairs, we entered a dim, high-ceilinged chamber. In the centre of the room was a large, old table with about twelve equally old chairs around it, and a ten-pronged candelabra in the middle. Only a few of the candles were lit. The walls were hung with thick, tatty (and somewhat moth-eaten) red and green tapestries depicting a castle of the standard fairy-tale type, with pointy-roofed towers, and soldiers on the battlements, and women in conical hats waving handkerchiefs at departing knights and so on. Perhaps that was how the ruin had once looked. But the most interesting thing was what I at first thought was a dressmaker's mannequin — rather an odd thing for a Dolor-ous Lord to have, I thought — standing next to the fireplace. It was wearing an embroidered dress, and otherwise seemed to be made of polished wood. It had no face, just a blank oval.

'See to the fire, it's going out,' the Dolorous Lord said, and I assumed he was talking to me, so I looked about for a poker, because although I don't know what you're supposed to do with a log fire to stop it going out, I know it involves a poker.

But he wasn't talking to me. He was talking to the mannequin, which turned out to be another of his mechanical creations. It smoothly came to life and put some logs on the fire, then found the poker that had so eluded me (it was on a little rack with a matching brush and pan), and used it to prod the logs, sending shivers of crackling sparks up the chimney, till the fire was lively and warm.

'Wow,' I said — at the mannequin, not the fire. I'm not a caveman.

The mannequin set about putting the rest of the room in order, lighting the unlit candles, taking the Dolorous Lord's cloak from where he'd left it on the back of a chair and hanging it on a hook near the entrance. She even came up to me and, using a very graceful pinching motion of the hands, indicated that she wanted to take my schoolbag. I gave it to her, and she left the room through a curtained archway.

'Um...' I said.

'She is taking your things to a place I have set aside as a guest bedroom, poor though it is,' my host said. 'I am assuming you'll want a rest after your recent adventures.'

'That'd be very nice.'

'Would you like to eat first or after?'

'Ooh, first please.'

The Dolorous Lord was heating some wine in a little cauldron-shaped pot over the fire, and adding spices and herbs from a selection of clay jars on the mantelpiece. 'I would like to hear about your adventures,' he said, 'but there is no hurry.'

'I've got loads of questions, too. I don't really know where I am, you see.'

'You are at the Edge of the World,' he said, in a rather distant voice. 'And, as I said, in the remains of my ancestral home.'

I spent a moment wondering if I should say what I needed to say, then went ahead and said it. 'Actually I don't — well, this is going to sound strange, but — I don't know what *world* I'm in. If you see what I mean.'

The Dolorous Lord regarded me for a moment without any expression. No doubt he was trying to work out if I was a nutter. All he said was, 'Would you like some mulled wine? It will warm you after the cold air and mist above-ground.'

'Okay,' I said, never having had mulled wine or any sort of wine before, but I know wine is what they drink in fantasy books. (And that's when it hit me, where I am. I'm in some sort of fantasy land. I mean, think about it. There was a forest with weird creatures in it. And a knight. (A mechanical one, yes, but still a knight.) And now a castle. (Ruined, yes, but still a castle.) And a lord. (Dolorous, yes, but still... and so on.) And now wine.)

My host poured some of the contents of his little cauldron into two goblets, then handed one to me. I waited till his back was turned before taking a sip, which was the right thing to do, because I couldn't help pull a face at how *bitter* it was. I swallowed (more because he would hear if I spluttered it out) and a moment later felt this warm glow emanating from my stomach, and soon I was taking another sip.

At this point the maid-mannequin returned and began busying herself with pots and pans, preparing a meal. The Dolorous Lord indicated that I should sit at the table, then sat down too.

'So,' he said sadly, 'you don't know what world you are

in.'

'Sorry,' I said, grinning rather foolishly, then taking another sip of wine.

The Dolorous Lord frowned. 'This presents us with something of a problem. Because, although I know what world I am in, it is the only world I know, so I have no name I can give it that might distinguish it from all the other worlds you must know. It is the Realm. That is how I know it. Does the world, or worlds, you come from have a name?'

'I call it the real world,' I said. 'And there's only one of it.'

'Interesting. Does this world you find yourself in now seem less real than your real world?'

'Um, no. But, as it's not the same place... Well, I don't know. I just thought... I'm not very phiso... phisloph... I mean, what's the word?'

'Philosophical.'

'Mm. That,' I said, quickly raising the goblet to take another sip so I could hide my blush. It's silly. I *knew* the word was 'philosophical', why couldn't I *say* it?

The Dolorous Lord, meanwhile, looked thoughtful. 'I wonder...' He frowned and shook his head. 'No. One mustn't allow oneself to hope. Hope is a burden I had thought to rid myself of.'

'Hope?' I echoed, then realised I was butting in on his entirely personal thoughts, but if he speaks them aloud, what can you expect?

He smiled that sad smile. 'These are, perhaps, matters we should discuss later. When you are rested. But I must admit I find it hard to believe there can be any other world than this, the one I've known all my life. It nevertheless opens interesting philosophical possibilities.' (He said that word 'philosophical' rather carefully — getting fumbly with words can be catching.) 'But have you not heard of, or felt the influence of, the — the Princess where you come from?'

Now at this point I thoroughly intended to say something sensible, but for some reason as soon as I opened my mouth everything changed and I came over all gushy. I grinned like a Cheshire Cat and cooed, 'Ooh, a princess? Is there a princess?' I immediately felt stupid, and wondered what was going *on*, but of course I'm used to my mouth behaving in a completely different way from how I want it to, only usually it says *less* than I want, not more. Anyway, I felt another blush rising to my cheeks, so I lifted the wine goblet again for another sip. To my surprise, it was empty.

My host refilled it. 'The Princess is, or perhaps I should say *was*, the very centre of our world. She is the reason for our being. It is her singing that causes the sun to shine, and now, alas, it is her lack of singing that makes it wane. She kept the land intact, but now it is fraying. She gave the people hope, but now...' He sighed. 'It was fated, I suppose. I always felt... It was fated.'

I sniffed, and realised embarrassingly that I was a bit tearful, only I don't know why. I quickly took out my hanky and blew my nose, and then the food arrived, two steaming platefuls of it. I can't, for some reason, remember what it was, but I do remember tucking in like a hungry hobbit.

I also remember saying 'Thank you' to the mannequin-maid, then finding it ridiculously funny that I was saying thank you to a person made of wood and cogs and springs, so at first I found it difficult to eat because I kept giggling, and not just giggling but actually going 'tee-hee, tee-hee' as if I was a cartoon character. Then I'd apologise to my host, because he was so solemn and dolorous and I didn't want him to think I was laughing at him, and then I'd feel so embarrassed I almost burst into tears.

And then... I'm not sure, but I have this vague recollection of suddenly feeling I really liked this doleful man who'd been so kind to me, and I wanted to repay him in some way, and the only way I could think of doing that, of showing how much I liked him, was to tell him everything that had happened to me. I can't be sure, but I do have this recollection of coming out with a torrent of words, telling him everything in one big girly gush. It's a bit embarrassing, now I think back on it. I mean, how much did I tell him? I hope I didn't go into as much detail as to mention, well, Simon Lawne. I hope I just told him about the stairs, not everything else. The thing is, I can't remember. Which is strange, but... Then again, there's how I ended up here, in bed, isn't there? Being carried. And now I have a headache...

You don't think... You don't think I was *drunk* do you? On one cup of wine? Or, actually, two, because he *did* refill my goblet when I emptied it. And that's just what I remember drinking. For all I know I finished the whole lot!

Oh dear.

I seem to have rather embarrassed myself.

Well, it's not the first time.

I think I'll have a snooze for a bit then get up and see if I can find my host. I've got so much to ask him. But not now. Too tired now. Yawny yawn yawn.

Na-night.

Day the next

We're going on a journey.

How exciting!

I don't have much time, but I've got lots to write down, so I'll probably have to leave most of it till my next diary entry, and who knows when that'll be, so here goes.

My host the Dolorous Lord is right now getting everything ready for our journey (for me, this only means doing up my shoelaces, otherwise I wouldn't even have time to write *this*), including winding up the mechanical maid so she's got enough oomph to keep the place in order till he gets back, and seeking out and polishing up his best formals (including a sword, which as a Lord of the Realm it's his duty to wear in case he's called upon, at any moment, to employ it in the service of the Princess, though he explained this is very unlikely to happen in his case as he's hardly the heroic type. His take on things: 'We philosophers seek to kill only illusions and misconceptions. And though it does not involve violence, it is just as perilous a task, though we are rarely, if ever, thanked for our efforts.')

So, a quick *précis*.

Where are we going?

To the Palace of Lord Paladin, no less.

(And who is Lord Paladin? I'll explain in a mo, if I have time.)

How are we going?

On a pair of real non-wind-up horses if you please, so this will be a genuine first for me (instead of the fake first of riding a horse which turned out to be clockwork).

But most importantly, *why* are we going?

Well, you see, it's quite exciting. It's all to do with the Princess, who I've already mentioned, and who my host told me more about yesterday. But what makes it all *so* exciting is that I may actually have some role to play in things. That episode with the glimmerlings, apparently — and this is all just *so* incredible I can barely get it down, but I really mustn't let myself get too excited, because it was only an idea the Dolorous Lord had, and it might not lead to anything, but then again it *might*, and if it *does*, well, what can I say, only that it may be the real reason I was born, it may be my fate, my destiny, it may explain why I never seemed to fit in back there in the world of 49 Willow Drive and school and so on, because all the time I was really meant to be *here*, and if you're thinking you're owed a full-stop by now, I'll oblige before I keep rambling on forever and ever. There. Full-stop. (Remember to breathe, Carol, remember to breathe.)

But here he is, all done up in his (black, of course) finest clothes, so I guess the explanation will have to wait. I'll just say that the next time I write in this diary things may well be very different. Very different *indeed*.

A few days later

Only, they aren't. Different, I mean.

But what can you expect? I'm only me. Not some wonderful wizard or anything.

Anyway, as I've nothing else to do, and I'm in this huge quiet all-to-myself library, I thought I'd write up everything that's happened over the last few days. It may take a while, so forgive me if I take a break or two, but I've got all the time in the world. (Though who knows how long that is. As Philosophus — which is what I call the Dolorous Lord now — said, the sun is dimming and the world is fraying at the edges. But I've got nothing else to do, and it may be years before those fraying edges close in on the Palace, which is where I am. Cheerful thought, but there you go.)

First of all, the crucial conversation that started it, back at Philosophus's family home (or what remains of it) at the Edge of the World.

Once I'd recovered from my (ahem) indisposition (I still felt my head was stuffed with straw and rusty bedsprings, but it wasn't bad enough to prevent me pottering about), I went in search of my host. I found him in the main room where we'd eaten the night before. He was sitting on a chair by the fire, deep in thought, watching the flames flicker and flit. His mechanical maid was standing perfectly still in a balletic pose by the table, as if any moment she might plié or something, though really she was more likely to mop the floor or dust the mantelpiece. Maybe standing on tippy-toes, though.

I gave my usual introductory 'um', and managed to bring a hint of embarrassed apology to it (I'm good at adding various shades of meaning to my introductory ums), as I still wasn't sure how much of a fool I'd made of myself the night before. (All indicators pointed towards a complete raspberry fool with cherries on top, and perhaps some chocolate sprinklings.) But if I *had* embarrassed myself, my host was far too gracious or well-bred (or lost in his own philosophical world) to give a hint of it as he came to and focused on me.

'Ah,' he said, as if I was not a real person but a reminder of one more sad thing to add to his already head-high stack of sad things to remember.

'Good morning,' I said. 'If it *is* morning. If it's not, then, um, good whatever it is.'

'I believe it is morning,' he said gravely, and seemed to want to add, as an antidote to any positive feeling the time of day might suggest, 'Though the world moves ever closer to its final twilight.' But instead he sighed and said, 'I have been thinking...' He lapsed into staring at the flames once more, till the pop of a bursting wood knot brought him out of it. 'But how remiss of me, you will be wanting breakfast.'

'Mm, yes please. If it's not too much trouble, I mean.'

Philosophus nodded, then indicated with a vague gesture that he would leave the practical details to his maid.

The maid didn't move as I approached her, which made me feel a bit self-conscious about talking to her (which is silly, because I'm always talking to inanimate objects back in 49 Willow Drive — mostly the kettle and the washing machine — and of course I always say hi to the weatherman on TV, but I suppose when I do those things I'm on my own, right now I had company), so I went back to my host and said, 'Sorry, but, what's her name?'

'Name? Whose?' He'd gone back to la-la land again.

'Your maid's.'

'She does not have a name. She is mechanical.'

Seeing I wasn't about to get any further help from him, I went back to the unmoving maid and said, 'I don't suppose you've got any, uh, Shreddies, have you?' I had no idea what they eat for breakfast in fantasy land.

The maid came to life, but only to tilt her head very slightly and give it a graceful shake before becoming absolutely still once more.

No Shreddies.

'Um, cornflakes?'

Again, no.

'Um, what *do* you have?'

But of course she couldn't answer that because she couldn't speak. Instead, she indicated I should sit at the table, then set about busying up a breakfast for me, which proved to be toast, jam, and a bowlful of porridge. (Not all mixed together, I should add.)

'Thank you,' I said as she set them in front of me. I cast a quick glance at my host, who was lost in his own thoughts, then whispered to the maid, 'Excuse me, but, uh, did you put me to bed last night?'

The maid nodded.

'I'm so, *so* sorry,' I said.

She gave no indication of how she felt about the matter.

'I didn't, um, do anything too stupid did I? Only I don't remember too well.'

The maid shook her head once, and added a graceful hand gesture to say, 'Think nothing of it.'

I felt a rush of gratitude that made me want to do something nice for her. But what can you do for a mechanical maid? I'd oil her cogs and springs, only she might not appreciate a stranger opening her up and poking about. I'd just get greasy blotches on her dress, anyway. The only thing I could think of was to say, 'Do you mind if I call you Tilly?' which is Princess Iyala's maid's name in *The Wizard of Eldara*.

Tilly thought about this for a moment, then gave a nod which somehow, despite the fact her face was blank as an egg, made me think she was pleased.

She returned to her waiting pose and I tucked into my breakfast. I was midway through my third spoon of porridge (which I've never had before, but it proved to be quite warm and filling, just what I needed) when I realised my host was looking at me curiously.

'You don't mind me calling her Tilly do you?' I said.

'It never occurred to me to call her anything. But perhaps it is better she has a name.' He sounded equally regretful about both these things. His voice turned thoughtful (or more thoughtful than usual). 'You seem to be able to give things names. The glimmerlings, for instance.'

'I just made that up.'

'Nevertheless, it fits. And a name that does not fit is no name at all.'

(Sort of like Selina for me.)

'That is partly what has set me thinking,' Philosophus said.

'Thinking?' I echoed, round a bite of toast.

'About the effect you had on the glimmerlings.'

'Oh, um, that,' I said, still with the vague feeling I'd done something wrong.

'The way you shaped them. The way you named them. The Princess...' He hesitated, then went ahead. 'The Princess used to do that. She named things effortlessly. She gave them form and purpose, a place in the world.'

He looked at me. It was not a normal look. At least, no

one has ever looked at me that way before. It was a look that seemed to be wondering if I was more than I seemed to be.

'Um,' I said, 'what do you... what does that... um...'

Fortunately, my host didn't attempt to unravel what I was trying to say (which is good because even I didn't know — I just felt I ought to say something at that point). He came over and sat opposite me.

'Perhaps,' he said, with the air of someone about to share a sad burden, 'I should tell you something of our world. Something of its history. It may help you understand where you are, and how this world differs from your own. But really it is by way of a preface to something I would ask of you.'

'Okay,' I said, feeling a bit nervous now. What was he going to ask? I mean, it's not as if there's anything special about me that someone — a *lord* no less — has to ask of *me* rather than anyone else.

(Meanwhile Tilly had come to life again and was taking my breakfast things away and replacing them with a pot of tea and two mugs, which she proceeded to fill. I gave mine a suspicious sniff before drinking it, just to be sure it wasn't laced with wine or anything. I wasn't about to repeat last night's performance. And I wanted to remember what my host was going to tell me. It might be important. (It was.))

The Dolorous Lord fixed his gaze on the table between us and adopted a slightly pained peak of the eyebrows, like a headmaster about to inform the parents of a troublesome pupil that it might be better for all concerned if the boy was removed from school and fed only bananas.

'When the Princess first came to our land,' he said, 'she was little more than a babe in the arms of Lord Paladin, her protector. From whence she came, and how far, I do not know, though it is said the armour of Lord Paladin was scratched and burned and bloody, and the man himself sorely wounded. The babe, though, was unharmed and swaddled in clean white cloth. Her parents and all her family had been killed, but of the perpetrators, and the reason for this terrible slaughter, Lord Paladin would not at first speak, nor would he talk of the hardships of his journey.

'Ever since anyone could remember, the girl's coming had been foretold. A Princess would arrive in the land, one day to be Queen, and she would be known by her singing. She would sing the sun to warmth and brightness, she would sing the fields to fruitfulness and plenty, she would sing the people to prosperity and purpose. There was no doubt that this child was the Princess we awaited. Even at the beginning, she sang beautifully, and the land, the sky, the people blossomed. Life became as it had never been before.' He smiled that backwards-into-the-past smile of his. 'All this, of course, I relate as my father told it to me. At the time of her coming, I too was a child, too young to be aware of such things.'

He picked up his cup and stared at the steam rising from it. 'Until such time as she was ready to assume the throne, her protector, Lord Paladin, took her place, ensuring the correct day-to-day running of the realm, and, of course, the safety of his ward. Meanwhile the Princess grew from a babe to a child to a young woman. The Palace, which had awaited her coming in silent emptiness for centuries, became filled with life and light and festival. Before her coming, ours had seemed an aged and dying land, but now it was young again. Every noble, however far from the Palace they lived, sent their children to the Princess's Court to grow up with her, to be near her, to be part of the new life of the Realm, not the old and dying life the parents had known. My father sent me when I was twelve, adjuring me to learn all I could from the Palace's famed library, and to make myself useful at court. Ours was a gloomy home, ever since the death of my mother, whom my father continued to mourn a decade after her passing. I sometimes wonder if he sent me away so he could consume himself entirely with that mourning. Indeed, it was shortly after my arrival at the Palace that I received the letter informing me of his death, a letter composed before the event and in his own hand. In it, he told me not to return to my ancestral home, which he called a place accursed, a place where the very stones seeped the sorrow of generations.'

My host smiled again his pallid smile. 'I was not intending to tell my story, but that of the Realm. However, I find that, in my mind at least, the two are entwined.'

He took a sip from his tea, then returned the cup to the table. 'At the Palace I did as my father bade me. I studied. I did not fit in with the fun and frivolity, the chatter and gamesome chivalry that surrounded the growing Princess. Instead I retreated daily to the library, there to study mathematics, philosophy and the principles of mechanics, which fascinated me. In my sixteenth year I completed my first automaton, and by my eighteenth had perfected the principles enabling me to create the likes of the mechanical knight. My efforts were treated by the other young nobles as an amusing diversion, but Lord Paladin saw their potential. He encouraged me, eventually providing me with my own workshop and laboratory. When I had perfected my art, he commissioned me to build specific types of clockwork mannequin: servants, guardsmen, and so on. For a while I was busy and, perhaps, happy — no, I will say *content*. But lost in my work as I was, I did not realise things were changing in the world.'

I was so lost in my host's story I almost jumped when Tilly came forward to refill our cups. I said a quiet 'Thank you' then went back to listening.

'Things had indeed been changing,' my host continued, in an autumnal tone. 'The air of fun and frivolity had palled. The young nobles had grown bored and listless. Some departed, others merely lounged around, seeking distraction in idle pleasures and passing fashions, never interested in any one thing for longer than it takes a star to twinkle in the sky or a snowflake to melt on the palm. But one day...' He sighed, narrowing his eyes again, and I realised he was completely lost in his own tale. I no longer existed for him, only the past did. 'One day she came to me. The Princess. She came to my workshop. I knew her, of course. I knew who she was. How could I not? She was the centre of our world. But she seemed... not as she was before, not as she should be. Sad, I might say, if she were anyone but the Princess. At first she simply watched me work. Inevitably her followers, those that remained, accompanied her. They joked and played, disturbing me, but I did not complain. Soon they grew bored and departed, as I had expected. But she — she remained. And she returned. Alone. Many times. She would sit and watch me for hours. I did not speak to her except to answer her questions, which were few.' He shook his head. 'One day she asked why I worked so hard. I said it was because it was the one thing I had found myself to be good at. "But," she said, "do you never ask yourself what you work *for*?" I confessed I had, and often. I come from a long line of philosophers and am named for my family's chief profession. How could I not ask such a question? But I had no answer. Perhaps I worked *because* there was no answer. Or because my work itself was the answer, an answer that could not be put into words.' He shrugged. 'I told her this. She seemed troubled, but said no more. That was the last time I saw her. For days, weeks perhaps, I remained in my laboratory, working on the pieces Lord Paladin had commissioned. When I finally emerged, and presented them to Lord Paladin, I learned that a terrible calamity had occurred. The Princess was gone. She had disappeared. No one had thought to inform me, but why should they?'

'Where had she gone?' I asked.

'It was said the Necromancer had taken her.'

I didn't ask who this Necromancer was. With a name like that, you don't have to.

The Dolorous Lord continued. 'A change had come upon the world. The sun rose dimmer and dimmer every day. The young nobles had departed. Lord Paladin spent his hours brooding. Storms gathered about the Palace and darkened the already gloom-shrouded land.'

'Was nothing done to try to get her back?'

'Heroes were sent for. They went in search of her. Heroes are still, I am sure, being sent in search of her. Heroes, and people who think they are heroes. None of them return, and the Princess remains lost.'

'You weren't tempted, then?' I said.

He shook his head, and said the thing about philosophers only killing illusions, which I've already written down. He continued with his story. 'Shortly afterwards, Lord Paladin suggested I return home. He said that as the young nobles were all gone there was no reason for me to stay. That had never been a reason for me to be there, of course, but I had no other reason, so I left. As I journeyed, I realised how much the world was failing now the Princess was gone. I could see it and hear it and smell it all around me, in the dimness of the sky, the wilting of plants, the staleness of the air. When I found my ancestral home in ruins, it was merely what I expected.'

'But what's going to happen?' I said. 'Surely the world's not going to just end? I mean, if it existed before the Princess came, surely it can exist without her?'

He sighed. 'Perhaps. But perhaps not. I sometime think it is... like love.'

'Love?' I said, a little embarrassed at saying the word, but also wondering what on Earth (or not-Earth) he meant.

Distantly, and, as ever, sadly, he said, 'It is possible to live without love, is it not? Yet, once experienced, those that lose it sometimes pine away and die for the lack of it.'

I guessed he was talking about his father, but there was a hint of something else. I've got a nose for tragedy (Miss Michalowski's particular young man, and so on), and I'm sure I was catching a whiff of it now — in the way he kept hesitating before he said 'the Princess', and how, in his story, he hadn't been able to speak to her, only answer her questions. But maybe that's just me, soppy as a sponge and soft as a sack of marshmallows.

'But someone's sure to find the Princess and bring her back, aren't they?' I said.

'Among those that hope, there is always hope,' was the inevitably dour reply. 'But as I have elected to forgo that illusion, I will not answer your question, but instead press on and ask, Lady Carol, the thing I have been thinking about. About you.'

'Yes?' I said, too distracted by wondering what he was going to say to take up that 'Lady' thing with him just now.

He pursed his lips for a moment. 'I cannot be sure, but the effect you had on the glimmerlings is as close as I know to the effect the Princess had on our world. I have not seen even a hint of it in anyone else, and I cannot help but wonder if you might have some of her power.'

Wow. I mean, what can you say to that? What can you *think*?

Well, what I said was, 'Sorry, but all that with the glimmerlings was just an accident. I mean, I'm only *fourteen*. I'm just *me*. I'm not special or anything.'

'Yet you come to our world from another. Is the ability to travel between worlds common where you come from?'

'No. Well, for all I know everyone does it, they just don't tell *me*. But not that I know of.'

'And yet you say there is nothing special about you.'

'But... But... I only came here because I was running away. If I was special in any way, I wouldn't have had to run away, would I? I'm a coward not a... conjurer.'

'In your world, perhaps. But now you are here. And here, you gave form to the glimmerlings and survived.'

I didn't say anything to that. I couldn't. He was right. But it *couldn't* be true, could it?

'I am not asking you to believe what I say,' he continued. 'I am only suggesting we investigate the possibility. The world is dying. It may be that you can keep it alive, perhaps not forever, but perhaps long enough for the Princess to be found and restored.'

'Um... Yes,' I said. I was feeling rather odd about the whole thing. And unreal. (Not surprising, considering I wasn't in the real world.) But I also felt something else, something new: excitement. What if it was *true*? What if I *did* have some magical power here, in this in-need-of-magic land? What if I *could* be like the Princess, even just a bit? What if I was *meant* to be here, not in that old school-and-home world, but here? And not just *being* here, but being magical and important and *someone*. It was all so confusing, such a mess of thoughts and feelings. But what could I do? I said, 'What happens next, then?'

'If you are willing, I will take you to the Palace, and present you to Lord Paladin. He will know what to do. It is not a long journey. And, if nothing else, at the end of it, you will have better quarters than I can offer.'

I bit my lip. 'Alright.'

I mean. I *mean*!

So that's what we decided to do. We started getting ready right away.

There's all sorts of rules for horses, apparently. I mean, I thought you just hoisted yourself into the saddle, said 'Gee up!' or gave a few clicks from the side of your mouth, and the horse took you where you wanted to go. But no. It's tons more complicated.

For instance, you're only supposed to approach them from the left side. This is because if they see you suddenly looming up at them from anywhere else (their eyes are very sensitive to looming, apparently) they get nervous (or 'shy' as the term is, though there's nothing shy about trying to kick you in the shins as far as I can see). But anyway, they're trained to let you loom (slowly) from the left, so you always have to approach from that side.

The trouble doesn't end once you're in the saddle, though. Mine, for instance, a young girl-horse called Even-star (my host can at least name horses), was quite patient in letting me get on her back in my usual klutzy fashion. I clambered belly-wise onto the saddle and wheeled my right leg round to the other side before hauling my way up her neck to sit straight. It worked, but not before I spent a rather sticky moment sliding head first over the other side of the saddle towards the ground.

Then it turned out the reason she'd been so patient was she wasn't intending to move today. She just stood there. I tried pushing myself forward, rocking-horse fashion, but nothing happened.

'Um,' I said, and looked at my host, who had of course mounted in one smooth movement then graciously averted his eyes during my struggles.

He seemed embarrassed. 'Do ladies not ride side-saddle in your world?'

'I'm not a lady, I'm a girl,' I said. 'And some girls don't ride at all, and I happen to be one of them. Last time I was on a bike I fell off. I thought this might be easier, because horses don't fall over. But this one doesn't even seem to move.'

'How does a "bike" differ from a horse?' Philosophus asked, obviously unfamiliar with the word.

'It's got two wheels instead of four legs.'

'Then I am not surprised you fell off it.' I could just *see* him readjusting his opinion of me and the world I came from, and not for the better. He didn't say anything more about it, though, and explained, very patiently, the basics of how to ride a horse, like how you poke the poor thing in the ribs with your heels to get her moving forward. I thought this was rather cruel. Poke me in the ribs, and I'll collapse in a giggling wreck, but horses, it seems, are rather more dignified. (I couldn't help saying sorry every time I did it, though.)

Anyway, we got going, and soon I realised that even once you're moving, things don't get easier. It takes a certain amount of effort to stay upright in the saddle, not a huge amount, but once you've been riding for a few hours, it tells. It also tells on your — how shall I put this? — padded regions. All that bobbing up and down and so on. Anyway, I won't go on about it, except to say I'm *still* a bit stiff and achy, and if I really have to do any more travelling in this world, I might just wait till they invent the bus.

Our journey, first of all, took us through the remains of my host's family home. There was quite a lot of it, about ten minutes' worth, all in ruins. I was preoccupied at first with trying to steer Evenstar past the potholes and collapsed walls and rubble and so on. Only, every time I pulled too hard on the reins she came to a stop and I had to spend some time summing up the courage to jab her in the ribs again. Finally, my host pointed out that she could avoid such hazards well enough on her own, and other than that would naturally follow his horse, so I didn't really have to bother steering.

'Does a "bike" need such constant steering?' he asked, seeming to have come to the conclusion that they were the main form of transport in my world, and sounding a bit contemptuous about the whole thing.

'Only if you're not travelling in a straight line,' I said, which is of course a totally stupid thing to say, but I only realised that, as usual, once the words were out of my mouth. I decided to shut up about bicycles, before he decided I came from a completely country-bumpkin corner of the multiverse and gave up on the idea of taking me to the Palace.

Instead, as my surroundings were pretty much the same as what I'd seen last night, with ruins and damp mist and the occasional mournful leafless tree, I decided to do some serious thinking.

About what?

Well, this world I was in, for instance. It seemed so real, but at the same time it was obviously some sort of fantasy world. It could have come out of any number of books I'd read. As I was going to spend some time here (and it might, even, become my new home), I ought to know more about it. I decided to ask a few questions.

First, the important stuff. 'Are there any dragons here?'

'Not locally.'

'But they *do* exist somewhere in this world?'

'I have never seen one, but of course have heard stories. Do they not exist in your world?'

'No,' I said, in a disappointing-isn't-it tone of voice.

'Yet you know of them, as you ask if they exist here,' he said. 'You know of them, yet they do not exist. A paradox.'

'Well, there are stories about them,' I said.

'How is it you can have a story about something that doesn't exist?'

'Well—' I said, but couldn't come up with an answer.

'It would seem,' my host said, 'that they at least exist in people's minds, otherwise there would be no stories about them.'

'Yeah, but that's not the same as *really* existing, is it?'

'How so?'

'Well, they're not, you know, real.'

'Is a thought real? Or an emotion?'

'Yes...'

'But a dragon isn't.'

'Mm,' I said, feeling a little less sure of myself.

'So what is the difference between a thought and a dragon?'

I blew out a long sigh. '*I* don't know. The wings?'

Mental note: never argue with a philosopher.

I decided to steer the conversation back to my original line of enquiry. 'Cause much trouble do they, dragons?'

'Not locally.'

Oh, ha ha. I mused for a while. 'What about unicorns?'

'Unicorns never cause trouble.'

'I mean, are there any around here? Will we see any?'

'I think it unlikely. I, certainly, have never seen one.'

'Only, um, I wondered because I wanted to know what I should prepare myself for,' I said. 'Like, will we meet any dangers on this journey? Like trolls or ogres or giants?'

My host turned to regard me. 'And how would you prepare yourself for meeting a troll, an ogre, or a giant?'

'I don't know,' I said.

He turned to face the front with no comment.

A moment later, I tried a different tack. 'What about magic?'

'Magic?'

'Yeah, you know. You said about the Princess singing and so on, but do spells and things work? You know, magic. The impossible being made possible, that sort of thing.'

'But the impossible is never possible. By definition.'

Like I said, never argue with a philosopher. (What's the point of making a mental note?)

A little while later, the ruins gave way to forest, and after a brief tussle with a thicket of bracken, we made our way to a track wide enough for us to pick up the pace and ride side by side. Gradually, the mist thinned and the day warmed.

Sometime after noon we stopped in a clearing for lunch. My host produced a loaf of bread and some cheese and made us a pair of crude sandwiches. I, meanwhile, had my first proper look at the sky of this world. Not having seen it before, except through a thick mist, it was difficult to tell if the sun *was* dimming, but certainly it wasn't too bright. (Takes one to know one, Carol.) The sky was mostly cloudy, so that might have had something to do with it. Other than that, it looked pale and wintry, but nothing to be too alarmed about.

There was something I wanted to try. My host had said the thing I'd done with the glimmerlings was the closest he'd seen to anyone doing what the Princess did. So could I make the sun brighter? I felt self-conscious about trying, but I needed to know. I mean, it would be great if I could arrive at Lord Paladin's Palace and point at the newly-brightened sun and say, 'I did that!' But equally it would be horrible to get there, have this enormous build-up about what I might be able to do to save the world only to find I couldn't do anything. (Yes, wouldn't it, Carol?)

And it would be *so* nice to be able to do something. To be able to *be* someone. I didn't want to take over from the Princess indefinitely, I wasn't after anyone's job or anything, but if I could fill in for her till she was rescued, that'd be great. Then afterwards I'd retire (on call for further emergencies, though hopefully there wouldn't be any) and I'm sure they'd give me a nice little cottage or quarters at the Palace, out of gratitude.

And wasn't that what I really wanted? I mean, I'd escaped from all that horrible stuff back in Mundania-Muggleland (Candice Cooper and Mum and so on) and now what I needed was a place to settle down so I could get on with the business of being me.

The trouble was, it all hinged on my being able to do

something magical.

Me.

Magical.

So, while Philosophus was making sandwiches, I took a wander round the clearing to stretch my legs, and when I was in a place where he couldn't see me, I looked at the sky and tried to *will* the sun brighter.

At first, nothing happened. Then a cloud passed in front of it and everything got a bit colder.

I tried not to feel disappointed. I mean, you can't help it if a cloud goes in front of the sun, can you? Unless I was a *negative* version of the Princess who actually made the sun grow dimmer?

I decided not to think about it. You can get into all sorts of muddles if you think too much about things you know nothing about. I went back to the centre of the clearing and claimed my sandwich.

For the rest of the afternoon we rode through forest, occasionally coming across a split in the track or a clearing, but really most of it was the same, hour after hour.

This is something you never read about in fantasy books: how boring it can be travelling long distances. I mean, I used to get bored going on long car trips (back in the days when we went on long car trips), but I'd always have a book to read or something. You can't do that on a horse. Plus, it was getting decidedly dark, and the forest was taking on its spooky night-time aspect. (Just like you or I might put on our pyjamas before bed, forests put on their spooky night-time aspect. Maybe with comfy bed socks.)

'Is this forest going to go on much longer?' I said, just above a whisper, because all that closing-in darkness was making me wary of making any noise.

'We should get out of the forest before we stop for the night, I think,' Philosophus said.

Hmm. Stop for the night. I hadn't thought about that.

'You mean at an inn or something?' I said.

'There are no inns between here and the Palace.'

Hmm.

'So we're just going to stop in the middle of nowhere and sleep?' I said.

'Yes.'

I'd been thinking we might get to the Palace, say, in the early evening (too late now) or at most last thing at night, with time enough for us to be ushered off to plush beds to get a good sleep and be all fresh for our audience with Lord Paladin in the morning. I hadn't considered the possibility of having to stop and *camp*. In the middle of nowhere. And anyway, where was our tent? We didn't seem to be carrying enough baggage to include a tent. Unless it was a magical tent that folded down to matchbox size and popped up on command into a nice warm bungalow, complete with central heating, electric blankets on the beds, and something nice just about to go ping in the oven. But my host had said he didn't know anything about magic.

I peered into the gloomy woods around us. I could hardly see more than ten feet into the mass of branches, brambles and undergrowth. There always seemed to be movement just beyond where I could see, making me think of trolls, ogres, and giants (small, foresty ones, anyway), not to mention wolves and bears and, I don't know, aardvarks. (I still don't know what they are.) Anything could be lurking out there, waiting for us to stop and sleep so it could nibble our toes.

'Should we start collecting firewood?' I said.

'Firewood?' my ever-distant host said.

'For a camp fire.'

'You think we should have a fire?'

'Don't we have to keep wolves at bay?' I said. 'And won't we need it to keep warm?'

My host considered this. 'Perhaps.'

'Well, what do you usually do when you go this way?'

'On the previous instance I travelled this route, I simply found myself a place to sleep and slept. I never considered the possibility of being harassed by animals. And, as for keeping warm, I simply wrapped myself in my cloak. However, it was warmer then... I am hardly a seasoned adventurer, I'm afraid. My journey to the Palace, and my journey back nine years later, represent the sum total of my travelling experience, and, for that reason, I did not think to bring tinder and flint for the lighting of fires.'

'But we can just rub two sticks together, can't we?' I said.

'We can?'

'Well... don't you know about this sort of stuff?'

'As I said, I am hardly a seasoned adventurer.'

I began to feel worried. And annoyed. My host, after all, was the responsible adult. Wasn't he supposed to think about these things? I felt the urge to turn round and go back, however long it took, and start the whole journey over again, only this time with firewood and a tent and matches and a first-aid kit and flares and an inflatable dinghy and, I don't know, everything we might possibly need.

Ten minutes later we emerged from the forest. It was night now, no denying it. The sky was dark and cold, with the occasional cloud drifting across the stars. (And I don't know what the Big Dipper looks like, so I couldn't do that visitor-in-another-world trick of seeing if the constellations were different and therefore really knowing this wasn't Kansas anymore. I just accepted that for a fact anyway.) The track took a turn downwards and to the right, wrapping itself round this huge rock that rose over us in a dark craggy hump. We followed it for a few minutes then my host pulled to a halt.

'This is where I stopped last time I went to the Palace,'

he said. 'It will do as good as any.'

There was a little indent in the side of that huge rock, deep enough for us to lie down in. A half-tree, half-vine had attached itself to the rock wall, and we tethered the horses to it. My host went through various end-of-the-day things with the horses, then wrapped himself in his cloak and I wrapped myself in the blanket he fortunately *had* thought to bring along, then we lay down and slept.

Or tried to.

What I mean is, my host slept but I didn't.

For a start, it was cold. It was also noisy. The forest wasn't that far away, and apart from the constant shushing of leaves in the breeze, making it sound more like a sea-shore than a forest, there was also the occasional hoot and the odd yelp, and all sorts of other sounds I have no word for and didn't want to think what might be making them anyway. But I *did* think about what might be making them, because that's what you do when you're as much of a scaredy-cat as I am. You think about what scares you. On and on and on.

I must have spent hours like that, trying to get comfort-able on the bumpy ground, trying to keep warm with this one blanket, trying to ignore the sounds, trying to sleep. At some point I drifted, and dreamed in that mixed-up half-dream can't-sleep way you do when you're ill. I thought I was back in my old bed in 49 Willow Drive. Only, it wasn't a pleasant dream with hot chocolate in my hand and a bedside lamp and a book to read. No, I lay there in the dark staring at the glowing blocky numbers on my bedside clock. It was 4:38 a.m., and I knew it was Monday morning, and soon I'd have to get up and put on my school uniform and go to school and face Candice Cooper.

Did I say I dreamed? I nightmared. I totally nightmared.

But that wasn't the worst thing that happened. I wasn't going to write about this, but it would be cowardly to leave it out, and though I'm a coward in most things, I at least don't want to be in my diary-writing, so here goes.

I pulled myself awake and lay there for a while trying to stop slipping back into that horrible dream. I had no idea what time it was. The night seemed endless. But I didn't care if I had to sit awake for every hour-long minute of it, just so long as I didn't have that nightmare again.

Then I heard a noise. A quiet noise, somehow making itself heard against all the other night noises. At first I told myself to ignore it, but I kept hearing it, again and again. It was close, and getting closer. It wasn't my host, who was sleeping snorelessly beside me, wrapped in his black cloak, and it wasn't the horses. It was coming from a little way off, in another direction. It was the sort of sound that stands out because it's trying not to be heard. A creeping-up-on-you sound. A furtive, shuffling, dragging step.

It came again, even closer.

I stared. Something moved against the stars, blacking them out, but wasn't it just a cloud?

The sound again. Closer than before. So close I could feel it.

My torch was right beside me in my schoolbag, but I couldn't move. I was terrified like I've never been before. Something was out there in front of me. Something that had tried not to be heard. Something I didn't want to see or hear or think about, but it was there, and I was really here, not in a dream, so I had to do something.

I heard that dragging step again, and it was so close now it was too much. I grabbed my bag and had it open and my torch out all in about a tenth of a second.

For a moment I just hugged it. I wasn't sure I wanted to turn it on. I couldn't hear anything now, and I was gasping in terror, shivering.

I turned the torch on.

Nothing. Nothing was there. Only night.

I could have laughed. I could have cried. I had just earned my B.A. in Cowardice from the University of Life, and that had been my dissertation, on Scaring Yourself Silly. Thank you, no ceremony please.

I shone the torch about, just to make sure.

And there it was. The thing I'd heard. Standing to the side, looking at me. It was skinny, impossibly skinny. Its limbs were bone-thin and sticking out at odd spiky angles, like it had been hastily put together or was trying not to fall apart. But it was human-shaped. Worryingly human-shaped. The one thing I most remember, and the one thing I most want to forget, though I doubt I ever will, is its face, because that of course was where I shone my torch. It didn't seem to have much flesh on its head, and certainly no lips, just grinning skull-teeth. Its eyes were dark holes.

I screamed.

I dropped my torch. I made a grab for it, but the way it rolled on the ground and flashed its light all over the place made me think the thing was coming for me so I just clamped up in a ball as tight as I could and waited.

Nothing happened.

A moment later I heard a sleepy voice. 'What is the matter?'

It was the Dolorous Lord. My scream had woken him up.

I grabbed my torch and shone it around. The thing was gone. There were only the horses and the stars and me and my travelling companion.

I said, 'It — there was a — just there — it — it made these noises — I saw it's *face...*'

Philosophus walked off to check the horses and look around.

'Was it a wolf?' he said.

'No, it was *not* a wolf.'

'What was it?'

'I don't know.' I tried to describe it, but made my usual mess of things.

My host nodded quietly, then thought for a while before saying. 'Perhaps we should journey on.'

'But what was it?'

'Probably a dream,' he said. But I could tell from the way he said it that he was really saying, 'Don't think of that now. Let's call it a dream and get going.'

But of course I couldn't help thinking of it, still out there in the dark, watching us. I got up onto Evenstar (and kept the blanket wrapped around me because I was shivering like a jelly on a washing machine) and all I could think of was that face.

Whenever I thought of that face I thought of something else, too. I thought of dead things, and the word 'Necromancer'.

Morning came slowly. I was knackered. Not only had I gone for most of the night without sleep, but that fright had taken a lot out of me. It was a real chore just to hang onto Evenstar's reins and stay upright. Every so often I'd find myself drifting off, then I'd wake with a start to find myself sliding out of the saddle. I'd grab on, Evenstar would give a hrruph that I guess is the horse equivalent of 'Tuh! Humans...' then I'd get myself upright and vow to stay awake, only to start drifting once more.

As it got lighter I woke up properly. We were travelling through country made up of low grassy hills with nothing on the horizon for ages except more low grassy hills. Every so often there'd be this sea of purple-flowered thistles, then we'd go over the next hill and there'd be nothing but long, bleached-looking hummocky grass again, with not a dot of colour. Quite often you'd see hares (Philosophus told me they were hares, otherwise I'd have thought they were big long bunnies) bounding around in search of, well, whatever it is hares eat. I thought it was carrots, but if they eat carrots, how come they have to run so fast? Unless maybe carrots here have developed wheels and thistle-juice-powered motor engines or something. Anyway, I didn't enquire into the ecology of the region, I had other things on my mind.

I waited till it was definitely day (the sun was up, though pale and cold-looking) before broaching the subject with my travelling companion.

'Will we reach the Palace today?' I said.

'Sometime after noon, if I remember correctly,' he said.

'Um, what do you think that thing was last night? Do you really think it was a dream?' I bit my lip, half wanting to suggest it might have been the Necromancer, half wanting to keep quiet, because if he agreed I'd be even more scared than I was now.

'*Was* it a dream?' he asked.

'I really don't think so.'

He frowned. 'Was it not something from your world, something that followed you here? This enemy of yours, this Candice Cooper you spoke of?'

Now that made me laugh, which was a nice feeling after all that scaredy glumness I'd been toiling through all morning. 'I know she's a fright to look at, but she's not *that* bad. Unless maybe that's her true face, and she wears a mask to cover it at school. But I don't think so.'

'Then I cannot think what it might have been.'

'Maybe I should just forget it,' I said. That little laugh had made me feel a whole lot better, and I wanted to put it all behind me. We'd reach the Palace today, so there'd be no more sleeping in the open. I had no need to worry about what that thing was. Already it was just a memory. Once we reached the Palace I could forget it entirely.

Didn't I have better things to think about, anyway? Like whether I was going to work magic on the sun and the rest of the world like the Princess did? I suddenly thought, 'You know, I'm *owed* a little magic after all that horrible stuff I had to put up with back in the real world. So maybe I deserve to be able to do something like that. To be important like that.' This made me feel better and I spent the rest of the journey thinking about that rather than what happened the night before.

A few hours later, about mid-morning, my host pointed out a little black speck that had appeared on the horizon. It was difficult to see because the sky there was mostly cloud, and black cloud at that, but as we travelled I could make out this dark point sticking up against the clouds.

'The Palace,' Philosophus said, and he actually sounded, if not happy, then certainly not unhappy. He might have been saying 'Home' and looking forward to being there. But even as he said it, he seemed to catch himself and quickly looked solemn again, as if reminding himself not to feel good about anything, which made me wonder why he was like that.

As we rode, the Palace grew closer but didn't fully reveal itself till we came to the peak of this one big hill that had been hogging the horizon for the past half-hour or so. Before the hill, all was pale grass and patches of heather, but on the other side, after a brief run of thicker, darker grass, it gave way to a down-slope of bare earth and scatterings of rock. The Palace was a tall spire set in a high outcrop of dark rock, which wrapped around it like a protecting hand. The Palace was built of rock that was darker still, in fact was pretty much black. That, along with the storm clouds gathered above it, and the bare earth and craggy rocks around it, made me double-take on the whole thing. It didn't exactly look like the home of some sweet magical wonderful Princess. It looked the opposite. But maybe that was because the Princess was gone.

We started down the slope of that last hill and picked our

way through the rocks, which I soon realised weren't rocks but ruins. I cast a look at my host, who was troubled. A little more troubled than usual, anyway.

'Are these ruins?' I said.

He looked at me blankly, then nodded slowly. 'There used to be buildings here. Homes and shops, traders, entertainers, people who had attached themselves to the life of the Palace. A town of sorts, growing into a city.'

'When you say "used to be"..?'

'The last time I was here.'

'A few *months* ago?'

He nodded.

'But can this really have happened in only a few months?' I said, because we weren't talking about abandoned buildings with sagging roofs and maybe the odd broken window, we were talking about fragments of walls and piles of rubble that only *hinted* at buildings being here, centuries ago.

Philosophus shrugged. 'It is the way the world is now. Fading, fraying, dying.'

We spoke no more about it, but picked our way down what was once the main street towards the Palace entrance. This proved to be a pair of enormous doors meeting in a pointy-topped arch. One of the doors had a smaller door set in it, about the right size for carriages and people on horses, while the other had an even smaller door set in it, this time just right for people on foot. Obviously they only opened the main doors on really grand occasions. (Or for really big people.) Around the edge of the main door was a carved design of roses and intertwining thorny stalks, which made me think of the wall of thorns around Sleeping Beauty's castle, an odd choice for a Princess's Palace, but there you go.

We dismounted (something I was just about getting used to) and approached the mid-sized door.

My host stood before it, doing nothing.

'Shouldn't we knock?' I said.

'Usually there is no need.' He looked a bit helpless at finding things other than how he'd expected. He raised his hand slowly, obviously hoping he'd be proved right before he had to prove himself wrong, and then, just before he knocked, the door swung slowly inwards.

'Ah,' my host said, a hopeful look on his face.

The space on the other side of the door was dark, and remained so until the door was fully open. Then a figure came forward bearing a warmly-glowing lantern.

'Ah,' my host said again. 'This must be...'

But whoever he was expecting, it wasn't. The figure was one of his blank-faced mechanical mannequins. It ushered us in and said, in neutral tones, 'I will inform Lord Paladin of your arrival.'

We entered the darkness of the Palace to find ourselves in a large hall or courtyard. It was cold in there, and dreadfully dark, but I could make out various doorways and staircases leading to other parts of the Palace (none of which had even a hint of light coming from them). The mechanical servant began climbing one of the staircases with a slow, regular step. There was no one else about, and no other sound.

We stood for a while in silence. Then my host suggested we see to the stabling of our horses, as the Palace servants who usually dealt with such things were obviously busy elsewhere.

I managed to help this time, and gave Evenstar a thank-you pat on the nose. I don't know, but she seemed to appreciate it, now our twin ordeal (me as inexperienced rider, she as patient ridden) was over.

We returned to the courtyard to kick our heels for a bit.

My host was silent.

'It's rather quiet here,' I said.

'Yes. Yes.' The first yes was of the 'let's pretend it's mildly curious not disturbingly odd' kind, while the second was more of the 'best not to think about it at all' variety.

I bit my lip. 'Was that one of your mechanical servants, then?'

'Yes.'

'Um... Are there any real-people servants here?'

'Yes. At least, there were.'

We waited.

After a while, against the vast dark silence of that huge courtyard, and all the other dark silences winding off it in the shape of stairways and archways and corridors, we heard steps approaching.

I began to feel nervous. My host looked hopeful.

It was only the mechanical servant returning.

She (it wore a dress, so I'll call it a she, but of course she was really an it) descended at the same slow, even pace she'd used to ascend. She came to a halt in front of us and said, 'Lord Paladin will see you as soon as possible. Please follow me and I will take you to where you can rest and refresh yourselves after your journey.'

'Thanks,' I said.

Philosophus said nothing.

We began the long tramp up the stairs. About halfway up, the servant said, 'Was your journey here a pleasant one?'

I looked at Philosophus, who said nothing. So I whispered, 'Should we answer?'

He shrugged. 'It was merely a pleasantry. This particular automaton does not pay attention to the replies, but asks so as to pass the time it takes to lead us to our quarters.'

'Oh,' I said.

A dozen or so steps later, the servant said, 'And what of the weather?'

We left the stairs and started down a corridor. The lamp

the servant carried started to flicker, and I was beginning to get worried in case it went out and the servant didn't realise (having no eyes), but just carried on walking in the dark, leaving us behind. There was no other light. The whole Palace seemed to be empty and dark.

The mechanical servant said, 'Do you intend to stay long at the Palace?'

It was eerie hearing these one-sided snippets of conversation, but it would have been silly to answer, so I stayed quiet, and thought that at least, if the lamp *did* go out, we'd be able to track her in the dark by these bites of chit-chat.

After a few turns, and another flight of steps, we entered a chamber where the mechanical servant set about lighting candles in four tall holders placed in the corners. Curtained archways led from the room, and a quick peek showed me that two led to alcoves containing beds, while the other led to a big brass bath, though without taps or any means of filling it.

'Should I fetch water?' the servant said.

I looked at my host.

He seemed lost to the world, so I said, 'Don't worry. How, um, long do you think we'll have to wait?'

'Lord Paladin will see you as soon as possible.'

'Thanks, then,' I said, and the servant left.

I listened to her evenly-measured footsteps recede into the dark, then turned to my host.

'There doesn't seem to be anyone else here.'

'That can't be,' he said, frowning and shaking his head. 'They must be...' But he couldn't think of what they must be, or where.

There were a few chairs in the chamber, and some things provided for us to amuse ourselves: a chess-like game on a small table, a tiny piano-like instrument with some disordered sheets of music, and a bookshelf with about twenty books on it.

I had a quick browse through the books, but even though the first one I picked out was this fabulously illustrated bestiary, I suddenly found myself yawning fit to drop, and realised that now was the time to take advantage of the bed not the bookshelf. I had to do just one thing before I went to bed, though. I flicked through the bestiary to see if it had anything about aardvarks in it. It didn't. So I guess aardvarks are one of those beasties that exist only in the real world, not in this fantasy one. Is that a good thing? I have no idea. Perhaps with a name like that, they're fantastic enough as it is.

I told my host I was going to lie down, but he merely nodded and went back to his thoughts. I was just thinking, 'I'll probably never get to sleep in this creepy place,' but the next thing I knew, Philosophus was standing over me saying, 'Lord Paladin will see us now.'

We were led, by the same servant (or so I assume — with eggs for faces you can't always tell), to an antechamber (or waiting room, as normal people call them), where again we found ourselves surrounded by chairs to sit on, only this time nothing to amuse ourselves with, which was a good sign, as it meant we weren't going to have to wait long.

The servant disappeared through a large, important-looking double door made of dark wood with great bands of iron studded onto it, which I guessed led to Lord Paladin's audience chamber.

As soon as we were alone I said, 'Are you sure we still *want* to see him?'

'Why should we not want to?' Philosophus said.

'*Look* at this place. It's all empty and dark. Everyone's gone. It's all ruins and dark clouds outside. What's going on?'

Philosophus shook his head slightly. 'It is what is happening to the world. Naturally, here it should appear much worse than elsewhere. This is the Palace of the Princess, the Heart of the World.'

'But what about all the people?'

'Lord Paladin doubtless sent them away for their own good, but has stayed to brave the storm himself. He is a Great Man.' (And he really did say it with capitals.)

Not knowing anything about Lord Paladin, I couldn't argue. (Anyway, remember that mental note?) A second later, the servant returned, curtseyed, and held the door open for us to go through to the next chamber.

I let my host go first, and kept an eye on him to see what I should do — you know, bow at every third step, or whatever. I was also on the lookout for signs that something was wrong, in case it meant we had to make a dash for it.

The chamber was long and high, and again mostly dark, though it had windows, the first I'd seen since entering the Palace. They were stained glass, but it was difficult to make out the pictures because it was so dark outside. The ceiling was a mass of straight and arching beams, making lots of dark corners up there.

Lord Paladin sat on a chair, or throne I should say, at the far end of the hall. It was raised off the floor on wide stone steps, and had a high back carved with the same roses-and-thorns design I'd seen round the Palace door. Here, though, the roses formed a circle near the top, where Lord Paladin's head would have been, had he been sitting up straight, not as he was, leaning forward with his head on his fist. In the centre of this circle of roses was a disc made of coloured stone. I didn't get a close look at it, but I think it was a map of the world.

Anyway, I was of course far more interested in Lord Paladin himself. He was a big man, broad and strong, a warrior-type — that much was obvious, not just from his size, but from the fact he was wearing full armour, including a helmet. He was entirely covered in metal. It was a dark, rough-looking metal that made me think each plate must be inches thick, and if you touched it, might sandpaper your skin away. His helmet was spiked at four points, like a thin and icy crown, and had an axe-blade ridge down the centre, ending in another sharp point just beneath his chin. The eye-slits, of course, were dark. (And there were no breathing sounds. With a get-up like that, you'd have expected something Darth Vader-ish, but I couldn't hear a whisper.)

Every part of him was mailed or plated. His gloved hands looked massive and heavy, and were weapons enough on their own, without the need of the huge sword resting against the throne by his side. That sword was taller than me, which I know might not be saying much, but it was probably heavier than me, too. It made me wonder how strong this fellow was. (I had absolutely no doubt he could not only lift it, but swing it around in all sorts of dramatic poses.)

I was, I must admit, both awed and scared at standing in the presence of this man (who hadn't said a word as we approached). You could just *feel* that he was a hero, a man who had been through lots of dangerous, difficult stuff and come out the other end scarred but alive and absolutely determined. There was, apart from his armour, a real *weight* to him, if you see what I mean, like the very air was dead-still out of sheer respect. But there was also the feeling that you'd never get to know him — all that stuff he'd been through, all that heroism and so on had made him utterly *different*, maybe better, maybe not, but certainly removed from what it meant to be a normal person. Isolated in his own inner fortress. I mean even I, who thought myself weird as a tartan mongoose, felt completely dull and ordinary in the presence of Lord Paladin.

'Lord Philosophus Dolorous,' he said, once we'd bowed. His voice, need I say it, was deep and powerful. It didn't ring around in his helmet, it rang around the *room*. But it also sounded tired, dry and, I must say, a little unwelcoming.

'Lord Paladin,' my host said, bowing again.

'I thought not to see you again, Philosophus. I bade you leave and not return.'

'And I would have done so, had I not found sufficient reason to risk your displeasure,' Philosophus said, with yet another bow (and this was thankfully the last of them — if I had to curtsey every time someone said something I might end up bow-legged). 'I find the Palace much changed in the short time I have been away.'

'The Palace has not changed. It is the world outside that dies and fades.'

'There is no news of the Princess, then?'

There was a pause long enough to make me wonder if this was one of those questions you weren't supposed to ask. Finally Lord Paladin said, 'None.'

'But what of the heroes? Have any returned or sent word?'

'None have returned. None have sent word.'

The Dolorous Lord shook his head sadly. 'More will have to be sent then?'

Again, that awkward pause. The silence became so oppressive it made me want to edge out backwards and hide somewhere. 'There are no more to send,' Lord Paladin said. 'No, Philosophus, now I await the Necromancer myself. He will come here. And when he does, I will face him, and face him alone. We are at the final play in this game, and this, the Palace, will be the final arena. You did not do well in coming back.'

This left Philosophus somewhat at a loss for words. He stared at the ground, blinking for several moments, then said, 'I see.' He said it in the resigned tone of someone who has realised things are so bad there's no point in feeling anything about them anymore.

And if that was so, what of Lord Paladin? I hadn't been able to detect any emotion whatsoever in anything he'd said. But how could that be, considering *what* he'd said? I just couldn't imagine. It was terrible. Like he was dead inside. Like everything was dead to him.

I realised his dark eye slits had turned to regard me. He said, 'I sensed, several days ago, an intrusion into our realm from outside...'

I took a dry swallow. Here goes, I thought. Now's where I have to explain myself. But I was suddenly so nervous I couldn't remember my name, let alone why I was here. Typical Carol. I *so* wanted to be able to do something to help this world, but my voice, faced with the challenge, took the coward's way out and I could barely manage a throat-preparing squeak of a cough, let alone say anything.

Fortunately, my host came out of his reverie (though dull-eyed and dull-voiced in a way that made me wonder if he believed there was any point in introducing me now). 'This is Lady Carol Selina Tanner.' (*Why* did I have to tell him my middle name?) 'She comes from another world. I brought her here because she has abilities that may be of use.'

If those eye-slits in Lord Paladin's helmet could have narrowed, they would have. He seemed to regard me even more intently than before, though of course I couldn't tell, because he was hiding behind that metal mask of his. But I certainly felt it. It was like he was X-raying me, dividing me up into atoms and interrogating each one. I couldn't breathe till finally he said, 'Abilities?'

'Shaping abilities, naming abilities,' Philosophus said, a little more keenly as his hope returned. 'She had an effect on the liminal beings who dwell in the Edgewood. She named them glimmerlings, and caused many of them to assume new shapes.'

'You saw this?'

'She told me the tale herself.'

'But you put it to the test?'

Philosophus stuttered for a moment. 'Ah, uh, no. Yet I see no reason to disbelieve her. She had no knowledge of what the liminal beings are, or what their nature is, when she told me.'

Pause. 'How long did the reshaping last? How many did it effect? How thorough was it?'

Again, my host was a bit flustered before replying. 'Ah, um, several dozen — I believe?' (He turned to me for confirmation, and I nodded, still dumbstruck by the whole situation.)

Lord Paladin sat back in his chair with the dull scrape of metal against stone. 'Untested, then. And unproven. A lapse in your usual philosophical rigour, Lord Dolorous.'

'Ah, yes,' Philosophus said, and bowed his head. He obviously wanted to say something more but couldn't put it into words, so in the end shook his head and went through that process of chiding himself for hoping, and reminding himself not to do it again.

Watching him, I began to sense what the relationship between my host and Lord Paladin was. Philosophus had left his home at the age of twelve and come here only to find he didn't fit in. The one person he'd connected with was the man in front of us, Lord Paladin. It was no wonder my host saw him as something like a father. And now he'd been shamed by him. It made me feel ashamed, too, because I felt it was my fault.

So, before that nervous worrying part of me could realise what I was doing and play its usual tricks, I said, 'Can't we at least try? I — I mean, I don't know if I can do anything to help, but it *is* true about the glimmerlings, and I'm willing to try anything, well, to do whatever needs to be done. I'm not trying to replace, um, anyone, I just thought, well...'

I ran out of steam.

At first Lord Paladin continued to regard me in silence as if I hadn't said anything, or as if what I'd said had come out in some garbled otherworld gibberish that didn't make sense.

But no, I'd said enough, and it had been understood. He rose (strangely quietly in all that armour) and stepped down from the throne. (Though he was so much taller than me it didn't make much difference.) He looked down at me for a moment, and I somehow gained the courage to look back into those dark eye-slits in search of real human eyes, and though I saw none, I felt a bit more sure there *were* some, somewhere in there, just as there must be a human heart beating behind that great metal breastplate.

He put a hand on my shoulder. (Not too heavily, thankfully, otherwise I might have collapsed. Not only must those gauntlets weigh a ton apiece, but I was as weak-kneed as if my legs had turned to slinky springs.) He didn't say anything, but turned me, gently, to face the wall with the stained-glass windows.

A gap must have opened in the clouds outside, perhaps at that very moment, because the stained glass windows were glowing with colour and I could see what they were.

There were four windows. In the first, a woman whose face you couldn't see was on her knees, bowing her head, while a figure in dark robes held a sword above her, obviously about to bring it down. In the second, it was a man who was on his knees, surrounded by horrible imp-like goblin creatures, all sharp eyes and teeth. In the next window there was a different man, dressed in armour — recognisable armour, for it could only be Lord Paladin — and in the crook of one arm he held a bundled-up baby, while with the other he swung that Carol-length sword that was now resting against the throne, and there were bright splinters of red glass glowing like fairy-lights in the sunlight, representing the blood spilled as he swung it. The fourth window showed that same man, Lord Paladin, tiny now, standing in front of the great spire of the Palace, alone except for the baby in his arms.

From behind me, Lord Paladin's dry, dark voice spoke. 'I see the events depicted in these windows every day. Not here in this room, but in the dark, before I open my eyes. I see them as I walk the corridors. I see them when I close my eyes to sleep. The slaughter of the Princess's parents. My battle to save her. My long, weary journey to this place. And so much more, so much more. Yet I lived through it. And I lived for one reason: to protect the Princess. She is the Soul of the World, the Heart of the World, the Life of the World. And every step of the journey from that far place where her parents were murdered, every painful breath I took against my wounds and exhaustion, I took because I had to protect her. I was dying, I was a walking death, yet I lived because I knew there was no one else to protect her. I survived through will alone, that she may live.'

The gloved hand left my shoulder, though I still felt the ghost of its weight.

'And now,' he said, 'something terrible has happened. She has gone. I have failed. Is there hope? I am alive. Therefore there must be hope. But it is a distant hope, unseen by me. And it is a terrible hope, a burden not a boon. I would die if I could, I would rest. But she must be protected. Therefore I continue as I always have, as when I travelled step by weary step, each seeming my last, to this Palace, bearing the child-Princess in my arms. You ask if we can try? We will try.'

'What, um, do we do next, then?' I said, in a very small voice.

'We will go to the chamber in which the Princess sang,' Lord Paladin said. 'There we will try you.'

It's now very late indeed. I would say everything's dark and quiet here in the Palace, but everything's dark and quiet here anyway, so that's no way to say how late it is. I've been writing all day. I just got to the end of that last bit and my biro died, so here I am with a fresh one, and I may as well push on and bring everything up to date. (It's either that or wend my way through the empty Palace corridors to the room I've been given to sleep in, but I don't fancy doing that, so writing in my diary is a good way of putting it off.)

So, back to a more solemn moment.

Lord Paladin led us through the Palace, up yet more spiralling stairs. He didn't walk, he *strode*, and even Philosophus had to give a little run every other step to keep up. (Fortunately my erstwhile host had also grabbed a lantern from the waiting room, otherwise we'd have been striding through the Palace in total darkness. Lord Paladin, apparently, doesn't need any light to know where he's going.)

The Singing Chamber, as it was called, was at the top of the tallest spire that rose from the top of the Palace. It was a round room, taking up that whole floor of the tower. A midnight blue curtain ran round the entire wall (we had come up through a hatch in the floor, so there wasn't even a break for a door). In the very centre of the floor was a white marble disc with brass compass-points on it, and Lord Paladin instructed me to stand there, so I did, feeling rather self-conscious, like I was in a spotlight. All that long walk to get here, I'd been trying *not* to think that this was the point where I'd find out whether I could do anything magical or not, whether I was going to be the one to help this world out of the darkness it had fallen into, and so find myself a new and wonderful home, and so on. I'd been trying not to think of these things, but of course they'd been whizzing round my head like a horde of roller-skated gremlins. Now I was actually here, standing on the spot I had to stand on, I was nervous. But, oddly, not as nervous as I've been in other situations. I mean, like that time I went up to Simon Lawne and gave him back his pencil case. (Simon Lawne! It's funny thinking of him. He seems so long ago and far away.) But anyway, I was less nervous than that. (Which I took, rather foolishly, for a good sign.)

Lord Paladin and Philosophus kept to the edge of the room, leaving me in the centre.

'It is here the Princess stands and sings every morning,' Lord Paladin said. Then, in a quieter voice, 'Where she *will* stand and sing again every morning when she returns.' He went to a tasselled rope close to the hatch through which we'd made our entrance, and with a pull made all the curtains gather themselves upwards to reveal that the wall of the room was made up almost entirely of windows, so you could pretty much see 360 degrees all around.

From here, the Princess looked out on the world as she sang her magic song. No doubt for her it was all bright morning sun and glittery dew. She'd have seen all the forests like thick fluffy carpets of green, with rug-ruffles of hills, and shiny lakes, and snail-trail rivers, and little blocky clumps of villages and houses, and patchwork farms, and rocky places like scatterings of gravel and so on. I saw nothing but black cloud. It wasn't right up against the window, it was just far enough away that I could see it as cloud, not mist, and see the way it was constantly moving. Sometimes I'd see a bright spot where, deep inside, lightning was crackling away. Thunder came straightaway, with no elephants to count, so you knew it was right on top of us. It shook the windows.

I looked at this great wall of darkness and for the first time admitted to myself there was nothing I could do. I mean, here I was, finally faced with it, and somehow I knew this was a really massive task, way beyond me. You don't just hum a little ditty or think nice bright thoughts and banish a writhing mass of storm-cloud that thick and heavy. You don't just wish the sun brighter, or the world better. Maybe the Princess can — could — but I can't.

I didn't say that. Instead, I looked at the Dolorous Lord and saw how much he was trying not to hope that I would come up with something really wonderfully magical, and how beneath that trying-not-to-hope he was desperately hoping. Lord Paladin's metal fizog, of course, was unreadable, but I guess he was going through something similar.

I said, 'What does she — I mean, what do *I* do now?' '

'The Princess sings,' Lord Paladin said, his voice less boomy than before, and perhaps a little awed (not by me, of course, but by his memories of the Princess). 'What she sings has not been written. It comes from deep within. It is new every time. It is pure.'

Right. Can you do that Carol? No.

But I said, 'Um, anything else?'

'No.'

Now, I *don't* sing. I may wail along with the radio a bit, but only when I'm alone. In Music, at school, when we sing, I never sing loud enough to hear myself against the racket everyone else is making. What I do, if I can't get away with mouthing, is one up from mouthing. I just *don't* sing.

I stood there for a while, looking out at that black billowing cloud, and it seemed to be laughing at me, mocking me.

I thought, 'I can't do it.'

'Um, does she, um, sing on her own, up here?' I said.

'Yes, of course,' Philosophus said. 'We should leave Lady Carol to try this on her own.'

'Um, just Carol,' I said. 'Not "Lady".'

Lord Paladin seemed reluctant, but turned and descended through the hatch, followed by Philosophus, who looked at me, maybe considered giving an encouraging smile, then decided against it and looked solemn as he disappeared through the hatch, which he closed behind him.

I sighed.

I stepped off the white marble disc and went to look through the window. Peering down, I couldn't see much of the Palace. All was darkness and cloud. Up was just as bad. I sighed again, misting the window.

I went back to stand in the centre.

I tried something. Something really silly. I tried singing. The only thing I could think of was 'Twinkle, twinkle, little star'. (Like I said, really silly.) Nothing happened. Lightning flashed, thunder growled, but the clouds didn't part and show me a twinkling star, nothing like that.

I told myself not to be so stupid. Nothing was going to happen. I should have realised it from the start. I'd thought, all the way here, that I deserved something magical to happen to me, but all that time I hadn't thought of the reality of the situation, I hadn't thought that at some point I'd have to stand here and make the magic come out of me. There *was* no magic in me. I wasn't 'meant' to be in this strange fantasy world, it wasn't my destiny, I hadn't been brought here by fate to be its saviour. It was a *mistake*. I'd slipped through a crack in reality and ended up here not because I was special or magical, but because I was so insignificant that whoever looked after reality hadn't noticed I'd slipped through. Or if they had, they hadn't thought me worth fetching back, and perhaps even felt reality was a better place for being rid of me anyway.

I sat down in the centre of the floor.

I stared at the clouds.

'Go away, clouds,' I said.

They didn't go away.

'Come back, sun. Shine brightly.'

It didn't come back. It didn't shine.

I wondered how long I'd have to sit here to make it seem

I'd really tried before I could bring Lord Paladin and Philosophus back up to tell them I'd failed. No doubt they were standing in the room below, eyes glued to the windows, waiting for some sign of change. How long before they realised I'd failed?

I decided not to wait. I went over to the hatch and hauled it open.

'I'm sorry,' I said into the dimness of the room below. 'I don't know what to do. I tried, but I can't seem to do anything.'

Nobody said anything at first. I actually didn't feel as terrible as I'd thought I would. I felt relieved. I thought, 'I'm me again. Just plain old me. At least I know how to *be* me. I wouldn't have known how to be a magical Princess, anyway.'

Eventually the Dolorous Lord's dolorous face appeared, a pale oval lit by the lantern he was carrying.

'Come down, then, Carol,' he said.

Lord Paladin wasn't angry, and he's not the sort to say 'I told you so'. Instead, he said I was a mystery that had yet to reveal its purpose. (Which is a nice way of saying I'm useless as a fishnet raincoat, but there you go.)

We went back down all those spiral stairs, and found two mechanical servants waiting for us. Lord Paladin told them to take me and Philosophus to rooms and give us something to eat and look after us. He said he wanted to talk to Philosophus at some point, but gave me the freedom of the Palace to amuse myself as I wished. All I had to do was ask my allotted servant to take me somewhere and I'd be taken there.

So we parted ways and I was taken to my room. I wanted to say something to Philosophus, if only 'sorry', but he disappeared down one corridor and I went down a different one, and I haven't seen him since. It's been a couple of days now, and for all I know he's gone back to his ruin at the Edge of the World, to sit on a damp rock and think about — what was it? — 'fate and futility'. But maybe not. I'd still like to bump into him again.

Anyway, my room is quite large, with a plush four-poster bed and a tall oval mirror and a couple of not-too-comfy chairs and a fireplace. There's a chest of clothes, none of which fit me, though I had a spell of dressing up all the same. My maid, who I've called Tilly Two (though she's far less chatty than Tilly One), accompanies me and does whatever I ask her to do. (She's right now standing outside the entrance to the library, where I asked her to wait.) She fetches food when I'm hungry, and lights the candles when it's dark (which is pretty much all the time). What she doesn't do is respond to anything I say that isn't an order. Even questions she ought to be able to answer with a nod or shake of the head. Sometimes I think she resents me being here, not because she doesn't like being ordered about, but because I upset the purity of all this darkness and silence. But that's just me being silly. She no more resents me than the kettle or the washing machine do back home.

See? Try as I might I can't help thinking of 49 Willow Drive as home. Even though I'm so far away it can't be measured in miles.

Do I want to go back?

No.

Do I want to stay here?

Well... I have a bed. I have food. I have the Palace's marvellous massive library to myself.

I never expected it to be this massive. It just goes on and on. There's double doors to get into it, but they don't prepare you for how big it is. You step through, and facing you are ten blocks of bookshelves. Each is about twenty Carol-paces long and so high you need a fifteen-step ladder to reach the top shelf. Between each pair of bookshelves is an aisle stretching off into the dark, and walking down each aisle you pass nothing but row after row after row of shelves, with every so often a table and chairs for study (or to rest from all that walking!).

The first time I came here, I was so wowed by how big it is, I had to walk right down one of the aisles, all the way to the back. It took me ages! I lost count of how many rows of shelves there were, and haven't tried counting again. (That was when I took the lamp off Tilly Two and asked her to wait outside, because her clickety-clack clog-feet were echoing round the room in a most unlibrary-like fashion.)

Of course, the shelves are packed with books. Not a gap to be found. Books on everything you could want there to be a book on — as far as this world's concerned, anyway. I can't read about motor cars or the British political system or Great Naval Battles, but I can read about the derring-do of heroes, the life cycle of the basilisk, the construction of castles, the potion-making properties of various wild herbs and flowers, as well as all sorts of wildly unscientific speculations about what the stars are, where the wind comes from, how birds fly, and so on — all sorts of really, really, really, well, useless stuff. But great all the same.

I thought I'd love it here. I *do* love it here. In this library. Surrounded by books. Packed in among them. But this world is dying. It's going away. With me in it. And what will happen then?

Yesterday I asked to be taken up to the Singing Chamber and tried once more to work some magic. The curtains were still raised from the last time I'd been, so, after sitting around for a bit and realising nothing had changed and I still wasn't magical, I let them down and closed the hatch and put all that behind me.

So that's it. Everything that's happened to me in the last few days, all written up. I don't know if I'm ever going to write much in this diary again, because I guess all that's going to happen is I'm going to stay here, haunting this library like a girly ghost till the Princess returns or (more likely) things end. And how they end might be interesting, but of course I won't be around to write it up. But I don't want to get all gloomy. I'm going to go to bed now and maybe, when I wake up tomorrow, I'll think of something else to do.

I don't know. Maybe. Maybe not.

Whatever. Goodbye.

Um, several days since my last diary entry

Can I start by saying 'eek'?

Thank you.

Eek!

No, I haven't turned into a mouse. Instead, I've tried to turn myself into the complete opposite: a hero.

When will I ever learn?

This is going to take some explaining, because even I am not sure how I landed myself in this mess — and make no mistake, I *did* land myself in it, and it *is* a mess.

It all started with a note I found in the margin of a book.

There's all sorts of notes written in the margins of the books in the Palace library. It seems to be something people do here. If they disagree with what the author has written, or agree but think it could have been said better, or if they just have some random thought that's nothing to do with anything, people in this world want to write it down in the margin of the book they're reading.

Sometimes these notes are useful. I was reading a book (don't ask why) on how to rid a house of unwanted fairies, goblins, kobolds and the like, when I came across a hand-written note at the bottom of a page that said, 'Just make a lot of noise. They don't like it, and go away after a day or two.' Like I said, really useful. (And that must be why vacuum cleaners are so noisy — they suck up all the dust and scare away the fairies at the same time.)

Sometimes, though, these marginal notes are funny. I was browsing through a book (again, don't ask why) on how to tell a basilisk from a cockatrice without looking at them (because looking at either kills you, and then you're not going to care which you were looking at), when I came across this whole conversation written in the margins. Two scholars, who obviously referred to this book a lot, started out writing little notes and counter-notes about some ob-scure point of basilisk-lore (does the gaze of a basilisk actually turn you to stone or does it merely paralyse you?) but ended up having a slanging match, with one scholar calling the other a 'plumped-up nitwit' and a 'simian dun-derhead' (he actually wrote that sixty-two times, filling all the white space on one page) while the other underlined words in the text like 'vile' and 'serpentine' and put an arrow to them saying 'That's you, that is' or 'They're talk-ing about you'. All very dignified and academic.

Anyway, this note was in a book of maps, something I'd been wanting to find for ages, because fantasy books al-ways have maps, but I'd yet to see one of this world (apart from the one above Lord Paladin's throne, but I hadn't had a chance to study that one, and anyway, what I like doing is tracing my finger across a map, imagining all sorts of jour-neys for myself). The book started with a long discussion on how difficult it was to map the world when all you had to rely on were travellers' tales, travellers being notoriously untrustworthy on the details of their travelings. Also, on how this task was even more difficult now the Princess had started to sing (it had obviously been written shortly after she appeared) because under her influence the world was changing, so these maps (the map-maker said) were more along the lines of a historical record than a useful guide. But I looked through them anyway, and found Philosophus's family home (it was marked 'Castle Lachrymosa, Seat of the House Dolorous'), and from there traced our route through the forest, round that big hump of a rock where we'd stopped for the night (and where I'd seen — no, don't think about that), and then the blank space where there had been all the grassy hills and thistles and carrot-chasing hares and so on. The Palace was marked by big bold letters declaring it to be 'The Centre of the World'. (The edges of the world were marked 'Formless' or 'Outside' or a rather off-putting variant on the traditional phrase, 'Here be Monsters of a Most Terrible Kind'.)

On one map, which showed the Palace and the land northeast of it (that's the top right corner for you compass-o-phobes), someone had traced a line, lightly, in pencil, and written a note in the margin. The line left the Palace for a series of dots heading east marked 'Ancient Roadway', then angled northwards into a portion of the map labelled 'Rocky Desolation'. After that, it entered a narrow space between two craggy lines which was marked, rather ominously, 'Manticore Pass', and then ringed around a tower or castle to indicate, I guess, that this was the destination of that particular journey. I realised exactly what that tower or castle was when I read the note: 'Here is the route shown me by Lord Paladin, whereby I must journey to save the Princess. Grant me strength to match my valour, luck to match my hope, and success to match the desperation of our need.'

It caught my breath for a moment, not just because it reminded me of the situation I was in — world dying, all hope lost — but because it made me realise that all those heroes who'd gone after the Princess hadn't returned, but had been lost, and here was one before he'd gone, full of hope and determination.

I put the map away and tried to think of other things, because I was getting a bit down about the whole dying-world thing. Whenever I passed a window, I'd stop to stare at the darkness outside, and wonder if I was about to see the final fall into endless night. But I knew there was nothing I could do about it, so I'd turn away and go to the library and immerse myself in a book that had nothing to do with anything.

Sometimes I'd find myself thinking about home. Just silly thoughts, really. Things I used to enjoy doing there, things I used to look forward to. Also, how I'd expected my life to turn out. Not that I had any grand plans or anything like that, but you have thoughts, don't you? And I don't just mean the fact I never finished reading *The Wizard of Eldara*, but things like maybe leaving home and going to university, maybe even really being myself there and having friends, things like that. Anyway, none of those thoughts had involved disappearing into a dying fantasy world, so I guess life has always got surprises in store.

On the same day as I found that note on the map (which was yesterday), Lord Paladin appeared in the library.

I was sitting at my usual table with a small pile of books either side of me (books to be read or browsed through on the left, books I'd finished with on the right — I'm a regular book-devouring machine) when I looked up and there he was, silent as a spectre.

How long he'd been there, and how he'd crept up on me, considering he's wearing enough metal to supply an entire orchestra with cymbals, drums and a modest brass section, I don't know. I almost gave a little scream. (I'm glad I didn't, because that would have been impolite.) I did jump a bit, though. I mean, who wouldn't, on looking up to find a suit of armour with nothing but dark metal slits for eyes staring at them?

'Oh, um, hello,' I said.

'Lord Dolorous is to return to his family home.'

'Oh,' I said, in a voice as small and squeaky as Lord Paladin's was dark and boomy.

There followed one of those horrid silences I remember from my first meeting with him. Then he said, 'Have you made any progress in your studies?'

I looked at the books in front of me, and realised he must have assumed that, as I'd failed to do any Princess-magic in the Singing Chamber, I was searching for an alternative. That made me feel totally guilty, because I was doing nothing of the sort. I was just reading randomly, with no purpose at all, other than to take my mind off things.

'Um, no,' I said, hoping he wouldn't look at any of the titles.

A short silence. 'Will you return to your world?'

'Um...' I swallowed, which was a surprisingly difficult operation. 'I don't know. I mean, I don't know if I... can.' But that was a lie, wasn't it? I'm dreadful at lying. I instantly bit my lip and blushed.

Lord Paladin was silent again. I stared, not at his eye-slits, but at his big metal chest. The metal was polished, but scratched, sometimes quite deeply, and I realised this must be the same armour he'd worn on his famous journey to the Palace with the baby Princess in his arms. Had he worn it ever since? Did he wear it to remind himself of what had happened? Or, perhaps, the state of the world being as it is, did he wear it as a comfort, a link to more hopeful times? But it's silly to think of Lord Paladin as afraid or in need of comfort. I think he wore it simply because it was part of him, and that was that.

He said, then, in a voice a little less boomy than before, 'We have entered the time of twilight. There will be no more morning, no more noon. Only evening and night. The dark has come, and soon, the Necromancer. Will you be here when he arrives?'

I swallowed but couldn't say anything. I knew he was telling me I shouldn't be.

He continued. 'And after that, if I fail in my task of slaying him, when the world enters perpetual night, and darkness seeps into the stones and the trees and the ground, and all becomes one nothingness, what will you do then? Will you return to your world? Will you write about the death of this one? Will you become the chronicler of our tragedy?'

Now this made me panic. He must have seen my diary to know I wrote about things. (I leave it in my room with my schoolbag when I come to the library.) *Had* he seen it? Had he *read* it? How much of it had he read? Or was he just one of those people who see right through you, and know you're the sort of person to keep a diary? I don't know, but it made me feel so small and weak and vulnerable, which is hardly necessary considering how small and weak and vulnerable I *am*, particularly compared to that metal-cased booming giant.

I didn't say anything.

Lord Paladin didn't say anything more, either. After another silence, he turned and left.

At first, I felt unreal. For half an hour I sat there, feeling guilty for having wasted my time reading pointless books, and simply for being here, in this dying world, when I wasn't part of it, and had no right to be a witness to its sadness. Then another thing he'd said sunk in: Philosophus was going. I hadn't known, before, whether my former host had already gone or not, but now I knew he was still here and *was* going, I had to see him.

I left the library and asked Tilly Two to take me to Lord Philosophus Dolorous. First, she took me to his bedroom, but he wasn't there, so I asked to be taken to his laboratory, which proved to be in a very dim and out-of-the-way corner of this labyrinth of corridors and stairs they call the Palace. There, I asked Tilly Two to wait outside while I knocked. (Asking her to go in, where she might see bits and pieces of her relatives strewn about, would have been rather insensitive on my part, don't you think?)

I could hear someone moving about inside, but as soon as I knocked, the movement stopped. There was a pause, then Philosophus said, in a who-could-this-be tone, 'Yes, hello?'

'It's me,' I said.

The door opened. Philosophus poked his head out, blinking like an unearthed mole, then stepped back, inviting me in.

The laboratory wasn't as big as I'd imagined from how proud he'd sounded when he told me about it. There were three wooden benches, two against the walls and one in the middle of the room, covered in saws, files, clamps, hammers, tacks, screws, rivets, bits of metal, bits of wood, springs, lengths of string and wire, and a whole host of esoteric measuring devices, some of which looked rather anatomical. Scattered among these bits and pieces were parts of mechanical people. There was an armless body on the middle bench, hollow and half-full of cogs and ratchets, and on another bench there was a pair of arms, hands open as if eager to grab onto the body they lacked. A stack of brass plates stood in one corner, like the voice-disc I'd seen beneath the mechanical knight's helmet. The one finished piece (or what I assumed was a finished piece) stood in the far corner, but I could only guess what it was because it was covered by a sheet. The place smelled like the craft-block at school: wood-dust, glue, and that tangy bitter hint of metal dust that isn't quite a smell and isn't quite a taste.

Philosophus pottered about, making a very half-hearted attempt at bringing a little order to this chaos of clockwork, then turned to look at me questioningly.

He seemed different here, as if he was no longer the sad lord who lived in a ruined family home, but had gone back to being the young noble who kept apart from his peers and was unsure of himself in all respects save his skill and enthusiasm in engineering. It made me like him all the more.

'Lord Paladin said you're going,' I said.

'I am to return to my proper place.'

I bit my lip and looked at my shoes. There were some twirls of metal shaving in the wood-dust by my feet that would have made lovely hair-ringlets for a mechanical maid, and I thought about picking them up and giving them to Tilly Two as a thank you. Then I remembered I was trying to think of something to say. 'I'm sorry I couldn't do anything, you know, in the Singing Chamber.'

'You tried. It is all we can ever do.' I waited for the inevitable 'we are all doomed to failure anyway' or something of that sort, but nothing came. Perhaps all that doomy gloominess was part of his older self, and not to be found within the bounds of this young-self workroom.

I played with a cog on one of the benches, circling it on its axis with my finger. 'Do you think... this is it, then?'

'Do I think this is the end of all things?'

'Mm.'

'It seems to be.'

'What about when the Necromancer comes, though? Won't Lord Paladin defeat him?'

'I do not know,' Philosophus said, though it sounded rather more like 'I think not.'

I tinkered with a small pair of weighing scales. 'Why do you suppose he doesn't go out and save the Princess himself?'

Philosophus looked uncomfortable. 'He has his reasons — that is, I'm sure he does.'

This made me think that not only did Lord Paladin have his reasons, but Philosophus knew them. But I couldn't exactly press the point. Instead, I said, 'Why don't *we* try to rescue her?'

Silence. Shocked silence. From both of us. I mean, *I* was as surprised as Philosophus at what I'd said. I hadn't been planning to say it, though I could feel, now, how it had been building up inside of me like a bubble in a mud bath, trying to be said. But now it was out. The bubble had burst and we were both covered in mud. (Figuratively speaking, of course.)

'We are hardly heroes,' Philosophus said.

'I know... I suppose I didn't mean as heroes. All the heroes have tried, and they didn't get anywhere. Maybe we could try in our own way. I don't know what I mean, but, maybe we could *think* our way through things rather than fight. I don't know. It was a silly idea.'

But the trouble was, now it had been said, it was difficult to get away from it. The world was dying, the Princess was in dire need, and here we were doing nothing about it except moping around the Palace. What excuse, what *real* excuse, did we have for doing nothing?

Well, we tried to find one.

'I suppose,' I said, 'there *might* be fighting involved, however clever we try to be, and really it would be pointless to go into danger knowing we couldn't handle it.'

But Philosophus went over to the corner where the sheeted object stood and pulled off the sheet, revealing a mechanical knight like the one that had saved me from the glimmerlings. 'I was working on this when Lord Paladin sent me home,' he said. 'It is, apart from a few rough edges, finished, and is a far better piece of work than the mechanical knight that you know. We could take it along, and it could do our fighting for us, should the need arise.' He looked a bit troubled, realising how we were talking ourselves into this, rather than out of it. Then he looked brighter. 'But of course we would have to consult Lord Paladin, if only to learn the location of the Necromancer's stronghold, and he would never allow us to embark on such a quest with the sole protection of a mere mechanical knight.'

'But we wouldn't have to tell him,' I said, apologetically. 'I know where the Necromancer's stronghold is. I saw it on a map in the library.'

'How providential,' Philosophus said quietly, making it sound more like, 'Damn! I thought I'd got us out of it.'

So we both sat in silence, squeezing the last drip of thought-juice from those dried-out sponges we call our brains (what charming images I come up with), but unable to think of a single excuse that would let us off the hook with our consciences intact.

'I suppose we should prepare for the journey,' Philosophus said, sounding rather bewildered we'd come this far without a get-out clause. 'Perhaps you can fetch the map you spoke of while I organise some supplies?'

So here I am. Still in my room in the Palace, but ready to go. It's early morning. I got up specially to write this down, because we're going to be on the road soon, and I might not have the chance for much diary-writing for a while.

(If ever again. What *was* I thinking?)

I told Lord Paladin last night that I was going to head home with Philosophus. Philosophus (who was with me) looked like he was at any moment going to blurt out everything, and perhaps I was hoping he would, because that would mean an end to it, but he kept quiet, and I kept quiet, so here we are.

I'm all packed except for my diary, which, now I'm written up, I'll put in my schoolbag along with my trusty biro, then shoulder the lot and set out on, let's face it, the stupidest, most foolhardy, doomed, hopeless, dumb-minded, laughable-if-it-weren't-so-pitiful adventure of anyone in this or any other world ever!

(Help.)

Day one of our journey

Well, nothing too terrible has happened so far.

I don't mean to sound pessimistic, but any journey that takes you through such dales of delight as the Rocky Desolation and the Manticore Pass and ends in a confrontation with a bod known as the Necromancer is bound to put you in a certain frame of mind, isn't it?

So what *has* happened today if nothing too terrible hasn't?

Well, we left the Palace first thing, without pausing for any more goodbyes from Lord Paladin. (I did give Tilly Two those curly metal shavings from Philosophus's workroom floor, but she just walked about with them in her hands as if unsure what to do with them. Or maybe she was waiting till I'd gone before chucking them in a bin, dusting off her wooden hands and muttering, 'Tuh, metal shavings! *So* last year.')

In the stables, Evenstar greeted me with a wary hruph, and I did my best to forget why I'd vowed to wait till they invented buses before making any more journeys in this world as I got into the saddle (which I managed with a bit less klutziness than last time, so perhaps I'd learned *something* on our journey here).

The Ancient Roadway at first didn't look at all ancient. Its paving slabs were intact, and there were regular milestones to mark the miles (or whatever measure they use here for long distances). But a few hours later, it became so old and uncared-for that half the paving slabs were missing, and half those that weren't missing were so broken they might as well not have been there, and whatever fraction was left was hardly worth getting excited about. (What *is* left once you take away a half then another? Pi, probably. Or the distance from your elbow to your ear.) Now it's pretty much nothing but dirt track, with only the occasional sagging signpost or corner of a paving slab to hint it was ever anything but.

It may be a bit unfair of me to say this, but I actually felt a lot better once the black spike of the Palace had disappeared behind us. For a start, the sky got brighter — never much more than an autumn silver-white, but it's better than that murky flock of black sheep crowding round the Palace all hours of the day. (They have the whole sky to themselves, why don't they take advantage of it? If I were a cloud, I'd scoot all over the place!)

I suppose the real reason, though, is it's just good to be away from those dim, silent, twisty corridors and staircases. And, I have to say, away from Lord Paladin too, because I'd become more than a little scared of him, even though he's a great hero. It wasn't till we got out in the open that I realised how gloomy I'd become, and how hopeless and depressing things had seemed while I'd been holed up in the Palace. Outside in the open light, things began to seem possible, even hopeful.

It made me feel all businesslike, so I said, 'What do we know about this Necromancer, then?'

Philosophus considered this. 'Very little.'

'Um, very little as in we have just this one really important piece of information we can use to our advantage, like he's terrified of frogs or allergic to cheese, or very little as in nothing?'

'I am afraid it is more along the lines of very little as in nothing,' Philosophus said. 'To tell you the truth, I had not heard of the Necromancer at all until he took the Princess.'

'Really? You mean he hasn't plagued this world for centuries with his evil plots and dastardly doings?'

'No.'

'Hmm. Very quiet necromancer, then.'

'You have necromancers in your world?' Philosophus said.

'Only in the same way we don't have dragons.'

We rode on in silence for a bit.

'Perhaps,' I said, 'he did evil things before, but under a different name. Evil people do that, don't they?'

'I have never met any evil people,' Philosophus said.

'Well, they do,' I said, hoping he wouldn't quiz me on it. I suppose I haven't met any evil people either, apart from Candice Cooper, who, you have to admit, is pretty minor-league evil. (Unless she has another identity she uses to do larger-scale evil things. But I doubt it. The whole point about minor-league evil people is they're too lazy to move onto the major league, which is a good thing for us minor-league good 'uns.) 'Are you saying,' I said, 'that there's never been any evil in this world?'

'Oh, I am not saying that.'

'It's just I'm wondering, if we examine the other evil people you've heard of, we might find this Necromancer fellow is really one of them in another guise, and we can use whatever happened to his previous self, how he was defeated and so on, to our advantage. Um, this Necromancer *is* a fellow, isn't he? I mean, not a she?'

'I presume so.' Philosophus seemed rather awed by my sudden burst of practicality about the matter, which I guess made up for all that nonsense about bikes on our first journey together.

'Right,' I said, 'let's go through the evil people who've been in this world. Who do you know of?'

He paused to consider this. 'Really, I can think of no one.'

'What about the people who killed the Princess's parents?'

'Ah, but those weren't people. They were beings from Outside.'

'Outside?' I said, sensing those tell-tale capitals and realising this might be important.

'Beyond the Edge of the World. Those were liminal beings that killed the Princess's parents. The creatures you call the glimmerlings.'

'*They* did it?'

'Or creatures like them.'

'But I thought they were all formless and useless.'

'Mostly. Sometimes, rarely, something happens and they burst into our world and do terrible things. They kill and wreck and terrorise. But it is not evil, anymore than the lightning that starts a forest fire can be described as evil, or the river that bursts its banks and ruins a field of crops. No, there has long been debate on what should be done about them. The Princess...' He paused, then sighed, as he so often does when talking of the Princess.

'Go on,' I said. 'It might be important.'

'The Princess,' he continued, in a quieter voice, 'spoke to me about it when last we met. She told me it had long been her wish to extend her influence not just over the world, but beyond its edges, to bring the creatures of the Outside into our world, to give them form and purpose, to make them as real as ourselves. She believed these out-bursts, these wild attacks, were caused by a frustration or boredom on their part, an excess of energy bereft of a natur-al outlet. She believed they were not evil, merely in need of purpose and form. She believed she could give them the purpose and form they needed to make them fit into our world.'

'Did she try?'

'Lord Paladin forbade it. He has always hated those

creatures you call the glimmerlings. To him, they are vermin, fit only to be exterminated. You must remember, he witnessed what they did to the Princess's parents.'

'Yes, but if the Princess can forgive them enough to want to help them...'

'It is her nature.'

After that, we didn't make any more progress on the Necromancer thing. (And the mechanical knight of course wasn't any help. He just clunked along behind us like a horse-load of pots and pans.)

It's evening now, and we're still on the dotted-line part of the map, the Ancient Roadway, and I've just lit my first ever campfire. This time on our journey into the wilds we brought some sensible, useful things, like a box of tinder and a flick-of-the-thumb flint-striking device. So, even though I didn't have to sit here for hours doing the Ray Mears thing, rubbing two sticks together, it still gives me an inner glow of satisfaction to know that the outer glow I feel is entirely down to my own efforts: I gathered the wood, I sparked the tinder alight, I persuaded the twigs and branches to join in the blaze. In fact, I was so pleased with the result, I would have kept piling on wood till our campfire was the size of a small garden shed, if Philosophus hadn't come back from tending the horses to point out that if we wanted to warm some food and heat water for tea, I ought to at least keep the fire small enough that we could reach over the top without being in danger of falling in. Also, so it wouldn't melt our kettle.

(We brought a kettle, too.)

Anyway, I sat there for a while staring at the fire (*my* fire), admiring the enthusiasm of the little flames (*my* little flames) as they danced their sprightly dance, till I realised if this went on much longer I'd start talking in grunts and perhaps walking around with a club in my hand, hoping for sight of wooly mammoth, so I got out my diary and began writing up day one of the journey. (As you can see.)

It's pretty dark now, and I'd better get some sleep. Living the life of adventure, you've got to pay attention to these things. Eating regular meals and getting a good night's rest suddenly seem very important, because you never know when you're going to have to do without.

(Hark at her, the adventuress, now!)

Day two of our journey

Today we left the Ancient Roadway and started into the Rocky Desolation.

Yippee for us.

Unlike our old friend the Ancient Roadway, which took a while to reveal its true nature (cracked, broken and missing paving slabs), the Rocky Desolation looked like a Rocky Desolation from the word go. We turned off the Ancient Roadway and started along a track through what I guess is desert. (Not a sandy desert, but a dusty one, which I reckon is worse, though I've never been in a sandy desert, so maybe it's just whichever desert you happen to be in that seems worst.) The track soon disappeared, and we were left having to rely on the mechanical knight's unerring ability to go in a dead straight line to keep us headed northeast. (He *can* steer himself round obstacles, but always comes back to the same straight line on the other side. Quirky, but useful.)

So what's the Rocky Desolation like? I can tell you're dying to know.

Well, there's these weird rock formations sticking up from the ground, like strange plants, or the sort of clay pots I used to make in Craft when it was my go at the potting wheel, which needless to say never looked anything like the sort of pot I had in mind when I threw the clay at the wheel, and in fact, once I was through with them, couldn't be used as pots, jars, plates, or any other sort of receptacle, or ornament, or anything at all. (By the time I was through with them, they were barely recognisable as clay.)

I'd tell you what kind of rock they are, only I know nothing about rocks. (I'm an igneous ignoramus.) They're yellow. And sometimes brown. What else can you say about rocks?

Well, Philosophus had a go. 'They are smooth, as if worn away by either wind or water. Perhaps this used to be the bottom of an ancient sea.'

The thought of sharks and other fishy beasts swimming about where I was riding made me go all spine-tingly, and when Philosophus dismounted at one point to investigate whether some half-buried bones we came across were the remains of an ancient marine creature, I just couldn't look, though he of course went on about it for hours afterwards.

As the day wore on, and in an effort to change the subject, I turned to my travelling companion and said, 'Hang on, I thought you said magic doesn't exist in this world?'

He looked at me blankly.

'*You* remember,' I said. 'I asked about magic and you said about the impossible not being possible. Well, if that's true, what have we got to worry about? If this Necromancer can't do magic, he's just a normal person, so why worry?'

'I did not say magic does not exist in this world,' Philosophus said. 'I merely forced you to provide a more precise definition of the word "magic" before confirming whether it existed or not, because "magic" is one of those words that has a different meaning for every person who uses it, rather like "truth" or "reality" or "love".' (There he goes, harping on about love again.) 'You gave the definition of magic as "the impossible being made possible", so naturally I responded that the impossible can never be made possible, by definition. However, I never said anything about sorcery, or necromancy, which is the correct term for what a necromancer does.'

'Oh,' I said. (Mental note: never argue with a blah blah blah.) 'So necromancy *is* possible?'

'It is. Strictly speaking, of course, necromancy is the art of forecasting the future through consulting the dead. However, we should assume that anyone capable of such a thing is capable of many other feats as well.'

'Great,' I said.

And that is as far as we got on the subject of the Necromancer on day two. Which is, as you can see, no further than we got on day one.

Day three of our journey

So what did we learn about the Necromancer on the third day of our journey?

Rather too much, as it happens, and now everything's changed.

How to go about explaining it all?

Well, call me controversial, but I think maybe an approach such as, say, begin at the beginning, then keep going till you run out of stuff to say, Carol?

Why not. Be a devil.

Know then, O diary, that on the third day of our quest, the Manticore Pass loomed. It was about midmorning when we saw it. For a while, those weird rock formations that gave the Rocky Desolation its name had been getting smaller, more worn-away, giving us a better view of what lay ahead. The sky this far from the Palace was pale but clear, and though we were in a desert, it wasn't all that hot (owing to the sun being so dim and weak), so things were pleasant enough, if only I could have forgotten where we were headed. Then this great wall of rock appeared. At first it was just a dim, dark band on the horizon, but as we got closer it rose like a solid wave of stone waiting to crash on us.

'A cliff to mark the edge of our ancient sea,' Philosophus said.

'Where's the pass?' I said.

We scanned the cliff both ways, and Philosophus spotted it to the south, a narrow split amidst the ruffles of stone, like the gap you get when curtains don't quite close.

We reached it, then dismounted while Philosophus made sure the mechanical knight was fully wound up, and gave him a quick check, telling him to draw his sword, assume a combat stance, and so on. (There was one thing he didn't check, but I'll come to that soon.)

I, meanwhile, prepared for the Manticore Pass as best I could, by getting thoroughly wound up myself. That opening in the cliff-face looked too much like a pair of monstrous jaws waiting to clap shut on whoever was foolish enough to venture between them.

'Do you think there'll be a manticore in the pass?' I said.

'I assume that is how it gets its name.'

'Maybe it's an ancient manticore, long gone.'

'Perhaps,' Philosophus said, though not as positively as I'd hoped.

'Or maybe the pass gets its name because the manticore likes to let people pass? Perhaps it's a nice manticore?'

Philosophus smiled his sad smile, which was as nice a way of saying 'and perhaps not' as he could think of, I guess.

The mechanical knight remounted, as did Lord Dolorous, but I took my time. Even once I was up on Evenstar again, I couldn't bring myself to move forward.

I had to admit it. 'You know, I'm having doubts.'

'Doubts?'

'About this whole heroism thing.'

'But you suggested, I'm sure you recall, that we face the task not as heroes, but as ourselves, relying on our wits rather than any prowess we have, or lack, with sword and other arts martial.'

'Yeah,' I said. (Arts martial, huh?) 'Well, I'm beginning to think my wits might not be up to it, either.'

'There is only one way to find out.'

I felt distinctly let down by his saying this. 'We *could* discuss it a bit more. You know, go over our plans, be that little bit more thorough.'

'What is there to discuss?'

'Well, what we're going to do if we meet a manticore in the pass, for instance.'

'What do you think we should do?'

'My idea is we should avoid the possibility of meeting a manticore in the first place. And the best way of doing that is not to enter any place named after one. You know, Manticore Meadows, Manticore Mountains, the Manticore Café on Manticore Street. And of course the Manticore Pass. What do you think?'

Philosophus nodded thoughtfully, and for a moment my cowardly self thought it had won him over. 'I understand, Carol. You have come this far, and that was a brave thing to do. Also, you instigated this quest, which took far greater daring than I have ever possessed. You have done enough. Turn back. I will continue alone.'

'I can't let you do it on your own!'

'I will have my mechanical knight with me. Unless, that is, you require him to guard and guide you back to the Palace?'

I felt awful. 'I meant we could *both* go back.'

Again, Philosophus nodded that all-too-understanding nod of his. He gazed into the distance and said, 'Over the last few days... How can I put this? I have felt so different. As if this quest we are on has introduced me to a whole new way of looking at the world. For too long I have wanted to do something to help the world, yet have done nothing. I told myself I *could* do nothing because there is no hope. But that is not true. I *decided* there is no hope. And why did I do that? Because it meant I could use it as an excuse to do nothing. It took you, suggesting we go on this quest, for me to face my cowardice and see it for what it is. And for that I thank you. But now I know this about myself, I am determined to overcome it and see this task through to the end. Even if it is the last thing I do.'

I felt rather ashamed of myself. 'Alright, let's go. But we should put Sir Bucket-Head in front. We might be trying not to be cowards, but that's no reason to be reckless, is it?'

Philosophus smiled, and we entered the pass.

'Sorry I called him Sir Bucket-Head,' I said, after a bit.

The pass was wide enough for the two of us to ride side by side, with enough room left for a quick about-turn, if only I were a capable enough rider to do anything quick, let alone something as complicated as an about-turn. With any luck, should it come to it, Evenstar would have enough instinct for survival to accomplish that sort of move on her own, though hopefully not so *much* instinct for survival that she'd realise she could get away a lot faster if she ditched her rider first.

I tried to keep my eye on every possible direction of attack: ahead, above, behind, and into every shadowy crease and crevice in the walls (of which, let me tell you, there were a good many), expecting any moment to see what I most didn't want to see.

Philosophus was a lot more calm. (Though I had a sneaking suspicion it was because he was stuck on that 'even if it is the last thing I do' idea, which to me is a rather unhealthy way of thinking.) The mechanical knight, ahead of us, was of course as cool as a clockwork cucumber.

We rode for about five minutes without anything happening. I was fit to explode. Half of me wanted nothing to continue happening, while the other half wanted something to happen just to get it over with — but only so long as, if we *had* to meet a manticore, it was about three inches long with all the biting power of a toothless kitten. I kept finding myself looking at Lord Dolorous's sword and wondering, if it came to it, if I could whip it out and — snicker-snack! — fell the foul beast with a mighty stroke. Then that practical part of me that's always ruining things would remind me that this was a manticore we were talking about, a wild beast that was used to killing heroes and eating their brains, and no doubt the rest of them too. If there was any snicker-snacking to be done, it was most likely to be by it, on me.

In the end, I shut my eyes.

Yes, I shut my eyes. Hardly the sort of instinct to get you marked down as one of evolution's favourites. But the worrying part of my brain just blew its fuse and decided the best way to get through this awful situation was to pretend it wasn't happening.

Then Philosophus said, 'Ah.'

'What? What?'

'The end of the pass is in sight.'

I stared, unable to believe it could be true. But it was. Ahead, about a minute away (we were going at quite a slow pace so as to make as little noise as possible, and to give us as much preparation time should the beastie we were expecting to meet appear in the distance and rush towards us) the pass opened out into a rocky area strewn with boulders.

Was that it? Had we got through the pass? No manticore?

A slight breeze, the first I'd felt since entering the Rocky Desolation, drifted between those sheer walls and for a brief second it felt cool and refreshing, till I breathed in and almost gagged.

'Ugh!' I said, pinching my nose. 'Whad's dat sbell?'

It was disgusting — hot and sharp, rank and foul, and so bad that even with my nose held I could taste it. I had to turn away and breathe facing backwards (which was still pretty bad) till the breeze died down.

'I believe,' Philosophus said in a hushed voice, 'that *that* is the source of the odour.'

'Whad?'

I concentrated on the end of the pass.

Nothing at first. Then something moved. It moved casually, loping on its heavy paws, a flash of mucky yellow fur passing from one area of boulder-shade to another, before slumping back into the dust.

'Oh,' I said. 'Oh dear.'

A long, long silence in which all was still.

'What do we do?' I whispered.

Philosophus said nothing.

I continued to stare, trying to pretend I hadn't seen anything, hoping that would give the world a chance to take back its decision of at last presenting us with a manticore. Then I heard a yawny lion roar, or perhaps a slow rumbling belch from a beast-sized stomach.

Maybe it's just eaten, I thought. Maybe it's sleepy and we can sneak past it.

Then the mechanical knight drew his sword. He might as well have scraped his gauntleted fingers down a blackboard while ringing a fire alarm. The metallic screech echoed down the pass like a flock of bats with loudhailers.

The dim, yawny-belchy thing scrambled to its feet and gave a full-lung roar.

Then it ran at us.

All those things I'd been planning to do — the about-turn, the grabbing of Philosophus's sword — went completely out of my head and I screamed (which was, I admit, not very useful) then sat there paralysed.

That thing, the manticore, was big. And fast.

Big and fast are not a good combination when they're not on your side.

It came charging down the pass, roaring, claws scraping the stones on the ground (and even from that distance I could see those claws, so they must have been about as long as my hand). Curled above its head was the heavy barb of its enormous scorpion tail, swaying as it ran, poised to strike. But the worst thing, the absolute worst, was its face.

Now, a manticore, in case you don't know, is mostly lion. Its body is the body of a lion. But like so many mythological monsters (and oh how I wish this one was *only* mythological), it's not just one thing. It's a potpourri of various creatures. (Though, as already pointed out, it hardly smells like the sort of potpourri you'd buy in Boots.) As well as a lion's body it's got a scorpion's tail (as already mentioned). But the other major part of it is the face. Manticores have a lion's mane and a lion's teeth but a human face.

This did not in any way make it less scary.

Quite the opposite. For a start, its head was bigger than a human's, so the face was bigger too, which made it look wrong. It was also horrendously dirty (that thing may have been mostly cat, but it certainly didn't have a cat's good habits) and something dark, a flaky reddish-black I didn't want to think about, was caked in the beard beneath its sharp-toothed mouth. One of its eyes was half-closed from an awful scar striking down the left side of its face like a red lightning bolt. But the worst thing was its expression. How it could look so human, yet be so wild, so angry and so *inhuman* froze me. I couldn't do anything but stare. And the sound I heard roaring down the pass, echoing fit to cause an avalanche (which, for a moment, I actually hoped for) was part angry lion, but part mad, scary human, too.

I *never* want to hear anything like that again.

The mechanical knight raised his sword above his head and said, 'I am but a messenger. Let me take you to my lord.'

Beside me, Philosophus said, in a dazed way, 'I put in the wrong voice-plate.' It was the thing he hadn't checked. Hardly a tragedy, but it was strange, to say the least, to hear the knight say, 'Please dismount,' as he pointed his sword at the incoming beast and urged his mechanical horse to a gallop.

The manticore didn't stop. It met the knight and charger in a crash that sounded like two cars colliding at full speed. The knight was launched from his saddle to slam into the side of the pass six feet off the ground, while the manticore went skidding the other way and took the horse with it. Claws and teeth screeched on metal. For a while the manticore lay with its fore-claws wrapped around the horse's neck, hind-claws pummelling its belly, jabbing with its scorpion tail and rending the poor creature's throat with its inhuman jaws.

There was a screaming sound I really thought at first was the horse, and for a second I went cold, thinking it hadn't been a mechanical horse at all and was really suffering, but it *was* a mechanical horse, and what I was hearing was the metal of its head tearing as the manticore ripped it off.

Realising this was not the fleshy morsel it was hoping for, the beast disentangled itself and got to its feet.

It was only now I realised, after that massive collision, that there was nothing between us and the manticore but a short dash. Realising the same thing, Philosophus fumbled to get his sword out of its scabbard, but it was stuck.

'The catch, the catch,' he said, and I wondered what he was blathering about till he popped the catch of a little leather strap keeping his sword in its scabbard and finally managed to draw it.

I felt a bit safer. For about half a second. Because Philosophus, unused to holding a sword, was taken aback by how heavy it was, and dropped it in the same movement as he drew it.

It clanged to the ground like a bell announcing dinnertime for manticores.

Our beastly foe gnashed its teeth. Its gums were streaming blood, no doubt as a result of biting into the metal horse, but it didn't seem to care. It leered an I'm-going-to-enjoy-this leer. It didn't charge, though. It obviously knew it was facing the soft centre of the party sent to face it, and that we'd be easy prey.

It started to pad towards us.

Then — and I may never be so glad to hear such a bizarre sentence spoken in such dire circumstances — I heard a tinny voice cry, 'Are you comfortable, my lord?' And suddenly, from behind the manticore, a sword rose in the air and came down.

The beast, taken by surprise (perhaps because it hadn't scented the scentless mechanical knight), screamed and wheeled, lashing with its claws. The knight thankfully hadn't been too damaged by his impact with the wall, and dodged back nimbly, then darted in and swung again, this time getting our foe in the face.

The manticore recoiled. Its right eye, the un-scarred one, was gushing blood.

The knight took immediate advantage, and drove forward with his sword. From that point on it was impossible to tell what was happening, as the manticore thrashed with its claws and tail, shrouding the two of them in dust. There were screams and roars and metallic screeches, as well as the occasional 'My lord', 'My lady', and 'Please dismount'.

Then the manticore was running.

Away.

It was running away.

'It's running away,' I said. Sometimes it can be quite

comforting to state the obvious, even if you do it in a voice about an octave higher than normal.

Yes, it was running away, and it was not running well. It careened into the wall of the pass, blinded by the wound in its eye. It fell, rolled, ran again, and was gone.

I could only stare at the suddenly still and silent scene of the battle. But no, it wasn't still. The mechanical knight, or what was left of him, was raising his sword slowly up, then down, up, then down, winding gradually to a stop. But he wasn't standing, or sitting, or lying. All that was left was the top part of his body, which was upright, but not attached to anything. His legs were a few paces away (no pun intended), motionless in the dust.

Philosophus dismounted, picked up his sword and sheathed it.

'Will it come back?' I said.

'Not for a while, I think.' He went forward on foot and did his best to gather the remains of our knightly saviour into as dignified a pile as possible. When I rode up, leading his horse by the reins, he shook his head sadly. 'There is nothing I can do. The damage is irreparable.' Then, I do believe, he smiled. 'But what a triumph. It is the first time one of my knights has been in actual combat. And it was a triumph.'

'Um,' I said, 'does that mean you never tested it before?'

'Oh, against straw dummies. But never in actual combat with an intelligent, or at least instinctual, foe.'

'Straw dummies?' I said.

'Against which it was most effective.'

I decided to let the subject drop, but made another mental note about philosophers that was not very complimentary.

Meanwhile, Philosophus looked into the distance, narrowed his eyes and said, 'We have passed the first test. How shall we fare, I wonder, in the next?'

'Yeah,' I said. 'Let's hope that whatever it is, it doesn't have breath as bad as that.'

It took some persuading to get our horses through the far end of the pass because of the lingering whiff of manticore (as well as several fly-caked dollops of what a manticore leaves behind), but eventually we emerged onto a broad rocky shelf. Either side of us, the walls that had hemmed in the pass opened to take in a dusty plain that began about twenty feet below. And slap-bang in the middle of the plain, about half a mile away, was a tower. It was square and squat, three stories high, tapering slightly towards its flat roof. It was built of large dull-brown bricks, with whitish ones at the corners. I could just make out a few arrow-slit windows, as well as some wider ones in the uppermost storey, but there were no signs of life — no smoke rising, no lights, no movement.

'There's a path down,' Philosophus said, nodding to where the shelf dropped away in a steep but not impossible slope on our left. 'I think the horses will manage it.'

'But is that...'

'The Necromancer's stronghold? We can only assume so.'

I stared at the tower. I'd been expecting something, I don't know, a bit more grand. You know, great dark arched windows like empty eye-sockets, pillars like ancient giant's bones, huge iron spikes and enormous lengths of chain and portcullises and drawbridges and flags flying the sign of the evil-eyed skull. But in a way, that unassuming tower was even more scary, if only for the simple reason that it was real, and in front of us right now. We would reach it in about fifteen minutes, and inside, waiting for us, perhaps looking back at us at this very moment, was the Necromancer.

I nudged Evenstar and she started down the path, which

she was eager enough to do as it meant getting away from that awful smell. But of course she didn't know what we were heading for. I did.

A little conversation started up in my head.

'Carol,' one half of me said, 'why are we doing this? It's not our world, why risk our life for it? We could turn around, go back to the forest, then the attic, then the stairs, and be home having a cup of tea in front of the telly in no time.'

'Look, Carol old buddy,' I said back, 'if we do, what happens? Everything will be exactly the same as when we left. You do remember why we left, don't you? So we're staying here. And to stay here we've got to save the Princess and save the world, okay? Any more dumb questions?'

'Just one,' first-half-of-me said. 'If we can go through all the fuss, bother and danger of saving a world, why not go to the same lengths to make things better at home, where at least there aren't any necromancers or manticores?'

I glanced at Philosophus, because sometimes when I have these inner debates my lips move, which I'm sure makes people think I'm a bit odd (or odder than they already think I am, anyway), but he was too intent on the tower. His eyes were narrowed and his face was steely. One hand rested, rather worryingly, on the hilt of his sword.

A dozen steps led up to a doorway in the side of the tower, one storey off the ground. To my surprise, there was no door in the doorway, it was just an opening for anyone to wander through. Was the Necromancer not at home? My heart gave one of those hopeful leaps it gives when it seems everything's going to be alright. Like in the Manticore Pass, when it seemed we'd got to the end without meeting a manticore. You know, just before we met one.

We halted at the foot of the steps. I looked at Philosophus. He looked at the tower.

'Should we, um, call out, or just go in?' I said, unsure of

the etiquette in this sort of situation.

'We go in.'

We dismounted. I was wondering whether we should tether the horses and take our gear off them, like we do each night when we camp, but Philosophus had already started up the steps, so I followed. I kept glancing at the roof in case the Necromancer was up there, about to drop a heavy stone or a barrel of boiling oil on us. I sort of hoped he might, because if a Necromancer has to resort to dropping stones or boiling oil on you, he hasn't got any mighty magic to use instead.

But no stone was dropped, no oil was poured. We entered the tower.

We found ourselves in a cool, dim, and very short passage. A set of stairs led down to our left, another up, to our right. Both disappeared into darkness, following the square angles of the tower's outer wall.

I took my torch out of my schoolbag and clicked it on.

'What's that?' Philosophus whispered, and I, quite naturally, darted the beam all around, trying to catch whatever it was he'd seen. 'What? Where?'

'In your hand.'

'It's my torch. Actually it's not strictly mine. I borrowed it from the kitchen, but as I'm unlikely ever to go back, I might as well call it mine.'

Philosophus stared at it. 'But how did you light it so quickly? And how can you move it about so carelessly of spilled oil? And why is it that odd shape? And how is it so bright?'

'Um, it's not oil, it's electric,' I said, handing it over as he was obviously interested.

'A lectric?'

I didn't correct him. I have no idea how to explain electricity. I mean, I barely understand it myself, and didn't want to make it obvious how ignorant I am of one of the major wonders of the world I come from.

Philosophus stared wide-eyed into the end of the torch. Then he had to look away, blinking, but as soon as his eyes recovered he was staring back into it again. 'There appears to be a tiny glowing worm trapped in a bubble. Is it a salamander? A sprite?'

'No, it's a light bulb. Don't you think we should have this conversation elsewhere? The, uh, Necromancer?'

'Ah,' he said. 'Yes.' He handed back the torch.

I shone the beam down to our left and up to our right. 'Which way?'

But Philosophus wasn't paying attention. He was muttering, 'So many wonders in the world — the *many* worlds...'

'Philosophus?'

He gave me one of his sad looks, something I hadn't seen since his telling me how much more purposeful he felt before we entered the Manticore Pass. 'I was thinking how unfair it is that I am about to put my life in mortal jeopardy when so much remains to be learned. So many mysteries. So many wonders. So many, many questions.'

I bit my lip, because that cowardly part of me was struggling to say, 'Yes, I agree, but there's still time to turn around, so let's go home, shall we?'

But Philosophus gave his head a little shake and looked steely once more. 'I would think that the stairs leading down—'

He stopped, listening.

Then he whipped out his sword and began charging up the stairs to our right.

I stood there for a moment, then ran after him, calling, 'I thought we were doing this *not* as heroes?'

I just caught up with him (his charge up the stairs in all that armour, and carrying that sword, had got him a bit out of breath) when the stairs, having taken two right-angle turns, passed an arched doorway on our left.

Philosophus passed the doorway, stopped, then dashed back and through it, shouting, 'Prepare to meet thy doom, foul Necromancer!'

'Oh no,' I said, and followed him.

The room we entered was quite large, with a high ceiling. There was a fireplace on the far side (unlit), while the rest of the room was taken up with seven or eight old wooden tables covered in the most ridiculous clutter I've ever seen. I mean, I didn't have time to stop and take it in, but as I'm in the same room now I can look around and give you an idea. There's hundreds of glass beakers of all shapes and sizes, as well as bottles of all colours, and tubes and clamps and stands and dishes and bowls and containers of powders and crystals and dried leaves and roots and fungi, not to mention a small library of books (half of which are lying open among the jumble, their pages stained or burned or creased or torn) and countless loose sheets of paper covered in writing, mostly on the floor. There are lamps and candlesticks, a small collection of mirrors, a case of glass lenses lying open on one bench, a case of tiny tools a jeweller might use lying open on another and, oh, all sorts of other stuff I don't know the names of or the use for. There's no sense of order at all. It's like a dozen absent-minded professors were working furiously at twice that number of experiments, then took a break and forgot to come back.

Philosophus barely paused to get his bearings before waving his sword and shouting more of that 'thy judgement has come!' stuff, while trying to get past all the clutter to an old man in the far corner, who looked rather startled.

I have to admit the old man didn't look how I expected a necromancer to look. He didn't look evil, you know? In fact, he looked rather harmless. He had frizzy white hair, and a beard that stuck out in all directions like the early stages of a firework explosion. He was dressed in a dull-coloured robe or habit with so many patches and repairs, it resembled the map of some small but warlike continent whose interior borders kept changing.

I thought, 'If this is the Necromancer, he needs an image consultant, because if you want to be taken seriously as the Greatest Force For Evil In The World, you really ought to look the part.'

Then I thought, 'Eek! It's the Necromancer! We really are here, about to face him... What *is* Philosophus doing?'

Trying to reach the old man (who had ceased to look so startled, and now looked a bit annoyed), Philosophus had gone round one bench only to find another blocking his way, and then, in his rush to turn and find another route, had slipped on one of the many sheets of paper scattered on the floor, and only just caught his balance by grabbing a table, sending half a dozen books flying.

'Do not try to escape thy fate, Necromancer!' Philosophus shouted, as if this slip had been the old man's fault.

I looked on helplessly, thinking this wasn't at all what we'd planned.

The old man's annoyance bubbled over. He rolled his eyes and threw his hands in the air. 'Young man, I am not, not, *not* a necromancer!'

'Prove it!'

The old man stared. 'Prove it? Prove it! Prove you're not a duck!'

Now it was Philosophus's turn to be taken aback. 'A duck?'

'Yes. Go on, prove it.'

'I have no feathers.'

'Then you're a plucked duck! Come on, come on, more proof.'

'I have no bill,' Philosophus said.

'So what?'

'Ducks have bills.'

The old man gave a little dance of delight. 'Oh, they do, do they? Well how do you know so much about ducks? Only a duck would know so much about ducks. Therefore, you're a duck! I, however, cannot prove I'm not a necromancer, so I present this very fact as proof that I am *not* one. There. Are you satisfied?'

Philosophus, obviously having forgotten his rush to kill the old man, shook his head. 'That does not make sense.'

'Oh, you want what I say to be true *and* make sense? You ask rather too much, boy.'

Philosophus couldn't think of anything to say to that, and the old man gave a triumphant nod.

'Um,' I said, 'you're not the Necromancer, then?'

'No, no, and triple no. I've been thinking lately I should make a sign to wear round my neck: "This man is not a necromancer. So don't bother asking."'

'But this *is* the Necromancer's stronghold?'

'No. It's a tower. It's my tower. And as I am not a necromancer, it's not a necromancer's tower, let alone a necromancer's stronghold. How can it be a stronghold when it doesn't even have a front door?'

I looked at Philosophus, who was completely deflated. 'Um,' I said, 'is the Necromancer's stronghold nearby?'

'Nearby? Young lady, this is a desert. There's nothing nearby but dust and rock, and the occasional underfed vulture.'

'Oh.' I turned off my torch and put it in my bag. 'I'm, uh, sorry we disturbed you, then.'

'Now that is the first polite word I've heard in months,' the old man said. 'And considering what I've been through with all these hero-types barging in every other day, waving their swords, accusing me of being a necromancer, not to mention all sorts of other things I wouldn't repeat to anyone of your age, I sometimes feel I'm owed a polite word or two.'

'Sorry,' I said again. 'Um, you say hero-types? Where are they?'

'I put them in the cellar.'

Philosophus woke up again. 'You killed them!'

'Calm down, young man. Of course I didn't kill them. I've never killed anyone in my life. I merely put a sleep spell on them till I could work out what to do.'

'A sleep spell?' I said.

'What do you expect me to do? They wouldn't listen to reason, they just kept coming. I thought they were bound to stop at some point, but it seems the world is more full of brainless do-gooders than I expected.'

'But, a sleep spell,' I said again, 'does that mean you're a sorcerer?'

'I prefer the term "wizard". "Sorcerer" always makes me think of, you know, silk robes and astrological symbols, gaudy jewellery, smoke and mirrors and all that gubbins. A wizard is more of your get-down-to-it, get-on-with-it, no-nonsense magic worker. We may not have the best dress-sense in the world, but if you want results, you'll get them from a wizard.'

'Wow,' I said.

The old man looked rather pleased at this reaction. 'Do you suppose your derring-do friend could put his sword away?'

'Philosophus, put your sword away.'

Philosophus did so, absently. I could tell he was still having trouble taking all this in.

I found a clear spot of bench and sat down. 'I suppose this means our quest isn't over then.'

'And what quest would that be?' the old man said. 'Nobody's bothered to tell me what all the fuss is about. They've been too busy waving swords and yelling about retribution.'

'We're looking for the Necromancer.'

'Thank you, I *did* gather that much. Though I've never heard of him, her, or it, whichever he, she, or it may be.'

'It's a he, we think. And he's kidnapped the Princess.'

The wizard, who had been tidying up the books Philosophus had upset, paused. 'The Princess? How could *that* happen?'

I gave a 'you tell *me*' shrug.

The old man tugged and twisted at his beard, which made me realise how it had got to be the shape it is. 'Hmm, well... In that case maybe I should tell you about... Yes, it might help. Um, this fellow *is* safe, isn't he?'

'Philosophus?' I caught his attention. 'The old man says he might be able to tell us something. So don't attack him, alright?'

Philosophus managed a nod, but no more. He looked rather depressed.

I shrugged at the old man again, this time apologetically. 'We had this discussion about not doing anything heroic. I mean, neither of us are heroes. I don't know what came over him.'

'Youth, probably. Being young has all kinds of side-effects. Still, no harm done. And you don't have to call me "the old man". I've got a name, you know.'

'Sorry. What is it?'

'What's what?'

'Your name?'

'Oh. I am...' He trailed off and looked puzzled. 'I am... um, sure I've got it written down somewhere, but for the moment it escapes me. Oh well, you'll just have to tap me on the shoulder if you want my attention. Or, if you're feeling inventive, try a few names and we'll see if one fits. Now, how about some tea?'

A quarter of an hour later we were sitting by a lit fire with our hands wrapped around some rather curious cups that had, for no reason I could fathom, three handles each. Philosophus had hardly said a word since his heroic outburst, and mostly sat staring at his shoes. His sword, scabbarded and unbuckled, rested against the wall near the doorway. The old man fussed about, lighting the fire, making the tea, trying to find some biscuits (which, when found, proved to be as blue and furry as a muppet jamboree), till finally he sat down with us.

He glanced at a nearby window, which was dark. 'Looks like we're in for a change of weather.'

A moment later there was the unmistakable patter of raindrops against the glass.

'I thought this was supposed to be a desert,' I said.

'Only when it's not raining.'

Ha ha.

The old man sighed and stared at the fire. 'It *has* been growing much colder lately,' he muttered. 'I thought it was an early winter, or that I'd lost track of time. So easy to do. One moment it's spring, the next it's bed-time. But the Princess, you say... That would explain... But how could anyone do such a thing? And why?' He looked up suddenly, and for a moment I thought he expected me to answer, so I shrugged. He shrugged back, took a loud slurp of tea, and began.

'I will tell you what happened to me. It may be connected. A few months ago, before this deluge of hero-types began, a man came to me asking to learn magic. I tried to fob him off with the usual, you know, "Go sit on a mountaintop for a year, then come back when you're ready" — teaching magic is such a bother, particularly as I don't really know how to *do* it.'

'But I thought you were a wizard?' I said.

'I merely do what seems natural to me. Apparently that's called magic. What other people do, what they do naturally, that, to me, is magic, or at least as incomprehensible and strange as what I do is to them. Waving swords around, for instance — can't understand it, can't do it, though I'm sure it must be useful in *some* way. No, I often think each of us has a magic unique to ourselves. If only we didn't spend all our time being jealous of other people's, we might, perhaps, realise the true value of our own, and maybe work together a bit better.'

'Wow,' I said. 'You really are a wizard.'

'On the other hand, I may be talking rubbish. There's always that possibility. I've spent a long time alone, talking to no one but myself. After a while you talk rubbish merely to hear something new.' He scratched his chin beneath his beard and gave a cat-like grimace of pleasure. 'So, I was telling you about this chap that turned up. Didn't take long for me to sense in him a motive I didn't agree with at all. You get a feeling from people, don't you? I could tell this chap wanted to learn magic for some specific reason, something with a bad feel to it. But the more I tried to put him off, the more abusive he became. I tried putting a sleep spell on him, but it didn't work.'

'Magic doesn't always work, then?'

'It's a contest of wills when it comes to things like sleep spells. Fortunately, I was successful with all those hero-types, but hero-types, as a rule, are rather one-dimensional, which always leaves a few weak-spots to take advantage of. But this chap had an incredibly strong will. He was so focused, so tightly controlled, I soon realised the best thing I could do was disappear for a while.'

'You can do that?' I said, impressed. 'Disappear?'

'Not literally.'

'Oh.'

'No, I levitated out of reach.'

'Wow.' Now *that* would be a useful thing to be able to do. Just think if I could have floated into the air when Candice Cooper cornered me down Sanders Close. Imagine the look on her face!

'Unfortunately, that gave him the run of my things,' the old man continued. 'He spent about three hours tearing the place apart, found what he'd come for, then left.'

'And what had he come for?'

'A book.'

'A book of spells?'

'Prezactly. Or, rather, a book containing one very complicated, very powerful spell.'

'A bad spell?'

'It's called the Death Spell.'

'Sounds pretty bad.'

'Which is why I never used it. I wish, now, I had destroyed the damn thing. Should have done it long ago, but you know how it is. You tell yourself knowledge is knowledge and has a value of itself, it may be useful at some point, you never know when you might need it. Then you forget you've got it and don't bother worrying about it till something like that happens, by which time it's too late.'

'So who was this man?'

'Never learned his name. Or I forgot it. I have a particularly bad memory for names. I don't remember much about his face, either. I think he was wearing armour. But so many people wear armour these days, particularly when they're on quests, as everyone seems to be round here. I mean, why come to a desert if you're not on a quest? Come to a desert, you're either trying to find something or lose something. I came here and lost my name. Well, about a month after his visit — which is, by the way, how long it would take someone of moderate intelligence and strong will to make some progress with the Death Spell — these hero-types started turning up, accusing me of being a necromancer and offering to trim my beard by way of my gizzard.'

'So this person who stole the book,' I said, 'is probably the one we're talking about when we say "the

Necromancer". Only he's not really a powerful wizard, just a man who knows one spell, one *bad* spell, and he's used it, I guess on the — oh no, on the Princess! Does that mean she's...'

'Dead? No. I know you might think it from the name, but the Death Spell doesn't mean instant death. It's like I said about a sleep spell, it's a contest of wills. To make someone sleep, it's a matter of persuading them they want to, then they do. The Death Spell is the same, only instead of persuading them to sleep, you persuade them to die.'

'But that's not likely to happen, is it?' I said. 'I mean, who wants to die?'

'The point about the Death Spell is you find, within your victim, some flaw, some rift — some part that finds life too hard, or too pointless, or too horrible. The caster of the Death Spell finds this flaw — it helps if he knows the victim first — and works on it, making it grow from a seed into a poisonous thing that has its roots entangled in every aspect of the victim's heart and mind, until it is all their wish to be rid of the world. Because that final step into death cannot be achieved by magic. It takes an active decision on the victim's part. All the Death Spell can do is lead them into taking it.'

'So the Princess isn't dead? I mean, she *can't* die, can she? She won't want to, will she?'

'As I say, everyone has a flaw of this type within them.'

'But anyway,' I said, 'I suppose the question is, what do we do? Can someone be rescued from the Death Spell?'

'Oh yes. It's merely a matter of reversing the process. However much the victim has been convinced they want to die, you must convince them to want to live.'

'Well, that should be simple enough,' I said. 'So the *real* question is, how do we find her?'

'Find the man who cast the spell and you find her,' the old man said. 'He must be close by, because he has to spend some time every day repeating the Death Spell, trying to convince his victim that little bit closer towards the moment of death.'

'So we only need to know who this chap is, or where he is?'

The old man nodded. 'And he shouldn't be that hard to find. Convincing someone to die is not a cold, detached process. The caster must become involved in every aspect of the victim's life and mind. He must walk a good way down the fatal path he intends for his victim, leading the way, drawing them on. The caster himself risks death, and will certainly have the air of it about him, if not the actual appearance. It's quite likely that, after all this time working the spell, he has become quite wasted, thin and emaciated.'

Then two things happened at once.

I said, 'But I've seen him! It must have been him! Do you remember, Philosophus? That night we stopped on our way to the Palace, that horrible figure with a skull for a face—'

But, just as suddenly, Philosophus got to his feet and shouted at the old man, 'Then why didn't you *do* something? Why did you not tell someone or say something? Why—' And then he walked out.

Silence, apart from the pop and crackle of the fire and the patter of rain on the windows.

'Sorry about that,' I said.

The old man waved the apology aside, then slurped his tea and leant forward to poke the fire.

I took a finishing gulp from my tea, then said, 'I'd better see if he's okay.'

I found Philosophus outside, tending to the horses.

'You're getting wet,' I said, though the rain wasn't heavy.

He said nothing. He continued removing our gear from

the horses, but kept dropping things because they were wet, and slipping in puddles, and at one point Evenstar shook her head and sent a spray of raindrops into his face. Philosophus tried to meet all this with as much affronted dignity as he could, but you know what it's like when you're in a high old huff, everything conspires to point out what a clown you are.

'Please don't be angry,' I said. 'The old man didn't know what was going on, with the Princess and so on, not till we told him. And even now we have, he still doesn't know who the Necromancer is—'

'But I do.'

'Oh,' I said.

He finished seeing to Evenstar, then joined me on the top step, just inside the doorway, out of the rain. The night was getting chilly, but he obviously didn't want to go back up to the old man's room just yet. Instead, he sat in silence while the rain pittered in the puddles on the plain and against the tower walls.

'I will apologise,' he said eventually. 'I was not angry at the old man. I was angry at myself.'

'But, you know who the Necromancer is?' I said.

He nodded distractedly. When he next spoke, though, he didn't answer my question. 'Did I ever tell you what my last commission for Lord Paladin was, before I left the Palace?'

'No.'

'When I had finished making the mechanical servants and mechanical knights Lord Paladin required, he asked me to construct one final device, something of a type I had not attempted before. It was not a wholly mechanical creation but something half-mechanical. A suit of armour a man could wear to enhance his strength and prowess in combat. I would be provided with the armour and the dimensions of the man who would wear it, so I would know how much room I had to work with in order to fit my enhancements inside. When the armour was brought to me by two mechanical servants, I recognised it immediately. Anyone in the Realm would. It was Lord Paladin's.'

'Oh?' I said, not sure what this meant.

'I had not known — perhaps no one had — but he had become ill, or old, or perhaps a victim of the wasting that has come over the land since the Princess's disappearance. I did not question him, but performed the task I was given. When it was finished, I had the servants take his armour back to him. I did not see him at all while I worked, but that was not unusual. After that, I left the Palace and returned to my family home, as you know. But as I went, I fell under a pall. Knowing Lord Paladin was sickening, I felt that all hope was gone, for surely only he could bring the Princess back, only he could save her, yet he was wasting away...'

He turned to me. 'When you saw that death-like creature in the night, when you described to me its terrible face and wasted limbs, I did not think it might be Lord Paladin. For, though I knew he had become ill, the adjustments I made to his armour were not so great as to indicate *that* degree of wasting. No, it did not cross my mind. Not, that is, until we returned to the Palace. Because, after your brave attempt at duplicating the Princess's magic had failed,' (pathetic, more like) 'Lord Paladin asked me to make further adjustments, to add further enhancements to his armour to make up for the continued ravishment of his body by the disease.'

He stared into the night. 'As before, I was not permitted to see him without his armour. It was brought to me by mechanical servants, along with a list of the measurements of the man who would fit inside, the man Lord Paladin had become. And as I fitted the mechanisms, as I laid them inside the armour and saw the space they left, I realised... The thing you saw could have been him.'

'Oh, poor man,' I said, or tried to, because my throat had

gone dry and it came out as a whisper.

'I completed the work and had it taken to him. When next I saw him, dressed in it, I told him what you had seen. He confirmed that it had been him. You see, before we arrived, he had felt an intrusion into our world from the outside — which was, I think, you — and he felt compelled to investigate it. But, as the wasting of his body made his armour too unwieldy for extended use, he ventured out unprotected, and so was seen by you as he truly is, or as he has become.'

'And I screamed at the poor man,' I said, thinking back to that awful face and body, trying to match that creature up with the image of Lord Paladin, so strong and imposing and brave and heroic, and feeling terrible about the whole thing.

Philosophus, lost in his own story, didn't seem to hear. 'Once he confirmed it, once I realised how bad things were, I felt our cause was even more hopeless. And so, when you suggested we set out to find the Necromancer and rescue the Princess ourselves, I knew we had no alternative. There was nobody else left.'

'So who is the Necromancer,' I said, 'if that thing I saw isn't?'

Philosophus looked at his clasped hands. 'But do you not see? Even after the old wizard has explained the effect on its caster of using the Death Spell? Even after you saw the Palace so empty? Even after we discovered Lord Paladin has been sending his heroes not against a necromancer, but against an old man whose only crime was to be robbed of a book? And who but the thief of that book would want its true owner silenced? And what is the cause of Lord Paladin's wasting but the working of that book's terrible magic?'

'But you can't — you can't be saying Lord Paladin is — is the *Necromancer*? Can you? He *protects* the Princess. He told me so — *you* told me so. It doesn't make sense!'

Philosophus looked shaken and determined. 'It makes

perfect sense. I can see now it is the only thing that does. There *was* no Necromancer until I heard about him from Lord Paladin's lips. There was no assault on the Palace that carried the Princess away. She is still there, in some dark room, held by the Death Spell that Lord Paladin has cast upon her.'

'But... why?'

'That, I do not know.' Philosophus stood. 'I will apologise to the old man. Please wait here. If we go up together it will only seem I am apologising because you are making me do so, and I feel he deserves more than that. I have been a fool in too many ways already, and must begin acting like the man I am supposed to be.'

With that, he went inside.

I sat on the top step, in the cold, listening to the rain, unable to believe what Philosophus had said. It was mad. When I think of Lord Paladin — I mean, yes, he scared me, but only in the way a really strict teacher scares you, because you know they'll shout at you if you don't pay attention or do your work properly, not because you expect them to turn out to be a murderer or something. But that's what Philosophus was saying Lord Paladin is. A murderer, or would-be murderer. The killer of the very girl he once saved from a terrible slaughter, and carried over who knows how many miles of wilderness to the safety of the Palace, and has looked after ever since.

It doesn't make sense!

The thing is, we still don't know for sure. But, whether it's true or not, it's obvious what we've got to do next: go back to the Palace and confront him. And that's the scariest thing yet.

I was just thinking about going inside, because Philosophus *must* have apologised by now, and as I couldn't hear any crashing of benches or shouting, I guessed it had gone okay, when I looked up and there was someone coming down the stairs. But it wasn't Philosophus, it was the old man.

'Has he said sorry?' I said.

The wizard nodded.

'And did he tell you his idea about who the Necromancer is?'

He sat on the step beside me. 'Yes,' he said, tugging at his beard again. 'He did.'

'And what do you think?'

'As with so much in life, I can think what I like, but the truth will be the truth, whatever it is.'

'Is that just clever-sounding nonsense or do you not know?'

'Both.' He sniffed and adjusted one of his sandals. 'Of course, there's only one way to find out. Go back to the Palace.'

'Mm, that's what I was thinking.' I bit my lip. 'I don't suppose you'd—'

'No,' he said.

'But you haven't heard what I'm going to say!'

'You were going to suggest I go with you.'

'Well, yes.'

'No.'

'Why? You could be really useful with all your magic.'

'I think we've established my magic is useless against Lord Paladin, if he is indeed the perpetrator of this awful crime. Not to mention the fact that he seems to want me dead.'

'But I mean for bringing the Princess back to life, out of the spell. I don't know what to do when we find her. You said we have to convince her to want to live. But don't we need some magic, too, you know, to counter the Death Spell?'

'No. You simply talk to her.'

'What do we say?'

'You remind her why life is worth living.'

'Well, yes,' I said, 'only, it might be difficult to, you know, find the right words. What would *you* say?'

'To tell you the truth, young lady, I don't know. Were I to find the Princess in the grip of the Death Spell, were I to sit beside her and have to convince her to want to live once more, I really, really, wouldn't know what to say.'

'But...' I said, but could think of no buts.

The wizard smiled a tired smile. 'I am very, very old. I'm almost done with life. Oh, I enjoy pottering about, tinkering with things, looking into this and that, but really I'm tying up loose ends, that's all. It's why I came to the desert, to this tower. I'm not part of things anymore. I was, once, and enjoyed it while I was, but now I'm not and I don't want to be. Slowly, gently, I'm making my departure. Don't feel sorry for me. This is how it should be. I'm happy. I feel I've done almost all I wanted to do. Only a few things remain. Perhaps this, your coming here, is one of the things I must attend to. Perhaps it's the last. I don't know. But I'm content.'

'Oh,' I said, disappointed.

We sat for a while, saying nothing, and I tried not to feel too sad because the old man was basically saying he was at the end of his life, though he didn't mind. I tried telling myself it might actually be nice to feel like that, but it didn't work, because I don't like the idea of dying, not when I haven't lived yet, not properly anyway.

And at that thought, I started to feel really unhappy. Not for the old man, but for me. Because here I was, in this fantasy world, but it wasn't my world at all. Everything I'd been expecting from life was somewhere else, back through a dark attic, down some stairs, in a life I'd run away from because it was too horrible. I thought, 'What am I doing here?' and almost said it, but at that moment I looked up and my eyes widened and my jaw dropped.

It was no longer raining. Instead, white flakes were falling softly through the darkness, seesawing and zigzagging and corkscrewing their way to the ground, and the patter of raindrops had been replaced by the gentle, muffled fuffing of settling snow.

I was amazed. Snow has always done something special for me, at least till you have to go outside and get cold and some kid throws a snowball at you and it hits your ear then melts down your collar, but the first time I see it I always think it's wonderful, magical — voorish — a reminder that the world can change completely in an instant.

The old man put a hand on my shoulder. 'I cannot tell you the words to use. You are young. You have your life before you, and so you have the promise of life *within* you. You must find that promise. It will tell you what to say to the Princess. Don't worry about putting it in the right words. Try your best, with honesty and passion, and you'll get across what you want to say. You simply have to be yourself.'

I tried to smile. But even all that wonderful snow wasn't enough to make me do that. It was no good. I had to be honest. 'I don't know what makes life worth living,' I said.

'Oh, come, now—'

'—And I don't have any passion. Or anything. I'm just miserable all the time. I ran away from everything because I hated it so much. But here I am and nothing's changed, it's all just as bad, with the Necromancer and the dying Princess. It's horrible. I hate it. I hate it all.'

I felt awful, and ungrateful, but it was true. I thought I'd escaped from everything I don't like, but I haven't, and realising that made me feel I'm more than halfway the victim of my own Death Spell, and certainly no help for the Princess. What had my running away up those phantom stairs been, after all, but running away from life, and what is running away from life but a wish you could end it all?

'You say everyone's got a magic all to themselves,' I said, 'but what's mine? Making people miserable? Making myself miserable? If it is, I'd rather not have any, thank you.'

'I can't tell you what your magic is. You must find it for yourself.'

'Well, where do I look for it? It's not at home, so I came here, and it's not here, because I tried being magic in the Princess's Singing Chamber and nothing happened. It's all rubbish!' I'm ashamed to admit I said that rather peevishly. The trouble is, I *so* wanted him to tell me that everything would be okay, and to work some of his magic to *make* everything okay, but he wasn't doing it, and I felt like stamping my foot and getting all moody, but I knew that was pointless, so there was nothing I could do but feel bad.

I was crying now, but fortunately not in that helpless blubby way that makes you sputter and sniff like a backfiring car. I took out my hanky and wiped my eyes. 'Sorry. I didn't mean to have a go at you.'

'It's alright to be angry sometimes,' the old man said, his hand still warm on my shoulder. 'Sometimes it's even necessary, particularly when you're young and find something worth being angry about.' He smiled. 'And there you are, saying you have no passion.'

'But that's not what I meant! I don't want to be angry. I just want to be happy. Not majorly happy, just happy enough, you know?'

'You may have to follow the darker feelings to find the lighter ones. But it's getting cold. Let's go back inside and see if your philosophical friend has kept the stew from burning.'

After I'd taken a moment to calm down and de-gloop my face, we returned to the wizard's room, which is where I am now, writing it up, trying to make sense of it.

Because there are big bits that don't make sense. Like Lord Paladin being the Necromancer and kidnapping the Princess, who he's supposed to have dedicated his life to protecting. But I suppose we can't be *totally* sure that's true yet. We have to find out.

And what do we do when we *do* find out? We (after defeating Lord Paladin, of course!) talk the Princess into wanting to live again. Me, Moping Millie of Willow Drive, and Lord Dolorous the professional miserablist.

While eating, we discussed how to confront Lord Paladin.

It was a rather short discussion. No one had any ideas.

Or, I had one, but it was short-lived.

'Hey,' I said, 'what about all those heroes?'

'What about them?' the old man said.

'Well, if we wake them up, we'll have our own little army, won't we?'

'Picture the scene, young lady,' the wizard said. 'The heroes wake up and see the man they *still* think of as the Necromancer, the man who cast a sleep spell on them and kept them prisoners in his tower while the Princess lies dying somewhere. They see him and he says, "You got it all wrong! I'm not the Necromancer. It's that well-respected pillar of all you think good and decent, Lord Paladin, who's the real evil round here. You've got to go back to the Palace and deal with him." What do you think will happen? Sliced wizard is what will happen. I know I said I'm almost finished with life, but I intend to go in my own calm, quiet way, not being mauled by the world's leading representatives of the Brawn Over Brain Club, thank you very much.'

So that was that. Philosophus and I are going back to face Lord Paladin on our own. I'm scared silly at the prospect, but Philosophus seems grimly determined about it, in his new-man persona. (He seems to be changing all the time, doesn't he? First he was the Dolorous Lord, then he had a brief but unsuccessful stint as Action Hero, and now he's — well, what is he? Perhaps himself? I hope so. *Someone's* got to come out of all this with something good happening to them.)

Anyway, my hand aches from all this writing, and it looks like biro number two is on its way out, so I'll give it, and me, a rest. Na-night!

Day one of our journey back

It's a bit like old times, isn't it, being back on the road? Here we are sheltering in a little hollow under one of the Rocky Desolation's weird rock formations, only without a campfire because there's no wood around, and it's actually quite chilly so it'd be nice to have one. But other than that (and a couple of other things I ought to mention) I could get used to this.

Hmm. That 'couple of other things'. I suppose they're rather important. The first of them is the sun, which ever since Philosophus told me was fading and dying I've been keeping an eye on, and except for that dreary episode in the doomy-gloomy Palace, I've always felt things aren't as bad as he made them out to be.

Till now. Because when I woke up this morning (this was back at the wizard's tower, where we stayed last night), it was still quite dark. I thought it was just really early so I rolled over and got a bit more sleep. Then I woke up again. Still dark. Wow, I thought, all this time I get to roll about in bed. (Actually it wasn't a bed, just a pile of blankets the old wizard put together for me, but it was comfy enough.) So I rolled over again and tried to sleep. But I wasn't tired. I sat up. The old man was in his chair by the fire, looking at an hourglass in his hand. I wondered if he was contemplating Time or something equally abstract and deep, like

Breakfast. Philosophus was in another blanket-pile bed in another part of the room and I could see he was just lying on his back with his eyes open, staring at the ceiling.

Then the old man said, 'It's morning.'

'Still early, though, isn't it?' I said.

'No. In fact, it may be quite late. I didn't sleep last night, I rarely do, and I turned this hourglass over each time the sands ran out. Eleven times. That means it has been at least eleven hours. I say "at least", because after counting the eleventh, I haven't bothered to turn it over again. Night has passed, and some of the morning, too.' He set the hourglass on the mantelpiece and turned to look at the window. 'It seems things have taken a rather sudden change.'

I got up, thinking it was probably just cloud making everything so gloomy. And there were a few clouds up there, but only a few, scudding around like stragglers at the end of a party, wandering in search of a bit of ground that hadn't been rained on yet. Most of the sky was clear. But it was grey. A grey, uncloudy sky. It's weird to look at. You keep blinking, to take the murkiness out of your eyes, but it isn't in your eyes, it's up there. The sun was like a thumb-print smudge on a grimy window, so pale you could stare at it for ages before remembering you weren't supposed to stare at the sun, then you'd look away but your eyes wouldn't hurt at all. Looking at the desert out there, I could have been on Mars.

'What's going on?' I said.

Philosophus, who had also got up and was standing behind me, said, 'Time is running out.'

We barely spoke a word over breakfast, then tidied up our things and went out to prepare the horses while the old man stood at the top of his stairs and watched. Before I knew it, we were mounted and saying our goodbyes.

'Farewell, sir,' Philosophus said. 'I apologise once more for my rash actions and stupidity.'

'Think nothing of it. Rash actions and stupidities are what make life interesting. I've certainly done my share, and avoid them now only because I'm old enough and slow enough to have to take my time about things, so I can think them through. I wish you many more.'

Then the old man turned to me and smiled.

I said, 'I don't suppose you'd—'

'No.'

'—reconsider—'

'No.'

'—coming... Oh well, goodbye.'

'Goodbye young lady. I wish you luck. Have faith in yourself, and I'm sure you'll come through.'

So we rode off and turned to wave every so often. The old man waved back, but I couldn't help feeling that as soon as we were gone he'd go up to his room and return to pottering about, 'tying up loose ends', and would forget about us on the instant. It makes me sad in a way, because he was such a nice old man and I wish I could know him better. But maybe we'll see him again. After all, we've got to come back once this is over (like, when we've faced Lord Paladin and freed the Princess from the Death Spell!) because we have to make sure all those sleeping heroes are woken up in a safe and wizard-friendly fashion. So there's no need to feel sad about it, is there?

Not when I've got so many other things to be depressed about.

Like Lord Paladin, for instance. He was the other thing, along with the state of the sun, on my mind.

We crossed the plain, which was now muddy in places, and even had lingering patches of icy snow, then re-entered the now Manticore-less Pass, and rode by the remains of the mechanical knight and his horse who had saved our lives only yesterday, and I found myself thinking, 'Yes, but was it worth it?'

Gloomy thoughts, Carol. Stay away from them.

We left the pass and set out again across the Rocky Desolation and it wasn't till then that Philosophus and I had our first, and only, conversation of the day.

'What I can't understand,' I said, 'is *why* Lord Paladin would do such a thing.'

'I cannot understand it either,' Philosophus said.

And that, my dears, was that.

Day two of our journey back

So here we are, on the Ancient Roadway again. The Palace is only a few hours away. Philosophus suggested we have a rest, finish our supplies, then press on, rather than camping for the night. I mean, it's late and it's dark, but it's been pretty dark all day, so that's not going to make much difference, is it?

All this journey I've been squirming out of doing anything heroic, and so far (amazingly) luck has been on my side. The mechanical knight defeated the manticore, and the man we expected to be the Necromancer turned out to be a kindly old wizard (never did learn his name), so there was no call for heroics in either case. But I've come to the end of my luck. I know what Lord Paladin's like. He's big and scary — even *more* scary now I know he's probably the Necromancer, and therefore evil as well — and he lives in a great dark tower surrounded by stormy clouds. (Which is exactly where you'd expect the baddie of the story to live, isn't it? Why didn't I suspect him before? Well, I *did* think something was up, but I never thought it could be *this*...)

I wish I was somewhere else. Home? In bed, waiting to go to school and face Candice Cooper? Almost. It's that bad.

Looks like we're about to go. What a way to end my

diary! I mean, presuming I never get to write in it again, which is a majorly probable outcome, considering we're about to walk into the dragon's den.

It's been fun. No, not fun, but... Well, it's been *something*. And (choose your last words, Carol) something's better than nothing, I guess.

(Way to console yourself, girl!)

So this is how it ends

Well, I was wrong. I do get one more chance to write in my diary. And what do I get to write?

We failed.

I knew we would.

Maybe not totally, not yet, but there doesn't seem much more we can do.

Anyway, I thought I'd write things up. As a warning to those who come after? No, just habit.

So there we were, riding along the Ancient Roadway in the dark. It wasn't totally dark, but we were definitely under that scum of cloud that clings to the Palace like bubbles round your big toe in the bath. Looking up, all you could see were silvery spider-web lines where the clouds were thin enough for what light there was (sun or moon, I couldn't tell) to get through. Sometimes there'd be a flash of lightning, oddly slow, so you could almost see it making its zigzag decisions on its way to the ground. (Left, right, left, then weee, crash! Must be fun being a lightning bolt, though brief.) Then thunder, cracking like an ogre grinding his knuckles. It rained one moment, snowed the next, then we'd have icy wind and sleet.

I was relying on the Roadway getting less ruined to let me know we were close, but suddenly we were there, and the road was still ruined. I thought I must have misremembered, but then we had a flash of lightning, and the Palace was this huge dark thing in front of us, and scattered all around were the ruins that had once been a growing town, and now were even more ruined than before. Really, it was nothing but rubble.

'How long have we been gone?' I said, thinking maybe I hadn't been told that time works in odd ways hereabouts.

But all Philosophus said was, 'Too long.'

We came to the Palace door. Philosophus reached out to push the smallest of those Russian Doll doors, the one we went through before, but it swung inward before he could, and a blank-faced mechanical maid ushered us inside that vast, echoey courtyard.

'I will inform Lord Paladin of your arrival,' she said, just like before.

'Wait!' Philosophus said, halting her. He turned to me. 'I have an idea. We cannot alert Lord Paladin to our presence just yet. We must endeavour to do two things before we confront him. First, we must uncover evidence that confirms our suspicions. Second, we must prepare ourselves to act, should they be true. Here is what I propose, if you are willing. I will work towards the second point. By this I mean that I will find what mechanical knights I can, and gather them together and make sure they are properly operational so we may use them if necessary.'

'Right,' I said, in a what's-coming-next kind of way.

'What I want you to do is try to discover if Lord Paladin really is the Necromancer.'

'How do I do that?'

'I have an idea by which this might be accomplished with no, or at least minimal, danger. This mechanical maid will be of use — or, parts of her.' He looked at me doubtfully. 'Here is what I suggest. You will dress in as like a manner to this maid as possible, so you can, in the darkness of the Palace, pass yourself off as her. This will give you the freedom to move around without suspicion. Doing so, you may be able to discover something.'

'But,' I said, trying to tell myself now was not the time for cowardice or doubts, 'what can I do?'

'You must find Lord Paladin and follow him.'

'Oh.'

He hung his head. 'I wish our roles could be reversed. But your build and size suggest you for this task. You are, perhaps, a trifle short, and will require padding to, ah, shape you correctly, but the mechanical maid is padded in those areas most characteristic of her form, so this is not a problem. I, however, am too tall.'

I was glad it was dark, because I must have been blushing some new shade of purple. But I guessed this wasn't the time for flattery, or for tiptoeing round the facts to spare my feelings, so I shrugged and said, 'Okay.'

'I am not asking you to approach Lord Paladin, or to confront him in any way. If you see him, remain hidden. Only rely on the disguise if necessary, and then only to make your escape.'

'Right.'

'Follow him. Listen to him. Observe him. But do not endanger yourself—'

'I said right,' I said, though not peevishly, just out of nervousness. If it had to be done, I wanted to get on with it. I could make up my own mind how brave to be, and how little of my cowardly common sense the situation called for when it came to it. 'Let's get me dressed up.'

What followed was handled with the utmost tact by all concerned. Philosophus had the maid go into the stables, and deactivated her in one of the empty stalls. I stood in the next stall, and as Philosophus removed various bits of her clothing, he handed them over the wooden partition and I put them on.

First there was a wig, which was easy enough, though it

felt a bit heavy and itchy. Then, after a certain amount of picking at threads and a ripping sound, came the dress, which actually proved to be a good fit, though I couldn't do it up on my own as it was laced down the back, so once it was on I had Philosophus come round to help. He grabbed the laces, wrenched them as hard as he could and tied them in a double knot, which I guess is what he did for the mechanical maids when he'd finished building them.

I, however am not a mechanical maid.

'How's that?' he said, turning me round.

'Can't — breathe,' I managed, and I don't know what colour I'd gone, but it was enough to make him whip me round and undo the laces in a trice. Once I'd got my breath back, he did them up again, bit by bit, constantly asking, 'Is that alright? A little more? Too tight?'

Then he removed the maid's face and turned it into a mask, cutting eye-holes and air-holes, and working out a way of fixing it to the wig so it would stay in place.

Now, I've never really been one for dressing up, or for wearing anything other than slouchy clothes, really. But suddenly here I was in a very feminine dress, with lacy frills at the collar and cuffs, and a skirt belled out by so many petticoats it would probably break your fall from a two-storey jump, and it felt quite nice. I'm not sure whether to say this or not, because it's a bit embarrassing, but I suppose it's silly to be embarrassed as I'm at the end of things and it doesn't really matter anymore, so I may as well say it. The dress, you see, was padded in certain places, so as to give the mechanical maid her feminine form. Padded in just the places that I, in my sub-adolescent bod, am not, if you see what I mean. (And if you don't, I'm not going into any details, right?) So I stood there looking at myself and thinking, 'I wonder if this is what I'll look like in a few years, if I ever actually grow up and don't remain a little girl all my life?' As I said, totally embarrassing. But the thing was it made me feel... Oh I don't know. I'm not going to go on about it. It's silly.

Philosophus came round with the mask and had me put it on. It took a bit of adjusting so I could see through the eye-holes, and even then I could only see straight in front of me. If I wanted to look sideways, or up, or down, I had to turn my head. Philosophus tugged at the sleeves and adjusted the wig, then stood back and rubbed his chin.

'Yes,' he said. 'I think... Yes.'

I waited. That was it. Well, what was I expecting, compliments?

I tried walking about, and Philosophus kept saying things like, 'Keep your head upright, mechanicals never look down,' and 'Yes, but with more grace,' till I had to stop and tell him that if I didn't look down I'd trip over my own feet, which was a very un-mechanical thing to do, and I was giving it as much grace as I could. If Lord Paladin got suspicious I'd just have to make a few spring-pinging noises and pretend I'd got a cog loose.

I put my clothes in my schoolbag and gave it to Philosophus, then we left the stables (where Philosophus had also seen to our horses while I'd been practising my mechanical walk). As we left, I averted my eyes from the maid, who was of course standing there with less than nothing on, cogs and springs out for all to see.

We started up the stairs, and almost instantly I tripped. I righted myself, readjusted my wig and mask, then tried again and tripped again, so after that I grabbed my skirts in one hand and raised the mask with the other and walked up the stairs like that. Philosophus gave me a look like he was about to say something, then thought better of it.

Once we reached the top, Philosophus said, 'I will gather as many mechanical knights as I can in my workshop. Meet me there as soon as you find anything out.'

'Right... Um, are you sure this disguise will work?

Mechanical maids have wooden hands. I don't.'

'Keep your hands hidden.'

'What if he asks me to do something? What if he asks me to fetch him something or go somewhere?'

'Leave him and come directly to my workshop. If you can, on the way, find a real mechanical maid and repeat his instructions to her. That way his suspicions will not be aroused.'

'But what if he asks me something? You know, a question?'

'Either nod or shake your head. The mechanicals have only a few limited responses, so he will not expect a verbal reply.'

'But what if—'

Philosophus held up his hand. 'There are a thousand possibilities in every moment of our lives, Carol. We cannot plan for them all. Be careful, be watchful, and if all else fails, take off the mask and run.'

'Right. See you soon — oh, hand me my torch from my bag.'

He did so, then walked off down the corridor and disappeared into the darkness.

Alone in the Palace with only a (probably insane) Hero of the Realm for company, I wasn't sure whether to be excited or nervous. I decided to pretend that the way my innards were writhing like a barrel of snakes was excitement.

I gathered my skirts and went up some more stairs. Spiral ones, this time.

I had to find Lord Paladin.

Where was I going to look?

Well, in my previous time at the Palace (before we'd gone off on our mad quest to save the Princess), I hadn't done much exploring, but I'd picked up enough to know how to find a few places. The library, for instance. So I started heading there. Then I realised Lord Paladin was hardly likely to be in the library, and I was only going there because I knew where it was, which was pointless.

So I stopped, midway up the stairs, and did some thinking.

My brain wasn't working too well. No doubt a result of all that 'excitement' I was feeling. So I sat down. It didn't help.

I took the wig and mask off. That didn't help either.

I turned off the torch. That just made me scared, so I turned it on again.

Then I heard something. Footsteps. Someone was coming up or down the stairs towards me. The thing is, the Palace is so echoey, at first I couldn't tell which direction they were coming from, and of course, the stairs being spiral, I wouldn't see whoever it was till they were on top of me, and that made me panic. I put the wig back on and made sure the mask was in the right place, but really I was in a tight spot, because those stairs weren't wide enough for two and if it was Lord Paladin coming towards me, at the close range we'd have to pass each other, he was going to see right through my disguise.

The footsteps were getting closer.

I realised they were coming from above. Stupidly, I shone the torch upwards to see who it was. The footstepper came into view round the corkscrew turn of the staircase.

It was a mechanical maid.

'Um, hello,' I said.

She didn't say anything.

Blown it again, Carol. Mechanical maids don't say hello to each other.

'Um, I'm going up,' I said.

Still, she said nothing and did nothing. I wondered if she'd been given orders by Lord Paladin to capture any humans she found wandering the Palace. Or perhaps strangle them. One look at those wooden hands and I could believe it.

I stood there for a few (very loud) heartbeats, then took a step towards her. She didn't do anything, so I took a few more, and this time she moved to one side to let me pass.

'Thanks,' I said, pressing my back against the wall and edging past, keeping an eye on her in case she was about to make a lunge.

Something caught my eye. A glint in the torch-light, coming from her hair. I peered closer. There was something shiny in her wig, something perhaps made of metal...

Metal shavings.

'Tilly Two!'

The maid curtseyed gracefully (despite being poised on the thin end of a wedge-shaped spiral step).

'You probably don't remember me,' I said, but she bobbed her head again, so I guessed she did (or was being polite).

I had an idea. 'I'm looking for Lord Paladin.'

Immediately, she turned and started walking back up the stairs.

'Oh no,' I said, 'I don't need you to take me to him, just tell me where he is.' But of course she couldn't tell me where he was, so I thought a bit more, and had another idea (which was good, because the other one would have been getting lonely). 'He's not in his throne room, is he?'

Tilly Two shook her head.

'Philosophus's workroom?'

Again a shake of the head.

'Is he in the library?'

No.

This was beginning to sound like a game of Cluedo, and I was running out of places I knew.

One last desperate try. 'The Princess's Singing

Chamber?'

A nod.

'He's there?'

A nod.

'Thanks!' I said, and rushed up the stairs.

It was only when I reached the top that I paused to remind myself what I was rushing towards.

The Princess's Singing Chamber, if you remember, is about the highest point in the whole Palace, which means there's lots of stairs-climbing to do to reach it. (Stairs, stairs, stairs. This whole thing has been about nothing but stairs!) Anyway, I took the wig and mask off and went up, keeping an ear out for any sign I was getting close to Lord Paladin. When I came to the final flight I paused to listen.

I couldn't hear anything. What was I expecting, him to be blasting out selections from *Guys and Dolls*? I guess not. The question was, what was he doing up there? Maybe he'd gone up to think about the Princess. If so, then I guess this was my best opportunity to find out whether he was the Necromancer or not, and what, if anything, he'd done with her.

But there were a few things to think about first.

Thing number one was the fact that those stairs were the only way of reaching the Singing Chamber. That meant they were also the only way of getting away once I'd done my spying. So, as soon as Lord Paladin gave the slightest sign of coming back down I'd have to scoot or get caught.

Thing number two was how to spy on him. The Singing Chamber has no furniture, nothing to hide behind. Beneath it is another chamber, but that's empty too, so nowhere to hide there either. The only thing I could think of was to crouch on the stairs as close to that opening in the Singing Chamber floor as possible, maybe poking my head up every now and then to see what was going on.

Thing number three. The wig and mask: put them on or leave them off? I mean, the mask was only going to get in the way of my seeing anything clearly. I decided that a mechanical maid had no excuse for being up here, so if Lord Paladin saw me he was bound to get suspicious and question me, and that would be that, mask or no mask. So I was going to not bother with the mask and just hope I wasn't seen.

Right. Situation thoroughly thunked through, I started up the stairs.

Immediately, I noticed something odd. My feet were crunching at every step. The stone stairs were covered in sand.

Sand? Up here?

It was quite dark sand, and some bits were more like gravel. But I wasn't about to do a Philosophus, linking it to marine erosion or whatever. Instead, I focused on the practical aspect. The sand was making my stealthy footsteps into unstealthy footcrunches. What to do? Well, apologies to the mechanical maid whose hair it is, but I decided to use the wig to brush the steps free of sand as I went, making them crunchless, and returning my feet to stealth mode.

When I came to the room below the Singing Chamber, I risked a quick torch-flash. The only thing different from when I'd been here last was all the grit on the floor.

Still no sound from above — no, wait, I could hear movement. I took a few more steps up and listened. Crunching. Just like my feet on the sandy floor, only these were harder, heavier feet, like a big man's encased in metal. (No prizes for guessing whose, then.)

I went as far up as I could, till I had to crouch to make sure the top of my head didn't show through the opening in the Singing Chamber floor.

He stopped moving. Utter silence.

Now was the moment to have a look. I poked my head

up, and ducked back down straightaway. All I'd seen was that he was standing in the centre of the room, facing off to my left.

I gave it a few seconds, then risked a longer look.

The curtains in the Singing Chamber were raised. Storm clouds were roiling outside like a troop of sooty tiger cubs. Lord Paladin was stock still, staring his lifeless eye-slit stare into the distance.

He raised his arms.

I ducked, but forced myself to keep watching.

Arms levelled in front of him, he looked like he was going to do a dive. He parted his hands, and the clouds drew aside like a pair of curtains. Light came through the gap, pale, weak, hardly recognisable as sunlight, or worth the name of moonlight. Then he let his arms drop and his head sag, as if the effort had tired him out.

After a brief rest he straightened, and this time raised only one arm, his left, lifting it with the hand cupped as if to grab at something. He remained standing like that, gauntleted fingers scrabbling at the air like whatever he was trying to grab was just out of reach.

I craned to see what he was looking at. What I saw was impossible: a castle on a steep grassy hill, surrounded by woodlands. What's impossible about that, you ask? Well, try this: there isn't a castle outside the Palace, and certainly not on a level with the Singing Chamber, which is about twenty stories off the ground!

So this was more magic. Lord Paladin had made the window focus on a distant place, who knows how far away. Maybe this was what the Princess used to do when she was up here. Maybe Lord Paladin was about to try and sing the world to life again?

Fat chance.

His outstretched hand reached a little further and *grabbed*.

On the instant, the closest wall of the castle in the window slewed away from the rest of the building, like it had just realised it was made of wet mud and ought not to be holding together. It cracked into huge fragments and smashed into the side of the hill, half-burying itself in the earth and sending off showers of smaller pieces. Dust billowed into the air, and I could make out a couple of people in the exposed inside of the castle standing there shocked. Then they ran for their lives.

Almost at the same moment, something even weirder happened. Lightning streamed through the Palace window, not breaking the glass, but heading right for Lord Paladin's clenched hand. It hit, bunching around him like a cage of light, then seemed to go inside him.

The air was electric. I'm sure my hair was standing on end. I felt this tingling all over my skin, and right inside me too, and I was jittery all over. The lightning continued to stream into Lord Paladin's hand, and that distant castle continued to crumble. One of its corner towers peeled away, sagging to flop against the ground as you'd never imagine something made of stone could, and taking more than half another wall with it. A whole section of the inside of the castle went, with floors and ceilings and fragments of staircases tumbling down the hill to crash into the trees and break or uproot them, leaving great gashes of raw mud in the hillside, and all the furniture in those rooms went too, to be dashed into fragments. Luckily, no people followed. None that I saw anyway.

The lightning coming through the window turned bright white and the Singing Chamber began to shake. At first I thought it was just me, shaking with fear, till I felt this sprinkling of dust come down on me, as well as a few larger fragments of stone, which of course explained all that sand I'd found on my way here. It wasn't sand, it was crumbled stone from the shaking of the Palace.

I fell back against the wall, not needing to watch now, just wanting to run. I couldn't get to my feet in all that shaking, even though I knew I had to get away, so I bundled into a ball. (Good to see the old survival instincts were back.)

Then it was over. I uncurled and risked a look. The clouds had closed up again, and were boiling even wilder than before, like they were angry Lord Paladin had been able to control them. The man himself was standing with his back to me, and at first he was sagging again, head down, shoulders bowed. Then he straightened, and raised his arms and gave a triumphant stretch, clenching his fists till they shook and little jags of lightning fizzled round them.

That made me realise what he'd been doing, and what I'd just seen.

I gathered my skirts and ran down the stairs as fast as I could.

'I know why everything's ruined!' I said, bursting into Philosophus's workroom.

I was so involved in what I'd just seen that I didn't notice there were no mechanical knights gathered in the room, nor did I see how defeated Philosophus looked, slouched on a stool in one dark corner.

I said, 'I found him — I had to ask Tilly Two — he was in the Princess's Singing Chamber — I went up and—' (pause to swallow) '—he was doing magic of some kind — making this castle appear in the window — then lightning came in — and he made the castle crumble — and he was tired at first then suddenly he wasn't, like he'd been filled with energy — he'd drained it from the castle somehow — and that must be why there're so many ruins all around, he's sucking life out of the world, just like the Princess used to sing life *into* the world, only he's sucking it out and using it to keep himself going.' I stopped, panting, and whatever reaction I expected was most certainly not what I got.

With the infinite calm of the beyond-all-hope, Philosophus said, 'It is too late. She is dead.'

'What? Who?'

Philosophus smiled his old, pale smile. 'I was not entirely honest when I asked you to seek out Lord Paladin. I did not expect you to find him. I thought, with your knowledge of the Palace being so limited, you would simply become lost in the corridors. I did not think it right you should become endangered in the battle for a world that is not your own. I did not, of course, anticipate that you would ask one of the mechanicals.' He frowned. 'I never built that ability into them. Odd, how they manage to constantly do more than I ever designed them to do.' He shrugged. 'Nevertheless, I thought I knew where Lord Paladin was, and where he would be keeping the Princess, so I made my way directly there.'

'Where?'

'The Palace dungeons, below ground. I had seen him enter them several times when last we were here, but of course thought nothing of it at the time. On our return journey, I made the connection.'

'But you didn't find him down there,' I said. 'I found him up in the Singing Chamber.'

'I found the Princess. The dungeon chamber where she lies was not locked. The door was open. She had been placed in an unclosed stone tomb.'

'But she can't be. Not... dead.'

'Yet she is.' He smiled again, as if to apologise.

'No,' I said. 'I don't believe you. I mean, isn't the world supposed to fall apart when she dies?'

'But do you not see? The sudden darkness of two days ago? The world may not fall apart instantly, but its final decline has begun.'

I sagged on a nearby stool. 'It can't be right.'

'It is *not* right. Yet it is true.'

I didn't know what to say. We sat there for a while.

Then I said, 'Did you check her pulse?'

'Her pulse?'

'In her wrist. Did you check it?'

'I did not touch her. I thought it unseemly. She is dead.'

'But you've got to check these things. Did you hold a mirror over her face? To see if she's breathing? Did you do that?'

He frowned. 'A mirror?'

'So you just *decided* she's dead by looking at her?'

'She was pale, motionless, and in a tomb. What other signs did I need?'

I stood up. 'I thought you're supposed to have studied these things, how the body works and so on.'

'I have studied its mechanics, its bone structure and musculature, but...' He looked a bit embarrassed. 'I have not studied how women's bodies work.'

'Well the breathing and heart-beating's the same! Though it seems the blood supply to the brain's a lot different.'

He began to look hopeful. 'You have studied these things?'

'No, but I've seen *Casualty* a few times. Come on, we can't give up yet!'

The dungeon, needless to say, was down some stairs, about three steep flights of them, as if whoever designed this place really didn't like the idea of keeping prisoners anywhere near the rest of the building, and maybe only stopped at three flights because the builders complained. The designer had also, rather thoughtfully, put plenty of gargoyle faces up in the corners, leering, gurning, and sticking out their tongues at the prisoners who had to walk under them, thus providing ample opportunity for your dungeon spider (they're a real variety) to set up home and build these huge ragged webs that hung all around us like a lich's laundry.

When the steps finally ended, we came to a hallway lined with doors, each of which led to a small, dingy cell. There were no prisoners. The only cell with anything in it was at the far end. It contained a long stone box with high sides. From the doorway, you couldn't see what was in the box.

'Is that where she is?' I said.

'It is.'

I noticed something. I clicked my torch off to be sure. 'She's glowing.'

It was true. A pale light was coming from the box.

'Perhaps the process of decay,' Philosophus said.

'Oh shut up.' I turned my torch back on and we went into the room.

It was cold. I took a deep breath, and when I let it out, it was a puff of mist. But there wasn't a bad smell, which was a good sign.

I realised I was nervous, not just because I didn't want the Princess to be dead, and not just because I didn't want to see some horrific sight staring back at me when I came to that box (*not* coffin) in the centre of the room. It was because, all the time I'd been in this world I'd been hearing about the Princess, how wonderful she was and how magical, and now finally I was going to see her. She would, of course, be beautiful, I knew that, as any reader of fairy tales would. I prepared myself to be jealous and humble, and stepped up to the box.

She was pale as ivory, and as still as stone. She was older than me, perhaps eighteen or nineteen, and had long dark hair, coiled in a plait on the cushion beside her. You could see, only just, the pastel green stroke of a vein beneath the skin of her temple. She wasn't breathing, but there was something about her, as though any moment she might wake up. I was sure she wasn't dead.

'I knew you would come back, Lord Dolorous.'

Lord Paladin was in the doorway. I glanced at Philosophus, scared he might do something rash, but instead he merely looked troubled.

'She is not dead,' Lord Paladin said. 'Not yet. She has reserves of life even I did not expect.'

'Then release her from the spell,' Philosophus said. 'Wake her up, put this right.'

'I will not wake her. She is infected with wilfulness and evil.'

'Evil?' Philosophus shook his head. 'I once thought there were two people in this world of whom that could never be said. Both are here now, before me. Yet I find, to my horror, that one has evil rooted in the very centre of his being. But even that cannot shake my belief that the other does not.'

'Oh, it is not a blatant evil, Lord Dolorous. She hides it beneath the mask of compassion. But it is an evil seed, and will bear fruit as evil as any other.'

'What do you accuse her of?'

'She would destroy the Realm.'

'She hasn't the capacity for destruction!'

'Oh, she would call it kindness. Kindness to our enemies. She would welcome them in. Yet folly is still evil if it has evil results, if it ignores the wisdom of its elders. I counselled her against this. She refused my counsel. She demanded I step down as Protector of the Realm so she could achieve her ends. She told me my time was over, and her time as Queen must begin. I could not allow that.'

'You are talking about her desire to welcome the glimmerlings into our world?'

'Pests! Demons! They are not living beings like you or I,

they are a plague! They are the evil against which we define our good. I live to fight, and I fight *them*. If I cannot fight them and live, I welcome the death of any world that will take them with it.'

'You are insane,' Philosophus said.

'Then let the sane die with their folly.' Lord Paladin stepped back and slammed the door. We heard the click of its lock, followed by heavy steps walking away.

'Hand me your lectric,' Philosophus said.

I gave him a blank look before realising he meant my torch, so I gave it to him.

He went to the door, muttering, 'A lock is just a mechanical device, a prentice-piece compared to my mannequins. It should be easy enough to...' He crouched before the door, but even I could see he wouldn't be able to do anything. There was no keyhole this side, just a blank metal plate.

He sighed and returned my torch.

'Look,' I said, before we got too hopeless, 'remember what the old man said about the Death Spell? You can bring someone out of it by persuading them to want to live. That's all we've got to do. There's no point getting out of here and going after Lord Paladin till we wake her up, right?'

'You are right.'

He stood one side of the stone box, I stood the other. We looked at the Princess, but neither of us said anything. I felt she ought to wake up of her own accord. I mean, she'd heard all that stuff Lord Paladin said about her. Surely that was enough to make her get up and have a go back at him?

Obviously not.

'What do we say?' I said, meaning, 'You go first.'

Philosophus coughed politely and leant forward. 'Princess? Your Highness? The Realm needs you. It is in great danger without you.'

No response.

'Lord Paladin is intent on destroying the Realm by destroying you.'

Again, no response. If anything, the light around her seemed to dim and her face looked that little bit less alive.

I felt suddenly desperate. 'Please wake up! Please? Everyone in the world depends on you. We need you. You can't die!'

Nothing.

Nothing, nothing, nothing. Everything we say, she just lies there. We've tried telling her about all the people who'll die without her, the way they'll be sure to suffer if she doesn't wake up and set everything right. We've tried telling her how the glimmerlings must want her to live, too. We've tried telling her how evil mustn't be allowed to win, how good must triumph, and how she is the greatest force for good in the world.

But, nothing.

It's frustrating. It's hopeless. It's pointless. She just lies there. Maybe it's not her fault. Maybe Lord Paladin's will is stronger than hers and there's no way she'll ever wake up. I can't believe that, but, well, it's not happening is it?

Philosophus has tried talking to her a few more times, but he gives up more and more easily. I just sat down to write in my diary, hoping for inspiration, and my torch finally faded out and died. There's still enough light to write by, coming from the Princess, though even that's getting dimmer. Anyway, now I've written it all up and I haven't got any ideas, so maybe the torch was right. It's the end.

Philosophus has been silent for some time. I think he's found himself a corner to sit down and give up in.

What else is there to do?

Later

Still nothing. Nothing to report.

Why am I writing in my diary, then?

Nothing else to do, really. I don't feel anything much, just disappointed it's all over and a bit fed up it's taking so long for things to end. (And how's it going to end? Is the Palace going to collapse on us? Is the world going to go out with a ping like a dead light-bulb, or a sigh like a punctured soufflé? Am I going to look up and find everything's disappeared, not just the Princess and the box she's lying in, but the room and the floor, and my hands and feet and arms and legs and everything else about me, too? (How would *that* feel? On second thoughts, I don't want to know!))

A moment ago, I took out my diary and leafed through it. It's amazing how much I've written. The pages have gone all inky-crinkly with biro'd loops, lines and dots. All those words! Hundreds of them. Certainly more than I've ever said aloud in my whole life. It's enough to make you dizzy. (Or give you wordigo, perhaps.)

But all for nothing.

No, it can't be for nothing.

Can it?

If only...

Oh, what's the point in saying it? Even my biro's running ou

Later, later, later

Say hello to biro number three.

'Hello, biro number three.'

Biro number three says hello back.

Circles, loops, lines and dots. That's what biros do.

You may have, by now, begun to wonder about my sanity. I can only say that I have, too.

Things have happened. Odd things. Strange things. Carolous things, and things un-Carolous.

What does biro number three make of them?

Biro number three doesn't know. He's just a pen.

I, however, am not a pen (thank you for noticing), and I don't know what to make of them either, so we shouldn't think any less of biro number three, particularly as he was in my schoolbag at the time, with his lid on.

I wasn't. I was out there. I may have even had a hand in making some of it happen.

The only thing to do, as always, is give it a run through, write it all up, see if it makes any sense. Maybe then biro number three will be better informed, and come up with some ideas.

So, I sat there on the floor of that dungeon/tomb (lovely place!), in the dimness, a bit cold, more than a bit fed-up, feeling this was the end and there was nothing more to do. Somewhere across the room Philosophus sighed, like a very unhappy clock tolling the hour. Nothing was happening. Nothing, nothing, nothing. I thought, 'I wish it would get on with it and finish. I don't want to die of boredom!' I meant it flippantly, but as soon as I thought it, I realised that was exactly what I was doing. I was sitting there waiting to die.

How *stupid*. I'm only fourteen! How did I get into this ridiculous mess? I suddenly had this vivid picture of Mum glaring at me, arms folded, foot tapping impatiently, saying, 'What on *Earth* do you think you're doing, Carol, dying in a *dungeon*, of all places, and in one of your silly fantasy worlds, not the proper world where you're supposed to be! I'm so ashamed. Why don't you snap out of it and become a *normal* girl?'

And then Candice Cooper, stepping out of the dark to

chime in with, 'Pathetic. Just pathetic.'

And then (I always thought those two were in league), Mum turns to Ms Ice and says, 'Why don't *you* be my daughter? I'd much prefer you.'

'Okay. How much do I get for pocket money? And can I have a new mobile phone?'

'As much pocket money as you like, as long as you *never* spend it on books. And a new mobile phone every month, so you always have the latest model...'

And off they walk into the darkness.

Odd.

Did I actually see that, or did I imagine it?

It was almost totally dark now. The harder I stared at the dungeon walls, the more I saw nothing but those swirling shapes you see if you stare too long at nothing. Swirling, swirling, swirling. Every so often I'd think I could see movement, as if something was about to step into view.

And then it did. A person stepped out of the darkness. At first I thought it must be Philosophus, but it wasn't. It was Dad! I sat up and actually felt a bit tearful, thinking he'd come to rescue me. But he was staring blankly, like he couldn't see anything. It was how he'd looked the last time I saw him. Blank and staring. It had scared me back then, but it didn't now. I knew what it meant. He was lost in darkness. I mean, he always comes across as so sarcastic and cynical, like he doesn't care, but that can't be true, can it? That can't be true of anyone. I felt really sad for him, and wanted to say something, tell him everything would get better, then I realised I was in exactly the same position myself. He turned away. 'Don't go, Dad,' I said, but he was gone, and I was alone again.

No, someone else was coming. Omygosh, it was Simon Lawne! Now *he* wasn't lost in darkness. He was bright with life. Seeing him made me feel how much *I* wanted to be like that, how really I *was* like that, or would be, if only I wasn't stuck in a dungeon waiting for the world to end, if only I wasn't such a coward about everything.

But he couldn't see me either. He went away, and I was alone again.

And then I knew I didn't want to be here, in the dark, fading away. I wanted to live, really live. I'd do anything — fist-fight Candice Cooper, re-paint the house, I'd even go up to Simon Lawne and tell him I really, really liked him. But what a time to feel all this, now I couldn't do anything about it.

Or could I?

I went over to the Princess.

She was pale and motionless.

I knew I hadn't said what I had to say to her. I'd been too embarrassed, or too scared. But what did that matter now? So I knelt down, and rested my elbows on the lip of that stone box, and did my best — my real best, this time.

'I think I understand you. Wanting to give up, I mean. It's what *I* wanted to do. It's what I *did*. I ran away from everything, and if that's not giving up, what is? But now I know I don't want to give up. I really, really don't. There's so much to live for. How could I have been so stupid to think there isn't? I don't seem to have any way of getting out of here now, but that's what I feel.'

I sighed. This was difficult, this — what had the old man called it? — 'honesty and passion'. But I was determined to go through with it.

'I just wish I could have one more go — a proper go this time, not being scared about everything, but really finding out what life's all about. Because it's *my* life, and I wish I'd realised that. Anyway, sorry this has all been about me, but I had to say it. So you know I understand.'

I felt relieved, and a bit exhausted, so I wasn't really concentrating when she moved.

The Princess moved. I was *sure* she did. Her lips parted

then closed again, as if she was about to say something.

I was just peering closer when Philosophus loomed out of the dark on the other side of the coffin. I'd completely forgotten him.

'I, too, have something to confess,' he said, head bowed over the Princess. 'It is a minor matter, unworthy of your ears, Highness, yet I cannot rest until I have spoken.' He sighed. 'You made the world alive. You were the centre of all things. So it was no doubt inevitable that I, coming from the Edge of the World, from House Dolorous where all is melancholy and sadness, should have loved you, yet I did.'

Now, part of me thought, 'I knew it!' All those hesitations before saying the Princess's name, and that talk of love from before — I just *knew* it. But the other part of me, the more decorous part, thought, 'I shouldn't be listening to this.' I wished I could slink away, but if I moved an inch it'd ruin the moment.

Philosophus didn't seem to notice me, anyway. He said, 'I hid away in my workroom, knowing I was unworthy of you. When you came and asked why I worked so hard, I thought you mocked me. When you disappeared, I became empty. I watched the heroes depart daily to find you, and finally offered my own services, but Lord Paladin sent me back to my family home. There, I spent my time in empty arguments, trying to convince myself that all action, all feeling, is futile. But that alone is the truly futile endeavour. For I know I love you still.'

'Philosophus...'

He looked at me, smiling his sad smile, though this time it wasn't only sad, it was, in an odd way, happy too. 'Forgive me,' he said. 'I did not mean to embarrass you.'

'But—'

'I will return to the darkness.'

'But—'

'Farewell, Carol.'

'It wasn't me who said your name!'

He frowned. 'I thought I heard...'

'Philosophus Soltharian Dolorous...'

He stared at me, but it wasn't my lips that had moved. We both looked down.

'Sol,' she — the Princess — said. 'I will call you Sol.'

Philosophus just stared.

The Princess opened her eyes. 'And you are Carol Selina Tanner. Carol.'

My mouth was hanging open like I was waiting for a truck to drive in with a delivery of new teeth.

'Tell me what has become of my world,' she said. 'I fear I've been so foolish.'

'Your Highness,' Philosophus said, bowing, but just continued to stare.

So I said, 'Everyone was told you'd been taken away by the Necromancer. Heroes were sent after you. But Lord Paladin was sending them to this old wizard in a desert who isn't the Necromancer at all.'

'The true Necromancer is Lord Paladin,' Philosophus said.

'I know,' the Princess said. 'I know.' She squeezed her eyes tight, as if in pain, then opened them again. 'Your hand.'

Philosophus held out his hand, and she used it to draw herself up into a sitting position.

'Things must be set right,' she said. 'I must face Lord Paladin and end this folly.'

'But are you up to it?' I said. 'You still look a bit weak.'

She turned and for the first time looked me in the eye. It was one of those looks that sees right through everything, every lie, every dodge, every self-deception. I felt she knew everything about me, and for a moment I squirmed, because I could see her turning over all my mental dirty laundry, like the ten pounds I took from the emergency money to buy *In Sleep a King*, and my absolute cowardice in running away here. All that stuff.

But she smiled, as if it didn't matter at all, and I of course found myself grinning back.

Her smile turned self-mocking. 'And now you'll see even a princess cannot climb from a bed like this and retain her dignity.' She hooked one leg over the side of the box (yes, it's a box now, not a coffin), and, still holding onto a dazed Philosophus's hand for support, raised herself over the lip and down to the floor, where she almost stumbled, but Philosophus caught her. She stood up straight and brushed her skirt down, sending a cloud of dungeon dust into the air. (She must have been lying there for quite some time.)

'Much better,' she said, then sneezed.

'Your Highness, what are you going to do?' Philosophus said, not noticing she still had hold of his hand.

'I am going to confront Lord Paladin.'

'The door to the cell is locked. We are prisoners.'

She turned to the door. 'I have no further need of this door,' she said, and there was no door. Fresh air came into the room, making me realise how stuffy it had been. 'This is *my* world,' she said, 'not my prison. Not any longer.'

'But you are tired,' Philosophus said. 'You cannot face Lord Paladin like this.'

'I must. Do not worry, gentle Sol. You must remember, his mind and mine have been twined for many years before he ever cast the Death Spell. I know him and love him, and that is all I need to face him now.'

'Yes, yes, of course,' Philosophus said, realising his hand was still in hers and looking uncomfortable about it. He tried to pull free, but she wouldn't allow it.

She smiled. 'I love him as my guardian, Sol. As my one and only parent since the death of my mother and father. I won't relinquish your hand. I need your support.'

'Yes, ah, Your Highness,' Philosophus said, totally confused now.

She took a deep breath and sighed a deep sigh, then said, 'He is in his throne room. And he knows I am awake.'

Lightning was flashing close to the stained-glass windows in the throne room when we entered, and the clouds were grinding and grumbling as if they were made of stone. Splinters of coloured glass crunched underfoot as we walked towards the throne where Lord Paladin sat, and I realised someone (I could guess who) had taken the figures of both the Princess and Lord Paladin out of the windows and smashed them on the floor, leaving only holes of twisted lead that let the rain and wind through.

Lord Paladin said nothing as we approached. He didn't move. His hands hung over the ends of the throne's armrests like heavy weapons. His head was bowed, but not, I thought, through exhaustion or defeat. It had that arched look vultures get when they watch their dying prey.

We came to a stop five paces from the throne. The Princess stood very straight, not stiffly, but regally, and looked into Lord Paladin's eye-slits without fear.

'My Lord Paladin.'

'Princess,' he replied, and he sounded weary, which gave me some hope. Maybe that burst of energy I'd seen him suck into himself had run out, and he'd be too tired to fight us. (His enormous sword, I could see, was leaning against the throne at his left side, where he could grab and swing it. Where we were standing was just out of range, though, so maybe the Princess had thought of that.)

'It seems,' the Princess said, 'we have a disagreement to resolve.'

Lord Paladin said nothing.

'You are my guardian, are you not, Lord Paladin? You took the throne in my stead while I was a child?'

Still, he said nothing.

'The last time we spoke — spoke as child and guardian, that is — I asked whether it was time for me to take the throne and become Queen. You told me it was not.' She smiled. 'I think you were right.' (That surprised us all.) 'At the time I asked, though a bare few months ago, I was still a child. But now I have faced death. I have faced the loss of all I love. I am a child no longer.' She turned to Philosophus and, with a wordless nod, had him release her hand.

She took another step towards the throne. Philosophus tensed, and I guessed he was thinking what I was thinking, which was she was now within range of that awful sword.

'You remember,' she said, 'the point of our disagreement? The creatures who come from Outside. The creatures who killed my parents. The creatures you fought so valiantly, to protect me. And that, my Lord Paladin, is how you still see them, as monsters to defend me against. Because you are a warrior, and a hero.'

She took another step forward.

'I knew how you felt, that they were monsters who had to be destroyed. And for many years I believed you were unquestionably right. I believed all you said, because you are my guardian, my protector, my beloved only parent. Can you imagine how I felt when, one day while I was singing to the world, while I was making it and shaping it, I realised that until I brought these creatures into my world, until I made them part of it, it would not be whole, and would always need me sing to it and heal it in this way? I rejected the idea. But it would not go away. I knew it was right, and had to be done. But when I did not act on it, when I went against my true feelings, it became a poison in my veins. It clouded my world with darkness. I kept it within me, hiding it for as long as I could, until it turned sour and began to devour me. That was when I came to you, seeking advice and comfort. And you set me straight. You told me the Outsiders could not be let into our world. You told me they are vermin and must be destroyed, and only a child would think otherwise. I tried to believe you. Yet the poison remained. Is this, I wondered, what it meant to be an adult? To be tormented every moment of my life? If so, then I was an adult, and should take the throne as Queen. There, I could resolve the issue, by ridding our world of these creatures, or by welcoming them in, because I'd have the power to do either. I was, at that moment, still undecided. And so I came back to you and told you I was ready to be Queen.'

She took one more step, and was now at the bottom of the few stone stairs leading up to the throne. Philosophus unclicked the catch that kept his sword in its sheath. His hand was shaking.

'But you refused me, my Lord Paladin,' she continued. 'And perhaps you did so because you knew me better than I knew myself. You knew that, were I to sit on the throne, I would instantly resolve the conflict within myself, but not in the way you wanted. I would welcome the Outsiders into my Realm, not wipe them out. And you were right. I have spent many, many hours in the darkness thinking about these things. The belief is strong within me, the belief that the exile of the Outsiders makes our realm incomplete. They must be brought in, to complete us, to heal us, else we shall be forever fighting them in their misdirected madness. For granting me the time to think about this, my Lord Paladin, I thank you. The Death Spell you cast brought me more into contact with life than I've ever been before.'

She raised her head. 'My Lord Paladin, I no longer have to ask you if I am ready to be Queen. I know I am. The throne is mine. You are my guardian, but you are not king of this realm. And so I ask, will you not stand and let me take my place?'

For a moment, everything was frozen. I'd been holding

my breath for most of that, and as the Princess spoke that last sentence, I must have been gawping like an idiot.

Lord Paladin reached to the side and grabbed his sword. Philosophus drew his, and rushed forward to hold it over the Princess's head, just in time to meet Lord Paladin's blade as it came crashing down and screeched, blade-edge on blade-edge, sliding off Philosophus's angled sword, spitting sparks, to clang to the ground and clatter there, dropped as quickly as it had been taken up.

Lord Paladin stared at his empty hands, then covered his metal face. 'My Princess,' he groaned, 'am I evil? The creatures, the Outsiders — to me they are evil. That is what I know. If you are right, then I no longer understand anything. I cannot live. I am unknown even to myself.'

The Princess, who seemed completely unfazed by the fact he'd just taken a sword-swipe at her, walked up the steps to the throne and took Lord Paladin's gauntlets from his face.

'You are not evil. What you did, perhaps, was necessary, and whatever evil was caused I forgive and will correct. My Lord Paladin, you speak so truly when you say you don't know yourself anymore. In time you will know yourself again, and it will be both the old self that I love, and a new self that can live in the world I will remake.'

'No,' Lord Paladin said. 'I do not want to live.'

'It is not necessary to die to change,' the Princess said.

'No,' Lord Paladin said again, so painfully that even I felt sorry for him. 'Please, my Princess. My wife, my child, all I ever loved save you... They died in the same attack that took your parents.'

'You never spoke of them.'

'I wished to scour their memory from my mind, to leave only a pain that would remind me of nothing but my anger and hatred for those that killed them. My Princess, I am tired of living with this sorrow. I wish to go. To be once more with those I loved.'

'Of course. For you, my guardian, I will do this.'

She reached forward and took his helm in her hands and raised it.

At first, I didn't want to look. I knew what to expect beneath that mask. But when it came to it, I couldn't move, I was so ensorcelled by the scene. So I saw that wasted face once more, that living, barely-fleshed skull, only this time, in this light, I could see it had eyes, and they looked human, and I felt sorry for the man who'd once been a hero and a lord of the realm, and was now so wasted and tormented.

'Farewell, my Lord Paladin.'

Something was wrong. Lord Paladin writhed, as if struggling. A darkness came to his eyes, like he had boiling black clouds within him. He reached out to where his sword had been, but where it thankfully wasn't anymore.

'Your Highness!' Philosophus said, raising his sword, but she held up her hand.

'My Lord Paladin,' she said, 'you must let go of the hatred within you, else you'll never fully leave this world.'

'I cannot,' he said feebly. 'It will not let me go. Help me.'

She leant forward and kissed his forehead. That violent thrashing took Lord Paladin again. But at that moment, though I can't be sure, something dark leapt from his mouth, like the darkness in his eyes set free. Then it was gone, and Lord Paladin was still.

The Princess bowed her head. 'It is over.'

The Palace began to shake.

A scattering of stone-dust fell on me, and I looked up to see a dangerously wide crack had opened in the ceiling.

'We must leave,' Philosophus said.

For a moment, the Princess ignored him, or didn't hear. She stood by the throne, looking at the drastically altered face of her former guardian as if she couldn't believe he was gone.

'Your Highness, we must leave,' Philosophus repeated, reaching out but not quite able to grab her hand and pull her away.

Somewhere, in another part of the Palace, there was an awful groaning sound, then a crumble-and-crash so loud it shook the whole place, sounding more like a series of explosions than falling stone, and for a moment I had one of those dreamy lurching feelings because I couldn't tell if the entire Palace wasn't falling over, and me with it. Then the shaking stopped and I realised I was still upright, not falling, but I knew we couldn't stay there much longer.

The Princess came to. 'Yes, we must go.'

We started to run through the corridors.

The Palace shook, sometimes so badly we halted, expecting the floor to fall away or the ceiling to come down on us. Sometimes we'd be showered in rock-dust and sharp little stones cracking free of the ceiling, and occasionally something a little heavier would come down and strike me on the shoulder or the hand (I kept both hands over my head, not wanting to be knocked out), and I've got more than one bruise and cut, now, because of that.

It had just started to seem like an all-surrounding endless nightmare when we came to the top of that long sweep of stairs leading down to the entrance courtyard. Philosophus and the Princess were slightly ahead of me. As we came to the top, the Princess stopped and looked back as if she'd forgotten something.

'Your Highness, we cannot pause,' Philosophus said. And he added, misunderstanding her, 'He is dead. We must live.'

But she said, 'Where are the mechanicals?'

Philosophus looked bewildered. 'Your Highness? Do not worry about them. We may not reach safety as it is.'

But she insisted, 'We must not leave them to be crushed

when the Palace falls.'

'But they are not alive, Your Highness,' Philosophus said. 'We are. We must see to ourselves.'

I felt pretty much as Philosophus felt, but at that moment, a movement caught my eye in the courtyard below us, and I shouted, 'There they are! They're opening the doors and leading our horses out!'

Even the poor maid who'd been stripped so as to give me my rather feeble disguise was among them, evidently having been reactivated by her fellows so she could get out. (She didn't seem overly concerned that she had nothing on, but you wouldn't exactly rush back into a collapsing palace for modesty's sake, would you?)

We began to run down the stairs.

'Is that all of them?' the Princess asked. 'Think, Sol, how many did you make?'

Now, most people would say, 'Yes, that's all of them,' just to get us out of there, but Philosophus being Philosophus, he started thinking aloud and counting them off on his fingers (still running down the stairs as he did so), saying, 'I made five mechanical maids, one mechanical butler, and four knights, of which one was destroyed by the manticore. One maid and one knight remain at my family home... Yes, that is all.'

'Good,' the Princess said, and then we were dashing across the courtyard.

We had almost reached the door when I heard this great resounding crack, so loud it seemed to punch in my eardrums. I stumbled and fell, and was lying on the ground thinking, 'I really ought to get up and run,' in a muffle-headed kind of way, when I felt this whoosh of air coming down at me from above. My brain was still thinking, 'Whatever could that be?' when my legs took matters into their own hands (or feet, I should say) and I was running again — just in time for an enormous section of ceiling to smash into the ground *exactly* where I'd fallen. The impact sent a shower of stones pitter-pattering against my back like horizontal hailstones, and a blast of air virtually carried me out of the Palace.

Even then we weren't safe.

The mechanicals were walking as fast as they could — they hadn't been built to run, but could really pace it up when they felt the need. The horses, being sensible beasts, had bolted as soon as they were outside, and Philosophus and the Princess and I just ran and ran, through the ruins around the Palace and up the surrounding hillside.

I was panting fit to drop, but kept moving, powered by the sound of what was going on behind me. I didn't have to look to know vast sections of the Palace were falling free and crashing to the ground. Great billows of dust blew against me each time, and at one point all I could see was choking grey.

Then those black clouds that had crowded for so long round the Palace towers released their rain. It came down in torrents and, catching the dust in the air, turned to mud as it fell.

I just went on and on, running through the slushy rain, till a hand grabbed my arm. I tried to pull free and keep running, but was too feeble. I fell over. My throat felt like it had been sandpapered. My legs felt like they'd been swapped for lead weights. My head swam like a goldfish in a washing machine.

'We're safe,' Philosophus said, panting too, and he pointed at the Palace.

It was difficult to make out at first, because the rain, which was limited to the bowl where the Palace stood, wrapped the whole thing in a curtain of muddy water. I guess there must have been something magical going on, containing all the dust and rock that would have been thrown out by the collapsing Palace. Lightning fizzled around it too, and I could see (now some of the blood had got back to my brain) that the Palace was barely a third of its former height, and still collapsing.

I thought, 'Alright, I've seen enough to be impressed.'

Then I lay back and closed my eyes.

'Compassion is all very well, Your Highness, but to endanger oneself, not for living beings, but for mechanical creations that can be replaced is... well...'

'Utter foolishness, Sol?'

I realised I'd been listening to this conversation for a while, and of course knew it was the Princess and Philosophus, but I had no idea what they were talking about. I was too happy basking in the sunlight with my eyes closed, while my hair was being combed.

Eh? Sunlight?

I opened my eyes, but at first all I saw (because I was lying on the ground facing up) was bright light, so I had to close them and wait for them to adjust before trying again.

A bright blue sky, so blue and pure you could have canned it and sold it to the ocean, and somewhere over there, somewhere I wasn't going to focus on right now, a dazzlingly white sun.

'The sun,' I thought. 'The sun is back.'

I looked behind me, and saw that a mechanical maid — in fact Tilly Two, because she still had those metal shavings in her hair (as well as enough Palace-dust to make it look like she'd gone grey with shock) — was kneeling by me, gently running her fingers through my hair, combing out the rock fragments.

I closed my eyes again.

'I would not — would never — say "utter foolishness" of you, Your Highness.'

'You wouldn't, Sol? I'm disappointed. Because if ever I was utterly foolish, I'd need someone to tell me. Wouldn't you like to be that someone?'

Philosophus faltered, obviously discombobulated by the Princess's inviting tone, then tried to bring the conversation back on track. 'Your Highness, I am merely saying your life is too valuable to endanger, particularly for things that are not alive.'

'Yet they are alive, Sol. That is what I realised. It came to me so suddenly, I forgot our danger. I realised something very important had occurred in my absence.'

'And what was that, Your Highness?'

'Sol, if you won't call me by my name as I've asked, I'll have to exile you. But to answer your question: I realised that, while I'd been wondering whether to bring the Outsiders into our world, and how it might be done, it had been done for me.'

'By whom?'

'By the man I intend to take for my King when I become Queen.'

'Ah,' Philosophus said, and I could just hear so much muted disappointment in that one little word I almost sat up and said, 'That's not fair!' Because I was there when Philosophus told the Princess he loved her, and *that* was the thing that made her wake up, wasn't it? So it seemed totally unfair she was going to marry this other person, whoever it was. Anyway, I'm sure Philosophus felt the same, but he was better at hiding it.

The Princess, though, sounded rather amused. 'Yes, the Outsiders have found a way to enter our world and become a useful part of it, a way of living among us without our being aware of them — certainly without Lord Paladin being aware of them, because the great irony is that, at the end, he surrounded himself not with his fellow men, but with the Outsiders he so despised.'

Philosophus, still sounding a bit grumpy, said, 'I do not follow you, Your Highness.'

'Exile, Sol, exile. But I'll explain, as you refuse to follow my meaning. The Outsiders are formless creatures. They seek a purpose as hungrily as anyone seeks a meaning in life. But these few found it. The few that are here, with us, now.'

'Where?' Philosophus said, and I also sat up and looked around, expecting to see glowing glimmerlings all around us, but there weren't any, only the mechanical servants and knights...

Oh.

'They found bodies, mechanical bodies, imbued with purpose but not with life,' the Princess said. 'And they entered them, giving them life. Here they are, the mechanicals, but merely mechanical no longer. They are as alive as you or I.'

Philosophus looked a bit dazed. 'I wondered how they could so exceed their designed functions.' Then he frowned and said, 'But, then, who..?'

'Who brought the Outsiders into our world, Sol? You did.'

'But... Not knowingly, Your Highness.'

'Exile, Sol... So say it now, or you're banished.'

'Your Highness — I mean, Luna.'

'That's it. Don't you see it now? Sol and Luna. King and Queen. It sounds right, does it not?'

I lay back, in the sun, and closed my eyes. I had a rather fuzzy warm feeling inside that I wanted to dwell on. Besides, I didn't want to intrude any further on that particular scene.

The day has seen enough marvels, surely, with the waking of the Princess and the return of the sun, but I saw one more before it was over, one more that accounts for where I am now.

So where am I now? I'm in a rather grand bedroom with

a wide arched window looking out onto a beautiful clear night sky, with all sorts of sparkly stars and a bright full moon peering in, like she's wondering what I'm writing. (Perhaps I'll read it to her, see what she thinks, because biro number three remains silent — though I can't blame him, he must be exhausted after all the writing I've put him through.)

Anyway, where is this rather grand bedroom?

In the Palace.

Now hang on, you say, I thought the Palace crumbled to ruins?

It did — the *old* Palace. When the rain had rained itself out and the lightning was discharged, all that was left was black rubble and a few sharp spikes of rock that barely hinted there'd been anything man-made there before.

Looking at it, the Princess said, 'You must design me a Palace, Sol, where you and I may be King and Queen.'

He smiled rather dazedly, obviously still getting used to the idea. 'Very well. It will be all that the last Palace was not, and all that a true Palace should be. It will be of airy white stone. It will not tower too high, though will of course have a singing chamber raised above all other rooms, from which you can see the world as you sing. It will have high arches and pillars of white marble that, at the designated hour, will blush with the colours of the sunset. It will have silver domes that shine in the middle of the day, and that will seem to weep silver tears in the rain. It will have open colonnades and galleries, and gardens with fountains and pools and streams, and a maze where people may stroll and talk, and sit at benches and discuss philo-sophy and other matters. And it will have one vast central hall, where a silver throne—'

'Two thrones, Sol.'

'—are raised by a single step above a floor made of that rare marble I have heard of, whose colour changes constantly in a thousand pastel shades, and which sometimes gleams with sparks of gold. And one wall of the throne room will be made of tall, clear windows, and the other will bear a mural depicting the saving of our Princess by Lord Paladin, and his terrible journey to the old Palace, and then the darkening of the Realm and the reawakening of our Princess, and her becoming Queen, and the renewal of the land.'

Now, while he was saying this, Philosophus was looking at the ground, as if seeing what he was describing drawn out in plans. The Princess, though, was looking behind him, into the distance, and I was looking there too, only I had my mouth in that position it's become rather accustomed to today: dropped open at the hinge, and round as a donut.

Why? Because as Philosophus described this wonder-palace he was going to design, and as he no doubt thought to himself of all the difficulties of actually building it and getting the right materials and fitting it together and so on, the Princess gazed at a flat patch of land a little way away and made it appear. It rose from the ground exactly as he described, all white stone and silver domes and one tall central tower. And as it was nearing the end of the day and the sun was setting, its white stones glowed orange and pink like the sky behind it.

At some point Philosophus must have realised he was no longer the focus of attention and looked at us, then looked behind him and saw the palace he'd been describing, the new palace where the Princess would be Queen and he would be King.

'Oh,' he said, and for a moment I'm sure I detected a hint of disappointment.

The Princess must have heard it too. 'Don't worry, Sol. I'll let you do some of the work. I merely thought to get us ahead, if only so we can have a place to sleep tonight. I, for one, am tired, and have had enough of sleeping on a hard surface.'

'Has it got any baths?' I said. 'I think I look like a mud-man.'

And yes, it has baths, as well as soft beds, and (fortunately) more than enough food, because as we reached the Palace and walked beneath its main arch my tummy rumbled and I realised I was starving.

Tilly Two seemed to instinctively know where the kitchen was, so I followed her, and we brought back a couple of trays of food for everyone. We had a quick meal in one of the smaller dining rooms the Princess has equipped her new Palace with, then we all went off to find a bedroom each, or at least I found one for me, I didn't enquire into anyone else's sleeping arrangements.

Anyway, after all the excitement, I found I couldn't sleep, so after trying for a while, and then watching the stars for a while, I got out my diary and wrote everything up.

And now it's done. And I feel, to put it plainly, knackered as a nut, so I'm off to bed again.

What a day! What a day of days.

Several days later

We're going on a trip! Yippee!

But before I get to that I should apologise. How many days has it been since I wrote in this diary? Three, four? I've lost track, but it must be that, if not five, or six max. Maybe a few more. Anyway, a long time.

But I've been *busy*.

Actually, that's a total and utter lie, because I've been about as busy as a sloth in slippers. It's everyone else who's been busy, while I've been wandering around watching.

(Except for one thing I did, which I'll come to in a mo, as it's part of the reason for this trip we're taking.)

First of all, who's this 'everyone else', because I don't just mean the Princess and Sol (which is what I call Philosophus now, because everyone else does — and there's that 'everyone else' again, so who *are* they)?

Well, it seems that loads of people in the Realm just got this feeling that things were changing, and changing for the better, and if they wanted to be part of it they had to be here, at the new Palace. So, right from that first morning they started turning up, and not just turning up, but turning up and getting on with things, like they knew exactly what needed doing. Apparently, this is the effect the Princess's singing has on people. She's not hypnotising them or anything, she just wakes them up to their natural sense of purpose and puts their talents to good use.

For instance, some people like gardening. Well, they got the urge to come here and get on with tending the gardens, which are probably the best in the Realm, so a real dream to people who like gardening (particularly as the old Palace didn't have any). Some are artists who've come to decorate the halls and corridors with murals and sculptures, and some are engineers and builders who are helping Sol with the bits of the Palace the Princess left him to do, while others are doing things like making furniture for all the empty rooms, or cataloguing the library, which is even bigger than that enormous hall of books I spent so many hours in at the old Palace. (And don't ask where the books came from, they seemed to have sprung up with the rest of the Palace, even though some of them look really old. I have a sneaking suspicion the Princess worked a bit of magic and saved the books from the old Palace library, but that would only account for some of them because, as I say, the new library's a lot bigger than the old one. Anyway, all I know is there's lots of books.)

At the end of most days, Sol and the Princess drop by for a chat, to tell me how things are going. (She's still the Princess, by the way, because she's not going to have her coronation and become Queen, and she and Sol aren't going to be married, till everything's fully sorted out. There's no rush, and she wants things done properly.)

But sometimes I do feel a bit left out, like the only guest at a hotel they haven't finished building yet. And this morning I really wanted someone to talk to, because I had a bad dream last night — *another* bad dream, I should say, because I've been having a few lately — but it was difficult to find anyone who was free, and I wasn't about to interrupt them while they were doing important work just to have a chat about something as unimportant as my nightly brain-twitches (which is I'm sure all they are).

I might as well tell you about these dreams. Not that they're important or anything, just to get them off my chest. (Or out of my head.)

They start with me and the Princess and Sol in Lord Paladin's throne room, and Lord Paladin is going through that horrible thrashing around he did just before he died. But that's not what makes it a nightmare, because for a moment after he dies, there's nothing but a feeling of relief and peace. Then I see (just like I did when it actually happened) something dark, like a shadow or a wisp of black smoke, come out of his mouth, as though his last breath was sighing out all that was evil in him. Then the Palace starts shaking and we have to run, but as I'm running, something's caught in my hair, and I'm trying to pull it free, and I realise it's the dark wispy thing, and it's all sticky, like a spider-web. And then I'm not running through the old collapsing Palace anymore, I'm in the new Palace, but I've still got this horrible dark sticky thing in my hair, and I can't get it out, and it's really quite scary because everyone else is so busy working that they don't notice me, or the trouble I'm having.

After I woke up from this morning's performance of the Nightmare Dreaming Company ('exclusive recitals uniquely tailored to frighten the socks off our select clientele'), I went looking for the Princess, but she was in her Singing Chamber, and Sol was up some scaffolding discussing the best way to interleave the tiles on a corner section of roofing, so I thought for a bit, and the only other person (if person is the right word) I could think of to go and see was Tilly Two. As soon as I thought of her, I realised I hadn't seen her or any of her mechanical chums for ages. I wondered if maybe they felt a bit left out because there were so many real people around. I decided to go and find her.

First, I wandered round the main bits of the Palace, but no luck there. Then I thought the mechanicals would have involved themselves in the kitchens or something like that, something they were familiar with. The kitchens are this huge series of rooms all joined by open archways, and each room has its own special purpose, but you can always see and hear (and smell) what's going on in the next few rooms, which gives the whole place a bustling community feel. For instance, there's one room given over to nothing but pastry-making, and next to it on one side is the room where they make the fillings for pies, and next to it on the other side is where they make cakes, so there's a constant to-ing and fro-ing, not to mention a lot of shouted gossipy conversations, songs sung in one room and harmonised in another (sometimes with several versions of the same song going on in different rooms, or even different songs in different keys, which is a real racket) and so on. The whole thing has the feeling of something between a marketplace and the waiting room for a talent contest, with a dash of circus thrown in for good measure.

I wandered from room to room, taking care not to linger

too long in case someone thought I was looking for something to do. Tilly Two, with her wooden arms and blank face, should have stood out like a day-glo ostrich playing the tuba, but I couldn't see her. I was just trying to think where I should look next when something caught my eye. It was only a glimpse, and it took a moment to sink in (by which time the thing I'd glimpsed had moved away), but as soon as it did, I was off and running.

Tilly Two's dress! I was sure that's what it was!

Dodging under a dangerously large tray of scones a man was balancing on one hand, leaping over the back of a woman scrubbing the floor where someone had spilt a jug of milk, I crossed the next room and saw it again, that swish of skirt, disappearing through another archway. I dashed after it through a room where sauces were being concocted by serious-looking men and women in what looked like lab coats, and then into a dead-end room where scores of people were washing pots and pans in this long trough of hot water that ran the length of three walls.

And there she was! She'd just squeezed into a gap at the washing-up trough on the far side of the room. Her back was to me, but the dress and hair were unmistakable.

I went over and tapped her on the shoulder. As soon as I did, I knew something was wrong. The shoulder I'd tapped wasn't made of wood. It was real flesh, with real bone beneath.

'Oh, I'm sorry,' I said as the young woman whose shoulder I'd tapped turned and looked at me enquiringly. 'I thought you were someone else.'

She smiled shyly, hid her face under her long hair, and turned back to her washing.

I of course felt a bit stupid (nothing new there), and was about to leave the kitchens altogether when I found myself thinking, 'But I'm *sure* it's Tilly Two's dress!' And I'd noticed something else, too. The young woman had had two silver streaks in her hair, in *exactly* the place Tilly Two had hung those metal shavings I'd given her.

While I stood there trying to puzzle it out, the young woman turned and looked at me again, wondering if I'd gone. As soon as she saw I hadn't, she whipped back round and bowed her head so low I thought she was going to dive into the dishwater and swim away.

I was obviously making her uncomfortable, so I left the kitchens and returned to my room, where I spent an hour puzzling it through, then gave up. By the time evening came, I was back to being bored, so I was glad when there was a knock on the door and the Princess and Sol entered.

'Have you heard the news?' the Princess said. 'Our heroes have returned.'

'Heroes?'

'The ones Lord Paladin sent to deal with the Necromancer. Apparently they woke up in the basement of the wizard's tower a few days ago, but could find no trace of the old man himself, so they returned. We're going to throw a banquet for them tonight, to which you are of course invited. Though I warn you, hero banquets can get rowdy. I intend to make my departure soon after the main course.'

'I guess the old man levitated out of harm's way,' I said, trying not to think about the other explanation, that he'd finally come to the end of his life, as he'd said he was going to. 'I suppose we've got no excuse for visiting him, now.'

'And how have you been spending your day?' the Princess asked.

I told her about my silly episode trying to find Tilly Two.

It didn't get the reaction I expected. Sol said, 'So that answers that question.'

'What do you mean?' I said.

'We have been intending to check up on the mechanicals for some days now,' he said, glancing at the Princess, 'but both of us have been too busy. Still, we did not expect things to have advanced so rapidly.'

Seeing my puzzled look, he explained further. 'Luna thought that, now they are free of the old Palace, and surrounded by people, the glimmerlings would change in some way. She even went so far as to suggest their mechanical bodies might turn organic, like ours.'

'You don't mean,' I said, 'that *was* Tilly Two, but as a real person?'

Sol nodded.

'Wow,' I said. 'I must go and find her! But why didn't she say anything? Why was she so embarrassed when she saw it was me tapping her on the shoulder?'

'Perhaps,' the Princess said, 'she doesn't want it known to her new friends that she was once mechanical and unlike them. You must remember, she and the other once-mechanicals are still unsure of themselves as people. They should be allowed to adjust at their own pace.' She looked thoughtful for a moment. 'But this confirms a feeling I've had for some time. I cannot leave it any longer to decide what must be done with the glimmerlings.' (She'd started using my word for them as soon as she heard it, because she thought it was far better than 'Outsiders'.) 'We cannot build mechanical bodies for them all. A better solution must be sought. I'm going to have to meet with them to discuss the matter.'

'Meet with the glimmerlings?' Sol said, worried.

'I will be in no danger.'

'No, of course not. But surely you do not expect to hold a conversation with them?'

'I will try,' the Princess said, and smiled at his puzzled look. 'There are more ways to communicate than words.' She turned to me. 'So, we are going on a trip. To the Edge of the World. To Sol's old family home, in fact. Would you like to accompany us, Carol?'

We're leaving early tomorrow. (Hence my need to write all this up, because now I'm off to the hero banquet, and I think I'll follow the Princess's advice and make a discreet departure before things get out of hand. And one glass of wine *only*. I'm not having a repeat of *that* embarrassing incident!)

Ciao for now.

Sunday

I'm back. Home. In the real world. Willow Drive.

I can't believe it, even though I'm sitting here.

The clock on my bedside table says 11:34 in luminous blocky bars, with a tiny 'PM' in the corner, so it's late. Wumpus is on my bed, and he hasn't moved an inch since I saw him last. My school clothes are still on the floor where I dumped them on Friday (which seems a long, long time ago). Everything's the same. Everything. But how can it be?

The thing that's making my head spin is how suddenly it ended. I wasn't ready. I didn't have a chance to say good-bye. There was that last conversation with the Princess, but I didn't *know* it was the last.

I have to write it down before it disappears like a dream. Soon I'll have to go to bed and then I'll wake up and it'll be school. And then it'll really seem nothing but a dream.

Oh dear. School. Candice Cooper.

But don't think of that yet, Carol. Just write down what happened.

Right. We left the Palace and spent two days travelling to Sol's old family home. The weather was pleasant, warm, sometimes breezy, with the odd cloud drifting across the sky like a great big billowy airship. There was just the three of us, no need for a guard or anything. Sometimes I'd be sitting there (on Evenstar again), musing, and I'd look up at the Princess and Sol and think, 'Isn't someone missing?' I'd try to think who it was, then I'd realise it was just one of those things that happens when you're with friends, you feel like there are more of you than there actually are. (Ha! Carol knowing what it feels like to have friends! Who says I wasn't in a fantasy land?)

We didn't talk much, just looked at the landscape as we passed, and at the hares in the heather frolicking because the world had come into a new spring, and that great big rock where we'd camped so long ago, where I'd seen that awful thing that had turned out to be both the Necromancer *and* Lord Paladin, but this time we didn't stop there, we stopped a bit further on, in a clearing in the forest.

There, while we had our evening meal, the Princess told us about her hopes for the glimmerlings, about how welcoming them in would bring a whole new life to the Realm. I wasn't paying attention, though, and I didn't understand it all. I just liked listening to her speak, how confident she sounded, and knowledgeable, and how happy she was things were going how she'd wanted them to go for so long.

We slept in the open, under blankets, and I lay awake for hours looking at the stars, hearing all those sounds from the woods that had scared me so much before, but now they didn't.

We came to Sol's old home the next day. It was still a ruin, still overgrown. The Princess offered to return it to its original glory if that was what Sol wanted, but he said no, some things ought to remain how they were, if only to remind us of how things used to be. 'My home is the Palace now,' he said, and smiled a genuine, non-sad smile.

We picked our way through the rubble and came to the entrance of the wine cellar where he'd lived, and where I'd stayed that night shortly after I first came to this world. Tilly (number one) was there, but she'd wound down and was standing by the fireplace with a poker in her hand, like she'd picked it up then forgotten what to do with it.

'The other mechanical maids stopped needing winding up,' I said, disappointed she'd been left out of whatever magic had happened to them.

'She has been here on her own,' the Princess said. 'The glimmerling that entered her, finding itself alone, perhaps got bored and returned to its people in the forest. If we were to take her back to the Palace, I think she'd wake up again, and soon enough become a real person. But there may be no need for that once I've spoken with the glimmerlings.'

Sol took us on a tour of his family home, pointing out how this ruined arch had once led to a magnificent ballroom where a dozen crystal chandeliers had hung over a marble floor so polished you felt there were as many lights below your feet as above your head. And this statue, he told us, was of his great-great-grandfather, only now its head had fallen off and a marsh-bird was nesting between its feet, which may be a far better use for such a big lump of stone anyway. And these stairs, which broke off after ten steps, had once led to a tower from which his grandmother mapped the stars.

After a while the stories dried up, but Sol continued to wander, every so often pausing to look at a piece of tumbled masonry, or a hole in the ground, and nod to himself, then smile and move on.

The Princess took my hand. 'Why don't we let him be on his own for a while?'

We found a fallen pillar free of moss and brambles, and sat down to watch as he occasionally disappeared behind a fragment of wall, then reappeared up some steps or over a pile of rubble. Then I realised the Princess wasn't watching her husband-to-be, but was looking at me, which made me feel a bit self-conscious.

'This is another thing I have left too long,' she said, and at first I thought she meant coming here, to Sol's family home, which I guess is as close as she's going to get to meeting the parents. But that wasn't what she meant. She said, 'There is so much I've been meaning to say to you, Carol, but I'll start with my thanks for what you did.'

'What did I do?'

'You woke me from my Death Spell.'

'But that was Philosophus, uh Sol, not me. You know, when he said he, um, loved you.'

'That helped, of course. But it wasn't what brought me back. The love of another is a wonderful thing, but even that is not worth living for if you cannot first live for yourself. And it was you who reminded me how to do that.'

'Oh,' I said, not sure what to say. I felt a bit embarrassed.

'You are an important person, Carol. A hero of our Realm.'

I felt like curling into a ball and disappearing. But I was rather chuffed, too.

'And I extend the thanks of the Realm, and an assurance that you will always find welcome here, and a home, and friends.' She (finally!) looked away, to where Sol was standing in front of a statue that had been reduced to a pair of legs. He was pulling aside weeds to read what was written on its plinth. She said, 'Sol told me the effect you had on the glimmerlings when you first came to our world, and your power of naming.'

'Not really a power,' I mumbled.

'Oh, but it is. And I believe that, when you named the mechanicals, when you called them Tilly and Tilly Two, it brought them a little more into our world. It gave them unique identities, which is something they had never had before. It may seem a small thing, but from such small things pearls are made. So that is another thing to thank you for. This time, I thank you on behalf of the glimmerlings.'

'Well, I didn't know what I was doing.'

'Then just think what you could do if you set your mind to it.'

I grinned, though I didn't really think I could do anything.

'But you have not been happy here,' the Princess said.

'Oh no, I love it here. Back at the Palace. Anywhere, really.'

'You seem bored, at times.'

'Not bored. It's just everyone else is so busy, and they know what to do. I enjoy it, though, seeing it all come together.' I bit my lip, because I wasn't sure that was entirely true. I *had* been bored, but I didn't want her to think that, in case she thought I was ungrateful or something.

The Princess seemed happy enough with my explanation, and for a moment she continued to smile at Sol, who was now so far away he was just a tiny man clambering over bits of rubble and poking his head through openings in half-tumbled walls and so on.

Then she said, 'You remember what you said to me, when I was lying in my would-be tomb?'

'Sort of.' I hoped she wasn't going to ask me to repeat it.

'You said you wanted to find out what life is all about. *Your* life.'

'Well, yeah...'

'Do you not still feel that way, Carol?'

'Yes, I do.'

'Then there's no reason to be bored, is there? After all, you are free to do all you could want to, aren't you?'

'Yes. I suppose.'

'But what is it you want to do? You don't have to tell me. I merely want you to think about it. I would like to help you. But I feel, Carol, I might not be able to.'

'Oh?'

'This is my Realm, and all within it is in my care. I have power over this entire land. I could, perhaps, make anything happen, make anything come true, here. But when you spoke to me of your life, of the life you wanted to live, I felt you were talking of a different place. You never expected to come to my world, did you? So your plans, your wishes, your ideas of what your life should be, are not about here. They are about the place you come from.'

'Oh,' I said, realising now what she was going on about. 'Are you saying I should go?'

'I gave you my welcome, Carol, and you have it unreservedly. But I love you as a friend, and I want you to be happy. You must ask yourself what it is that will make you happy. And then, Carol, I want you to make it happen, because I believe you can.'

'Are we talking magic here, or..?'

She smiled. 'I don't know the workings of your world, so I cannot say. But there is no great rush. Take your time. And if you want, we can talk about this again, as many times as you wish. Now, though, while Sol is busy with his past, I will busy myself with the future. I am going into the woods to meet with the glimmerlings.'

'Okay, then,' I said. 'Good luck.'

She got up and placed a friendly hand on my shoulder, then left. Sol was still off in the distance. It was the last time I'd see either of them, but I didn't know that. I sat there for a while longer, then decided I wanted to go back inside, so I picked my way over the rubble, heading for the wine cellar where my things were.

I knew what the Princess was saying. I could remember what I'd felt when I sat in the darkness of that dungeon and said all those things. And she was right. Everything I'd planned and wanted, all those silly normal things like having a home of my own and so on, were all back in my world. The fantasy world I was in was exactly the sort of place I'd spent so many reading hours escaping to, and I loved it. And I had the invitation to stay for as long as I wanted. But part of me wanted to go back where I belonged. Of course, going back meant facing all those things I'd run away from. It meant Mum and Candice Cooper and Dad and school and no-friends and no *In Sleep a King* and all that. But, wasn't I supposed to be a hero of the Realm? Hadn't I saved a world, and helped to wake a Princess and defeat an Evil Lord? Were those other things — Candice Cooper, school, and so on — the sort of things heroes of the Realm were afraid of?

'Yeah, but I'm not your average hero,' I said, then realised what I was saying, and laughed.

I *would* go back. Maybe not now. Maybe when I'd had time to plan and think things through. Maybe, even, when I'd grown up a bit, so I could go back to that other world and find there was no need to go to school, but could short-cut all that. (And I thought, rather wickedly, 'I wonder if they'll let me take any of the Palace riches with me. You know, a few gold coins or something, to set me up in life when I get back. That'd be nice and I'm sure it'd be okay.')

I came to the wine cellar entrance and went down the stairs. The main room was dark, so I lit a candle then got my schoolbag. I was planning on writing in my diary and setting down the decision I'd come to, but I didn't get to do that. Instead, I found myself staring into the darkness thinking someone else was there.

'Hello?' My first thought was of Tilly, that maybe she'd come to life again now there were people about. But she was motionless by the fire. (Sol had taken the poker out of her hand in case there was any spring-energy left, and she gave one of those winding-down jerks and threw it at someone.)

But it wasn't her.

I told myself I was being over-imaginative, and pulled a chair from under the table to sit on, then froze, because I had the real feeling that something had used the scraping of the chair-legs as cover to move towards me.

Now *that* is a spooky feeling. I whipped round, but

nothing was there. I held up the candle and stared. Candles are really not that great for light (not when you're used to light-bulbs, anyway). They flicker a lot and don't reach the corners in anything but the smallest rooms, meaning you always have the feeling the darkness is moving.

I told myself I was only spooking myself.

But, no, this time I really did hear something. It was a sigh, a breathy sigh, only it didn't remind me of someone flopping into a comfy chair and kicking off their shoes. It reminded me of Lord Paladin's dying breath, when that darkness had come out of his mouth, and I'd had to run through the Palace trying to get that sticky shadow-cloud out of my hair.

'No, you dreamt that,' I said, but my heart was thudding like a miniature blacksmith on a padded anvil, beating out some frightful mask to scare me with.

I decided to get out. Even if it was only imagination, there was no sense in letting it get the upper hand. (I had now forgotten all about being a hero of the Realm.)

I shouldered my schoolbag and walked to the stairs, sideways-on, so I could keep watching behind me. I'd left the candle, in its holder, on the table, which meant there was enough light to see. As I reached the point where the stairs would take me out of sight, I paused, and stared, and then I saw it — a dark shape at the edge of the light.

I was spooking myself again. If I stared it out, I'd realise all I was seeing was a cloak thrown over a chair, or a pile of books. But no, it wasn't that. It was a man-shaped thing, short and stick-thin, with an overlarge head like a bloated, poison toadstool ready to burst.

My stomach gave a lurch as if to say, 'This is real, Carol.'

'You're dead,' I managed to say, feeling cheated and afraid at the same time. 'You died with Lord Paladin. You *were* Lord Paladin. But he's at peace now, you can't be here...'

A voice came out of the dark — a gloopy-sticky hissy voice, as horrible as anything I've ever heard. 'In the end, it was *he* who came to look like *me* and do *my* bidding. Now I need a new tool to work with. And I see one — one who can walk between worlds...'

'No! Not me! Go away! I'll never—'

But suddenly he — it — was moving towards me, running on stick-like legs, tickering over the floor like a spider. It was too much. I bolted up the stairs.

The day was darker now (had it really become evening in the short time I'd been downstairs?), but it was light enough for me to stop and look back, thinking surely that dark thing wouldn't follow me into the daylight.

But it had. It was slinking from shadow to shadow, using even the tiniest lightless patches as stepping stones. Occasionally it would find a real patch of darkness and just zip into it, getting closer all the time.

I had to find the Princess. She'd deal with it. She was in the forest, so that's where I headed.

Scrabbling over rubble and through sprays of rough-edged grass, I found myself on a path I recognised, the path I'd taken into this waste of rubble in the first place, when I'd followed the direction of the mechanical knight (and where was he now I needed him?) to Philosophus, the Dolorous Lord, and the start of this whole adventure.

But there was no time to think of that now. And I didn't need to hear that thing so close behind me, with its skittering-over-rubble and slithering-through-shadow sound, to push me on as fast as I could go.

I came to the clearing where the mechanical knight had wound down. The true thick of the forest wasn't far away. Soon I'd be with the Princess. I could have called out her name or screamed and she might have come, but I didn't do that, because I didn't want to admit how scared I was.

I glanced back. That thing's rubbery arm was stretching out from its last hiding place to grab a patch of shadow under the bricks of a crumbling wall, and then suddenly the rest of it followed, pulling itself into that tiny crack of darkness and not pausing before reaching out again for the next shadow, this time under a tree a few paces away, and that much closer to me.

The forest I was about to enter was completely dark. Wouldn't it move a lot faster once we were in there?

No time to think about that. I dashed ahead.

Under the trees, there was still the occasional glimpse of sunlight through the breeze-blown roof of leaves, and I could see well enough to avoid the foot-tripping roots and low, head-knocking branches.

How deep would I have to go before I found the Princess? I thought back to that nightmare dash through the forest on the mechanical knight's horse which had taken me from my first meeting with the glimmerlings. It had seemed to go on forever. I'd never thought I'd ever be in such a rush to get back to them. But it wasn't them I was trying to find, it was the Princess. She'd be with them. She'd save me.

It was only then I realised there was no reason why she'd have come this way to find them. Just because this was where I'd met them, didn't mean she'd come here. She could have gone into the forest at any point, and headed in any direction. I might be moving further from her with every step.

'No, no, that *won't* be true,' I said, and kept running.

The forest ahead was getting darker.

Perhaps the glimmerlings would save me? Perhaps I could do what I'd done before, changing their shapes as I touched them, only this time making them into knights and heroes who'd defend me from the darkness-thing chasing me?

(And what *was* that thing chasing me? The glimmerlings were all glimmery light, but this thing was darkness itself. Were they somehow linked? Was the thing chasing me some kind of darkness-glimmerling, a hate-glimmerling, and perhaps the cause of those evil things the glimmerlings were supposed to have done in the past, such as killing the Princess's parents? I was suddenly sure of it.)

The forest was getting darker and thicker, but I couldn't turn round and run back to the light. Any swerve either way would mean the thing chasing me could get that much closer, and I already felt it must be gaining in the increasing darkness, because that was how it moved.

I stumbled, but caught myself and kept running. The tree roots were getting thicker beneath my feet, and as it was getting darker, it was more difficult to see them.

I stumbled again, and took several lurching steps to catch my balance. I was in total darkness, now. I wasn't running over a forest floor anymore, either. I was running over horizontal beams, regularly spaced. The darkness felt open and empty. No more trees.

I was in the attic.

I felt this wrenching, sinking feeling as I realised I was leaving the Princess and Sol behind. But there was nothing I could do! I had to keep running — had to push myself even faster — because it was totally dark now, and that thing must be almost on top of me.

I got into the rhythm of running over those beams, and for a while concentrated totally on that. There was no point looking back, it was too dark to see anything, and anyway, I didn't want to find myself staring into some nasty grinning face only inches from mine.

Instead, to tell how close it was, I listened. Of course, at first all I could hear were my own feet pounding on the rafters, and my panting breaths. But beyond that I could hear something else. A distant voice. Not the hissing evil

voice of the thing chasing me, but something a bit more...
familiar? Someone was asking, 'What am I doing?' Then,
'Why am I here? And where is here?' And, 'What shall I
do?'

It was *me*. That was *my* voice, and those were things *I*
had said, ages ago, in this very attic. It was as if they were
only now echoing back from some distant roof.

I heard, 'What shall I do? What do I want? What do I
want? *What* do I want? What do I *want*? What do *I* want?'

I almost laughed, though in a rather manic-and-mad way,
and said, 'I know what I want. I want to live the best I can,
that's all!'

And I couldn't be sure (I didn't want to be sure), but I
think I heard a very nasty chuckle close behind me, so I
pushed myself faster still.

I saw light. Just a splinter of it, a sliver, a squashed
square... Yes — the hatch! And, as I ran, the squashed
square widened into a full square of light.

I didn't slow down. I kept running till I was a pace away,
then threw myself, feet-first, onto the landing below with a
thud so hard I fell on my bottom.

I lay there looking up. I wasn't home yet. This was the
top of that endless set of stairs I'd climbed. There was no
carpet, just floorboards. There was light, but only a dim,
golden glow that seemed to be on the verge of becoming
night at any moment. I stared at the black square of the attic
hatch, exhausted and stunned.

Then a spidery hand reached out of the dark and felt
around for a patch of shadow. It slithered across the wall
towards me, and I realised *I* was casting the closest shadow,
and in a moment it would slink its way under me, and then
I'd never be free of it.

Instantly, I was up again.

The thing's questing hand had found another shadow,
this time under the sill of the landing window, and in one

slithery movement the rest of that dark thing joined it, to grin at me evilly.

The chase was on again.

I pelted down the stairs. If Mum had heard me making that racket she'd have given me an earful. But I didn't care. Something like death was chasing me, and I pounded down the stairs like some super stair-stepping machine. Bru-du-du-du-du-du, then a dash down one length of the landing, a hairpin turn, then more stairs, more bru-du-du-du-du-du, again and again and again.

I found myself thinking, 'What's going to happen when I get to the bottom and it's chasing me still? There'll be nowhere else to run, so what am I going to do? I'm going to have to fight for my life. So why don't I turn round and do that now, before I knacker myself out? Because if I can't fight for my life, my life isn't worth living. But I know it *is* worth living, so I *will* fight. I don't know how, but there's nothing else for it.'

But at first I kept running.

The landings became carpeted. (And again I missed the moment it changed, but I wasn't going to go back and look!)

I kept running. And I kept thinking that at some point I was going to have to turn and fight, and the sooner I did, the more strength I'd have. But it was scary, so scary, the idea of turning and facing — that.

Then I thought, 'It's no good. I'm going to have to do it!'

So I stopped. I was on the last step of I didn't know which landing, but I stopped and turned.

The shadow thing was at the top of the stairs.

'Okay, I'll fight you,' I said. 'I'm fed up of being scared. You're no better than Candice Cooper, you know that? So come on, let's fight. And I may look small and pathetic, but I bet I'm stronger than I look.'

I stood there panting, and the shadowy thing paused for a moment, then slunk down a step or two.

It paused again, as if unsure.

'Oh come, on,' I said. 'What are you, a coward?'

I stared into the pits of its eyes. This thing had taken me away from the Princess and Sol, my friends, and now it wanted to take away my life. Well, I wasn't going to let it. And if a stare could say that, then that was what my stare was saying. And I think it must have realised I wasn't going to be as easy as it had thought.

It hesitated, took another step—

And then, suddenly, from the side, this furry fury leapt at it.

I was as shocked as it was, because for a moment I had no idea what was happening. It was writhing on the stairs with this growling monster on top of it, being clawed and bitten and, finally, grabbed like a rag and shaken and thrown.

It lay there for a moment, tattered and torn, much smaller than it had been before. Then it picked itself up and scampered away, back up the stairs, and I'm not sure, but it seemed to get smaller with every step, till it disappeared into nothing.

'Tollers,' I said, blinking at my furry saviour. 'Is that you?'

Tollers sat down and licked his paw as if to say, 'I knew I could do that sort of thing all along.'

'You manticore, you,' I said, and scratched him behind the ear.

He let me do that for a few moments, then wandered off, no doubt having far more interesting things to do elsewhere.

I stepped off that final step, and realised where I was. I was back on the real first-floor landing. It was dark. It was night. I looked behind me and the phantom stairs were gone.

The house was silent.

How long had I been gone? Had Mum and Dad sent the police out looking for me? Would they be angry? Would they cry? Had they moved house so as to forget me, and was I now in someone else's home?

I went to my room, wondering how it would have changed. Had the police been through it looking for clues? Had Mum taken all my clothes and given them to charity?

No, it was exactly the same. Creepily the same.

So how long had I been gone?

There was only one way to find out.

I went to Mum's door and knocked lightly. She was in bed, but still awake.

I said, 'I'm back, Mum.'

I don't know what I was expecting, but it certainly wasn't for her to say, 'You didn't tell me you were going out.' Then she looked at her bedside clock and said, 'Carol, it's past eleven. It's school tomorrow. Go to bed.'

So I backed out and closed the door, then stood for a while on the landing, looking at where those phantom stairs had been but weren't anymore, wondering, well, all sorts of things. Like was *this* a dream, or had *that* been a dream, and if it wasn't, how had it happened, and what *was* it that had happened, and how I was here now, and so on till my head was spinning.

Then I came back to my room and put on my bedside lamp and sat down with my diary and looked at all these pages I've written, all about the Dolorous Lord Philosophus who I came to call Sol, and the Princess, and Lord Paladin, and the old man who lived in a tower in the desert, and the weird glowy glimmerlings, and that whole fantasy world that maybe didn't exist at all. But it *did*, because I had been there, and had written about it, and I couldn't have written it all in one Sunday evening. But it *is* still Sunday, the same

Sunday as when I left this world for that one. All those days — so many I've lost count — it must have been at least a couple of weeks, if not more, but here nothing's changed, and barely any time has passed. Only a few hours. Mum didn't even know I was gone.

Wumpus knew. There's a sort of kink in that lopsided mouth of his, like he's saying, 'I know you've been somewhere different, and things have happened, but I'm happy to wait till you feel like telling me about them.' And I will tell you, Wumpus. I'll read you this entire diary, if only so I can hear it again myself and work out whether it happened or not.

But it *did* happen. It did.

But also, *everything's the same*. The same as when I left. And that means Candice Cooper, Mum, Dad, school — all that — *all the same*.

It's really late now. I don't want to go to bed, even though I'm really tired, because when I wake up, it'll be Mum then school and it'll all be back how it was.

But I'm too tired to do anything else.

Monday

What a day!

I'd say words couldn't describe it, but as I'm about to try, let's hope they can.

(Go, words, go!)

I woke up early, despite my late night with all that diary-writing, and looked at the clock and thought: 'Monday. School. Candice Cooper.'

Three levels of awful.

I rolled over and tried to sleep. I rolled over and tried to not *be*. Then my alarm clock went off.

I hated that alarm clock. Beep beep beep. Is that all you

can say, you stupid alarm clock? Such a lack of originality. If *I* were an alarm clock, I'd at least vary things by adding the occasional 'ka-proot, ding, ba-boing.' But no, you say beep beep beep, on and on, like someone who *knows* they're right about everything.

There's no point arguing with an alarm clock.

I got out of bed and went downstairs.

Mum was in the kitchen, doing her usual breakfast-time faffing about.

'Morning Mum,' I said.

'Mm,' she said — her way of announcing she was *already* having a bad day, so I shouldn't even *think* of trying anything.

I poured myself some Rice Krispies and ate them in silence. (Actually, you can't eat Rice Krispies in silence, but you know what I mean.) Mum made herself some coffee and drank it while staring out the window at the garden fence.

Silence. Pop, crackle, crunch. Silence.

Things were the same. The same, the same, the same. But how *could* they be? I'd been to a fantasy world. I'd helped defeat the Necromancer and rescue the Princess. *Something* had to be different.

I went upstairs and got into my school uniform, then came back down, shouldering my bag, said 'Bye, Mum,' and walked out the front door. I was halfway up Willow Drive before I realised I'd forgotten to do my usual thing of waiting till the last minute before setting off. Then I thought, 'What does it matter? If I have to face Candice Cooper, why not get it over with?'

It was a dullish morning, with enough of a hint of damp and cold to suit my mood. A few other kids were walking to school, some in pairs, some on their own. I could have walked up to any of them and said, 'I was in a fantasy world yesterday.' And why not? Maybe everyone had been on a trip to a fantasy world last night. I looked for signs. Is playing games on your mobile phone a sign? Is chatting loudly about what Ginny Carlson did at Trish Tarrant's party a sign? Hmm. Maybe best keep quiet about it then, Carol.

Through the school gates, I headed for my classroom.

A few other people were there, but I didn't register them. All I saw was Candice Cooper. I could just see myself through her eyes, a tiny, helpless girl framed in a doorway, and (this being Candice Cooper, the Half-Terminator) she no doubt had twin cross-hairs closing in on me, as well as all sorts of digital read-outs like body-temperature, pulse-rate, and likelihood-to-collapse-in-a-blubbery-mass-when-bullied.

I could have turned and ran. I could have burst into the staff room and claimed asylum. I could have put my school bag on my head and danced like a mad thing. I could have done all sorts of things. But I didn't. I thought, 'Let's get this over with,' and went in.

'Oh look, it's Carol Tanner,' Candice Cooper said.

I picked my way, very self-consciously, to my desk, doing my best not to trip over and make a fool of myself now everyone's eyes were on me.

'Aren't you going to say hello to your friends, Carol?'

I was blushing. I knew I was. Obviously my adventures had done nothing to make me into a hero. I was still scared and flustered by this one stupid girl. I put my bag on my desk.

'No hello's?' Candice Cooper said. 'Or is it no friends?'

But I wasn't listening. Something odd had happened. When I put my bag on the desk, it didn't make the sound I'd expected it to make. It made a clonk. And then I realised — the torch! I'd forgotten to take the torch out. I couldn't help but smile, because it made it all real again, the Dolorous Lord, the Princess, that wizard in the desert, Tilly Two and everything else, and it seemed so ridiculous to be scared of someone as pointless as Candice Cooper. I mean, a manticore tried to *kill me*. Candice Cooper is nothing.

'Or are we too scared to say hello?' she was saying, in an ah-diddums voice.

I sighed, then turned and looked her right in the eye (nothing like a manticore's eye, and nothing like Lord Paladin's dark eye-slits) and said, 'Yeah, I'm such a coward. I only pick on people smaller than me. And only when they're on their own.' Then I sat down.

You could have heard a pin *thinking* about dropping.

Someone sniggered.

Then someone started talking about TV.

I sat there, thinking, 'I did it. I did it and it was easy.'

Then the bell went and Miss Michalowski came in to take the register.

First lesson of the day was English. As was the second. Double English with Miss Michalowski. In the second half we got our Winter's Tale stories back. Mine had the comment, 'Very voorish!!!' in red at the bottom. (Miss Michalowski seems rather fond of exclamation marks. I know I use them a lot, but *three* in one go? That's sheer extravagance!!)

The lesson went on, and every so often Miss Michalowski would give me a smile, as if to say we had our little joke, and that made me think how much I liked her, and how sad it was about her particular young man. I wished there was something I could do. Then I realised there was, and after the lesson I went up to her desk.

'Hello, Carol,' she said.

I bit my lip, then decided to dive in. 'Miss Michalowski, I was wondering if you enjoyed *Winter's Ragged Hand*?'

'Oh, yes. It was very fantastical.'

'It's just, if you wanted to borrow the other books in the

series, I don't mind lending them to you. I mean, I'm going to read them again once I've read *In Sleep a King*, which is the last one, but I don't know when that will be.'

'Why, thank you, Carol. I may take you up on that offer.'

'Fantasy's rather good when you want to get away from things, isn't it, miss? I mean, I want to do that sometimes, and I'm sure you do, because of, you know...' I trailed off, thinking maybe I shouldn't say what I'd meant to say after all.

But Miss Michalowski was looking at me curiously. 'Because of what, Carol?'

'Um, your particular young man. The one you liked when you first came to England. Because, when you told me about him, you know, I thought how sad it was, because you're, um, *Miss* Michalowski, so obviously you didn't marry him.'

I couldn't believe I was actually *saying* this!

Miss Michalowski smiled. 'You're right. I didn't marry him. He turned out to be rather shallow, so I'm glad I didn't.'

'Oh...'

'Instead, I found myself another man I'm far more happy with.'

'Oh.'

She leant a bit closer and whispered. 'So, you don't have to worry about me on that score, Carol. I'm quite happy as a Miss.'

All that time I'd spent thinking she had a tragic sorrow in her life! She was perfectly happy, and the fact she was a Miss not a Mrs was neither here nor there. (That's one of the troubles with us fantasy fans. We're rather old-fashioned, and sometimes forget it's possible nowadays to, you know, be called a Miss while having all the advantages of being a Mrs, if you see what I mean. Or, to put it another way, Misses don't have to miss out.)

So I said, 'Oh! Um, I'd better go, then.'

But Miss Michalowski said the strangest thing. 'Just a moment Carol. I believe Simon has something he wants to ask you.'

'Um, who?' I said, because she couldn't mean the only Simon I could think of.

Then I realised everyone had left the classroom except me, Miss Michalowski, and Simon Lawne, and Simon Lawne was smiling at me.

'Um, me?' I said.

'He's hoping you can help him with something,' Miss Michalowski said. Then she picked up her loopy bag and left.

Me and Simon Lawne, alone in the classroom.

So I said the only thing you *can* say in this sort of situation.

'Um...'

'Miss M told me about the word you used in your essay,' Simon said.

'Miss..?'

'Miss Michalowski.'

(And for a moment I felt totally jealous he called her Miss M.)

'Oh,' I said.

'She knows I read a lot of fantasy too, so she asked if I knew where it came from.'

'Oh,' I said, again. I mean, if it works, stick with it.

'And I knew it was in *The Wizard of Eldara*, so I told her. You must like *The Wizard*, too?'

'Yeah.' One word at a time was my breathable limit right now.

'Great,' he said. 'But it's something else I wanted to ask you.' And he took out that mysterious notebook I'd seen him making ticks in the other day. 'I've been carrying out this survey. Can you answer a couple of questions?'

'Mm,' I said, though it came out slightly squeaky. What I'd really liked to have said was, 'Yes, as long as they can be answered "um", "mm" or "oh".'

He took out a pen. (The black biro from his pencil case. A guilty moment of recognition passed between me and that pen. Fortunately, neither of was about to say anything.) 'Great. First, how often do you use the school library? Once a week? Less? Or more?'

'Mm,' I said, with a nod, at 'more'. I go there every lunch break. That counts as 'more'.

'And second — though I know the answer to this — do you read fantasy?'

'Mm,' I said, with another, more enthusiastic, nod.

'Great.' He made a couple of ticks. So that was what the notebook was for. Sort of disappointing, really, though it was nice to be included in his survey.

But that wasn't it.

'There's something else,' he said. 'A sort of favour. Just a little thing, but it would be a real help, cos you read fantasy, too.'

'Mm?' (I can vary my mm's.)

'It's this project thing I'm doing. For Mrs Barker, in the school library. If I could have someone's opinion — someone who reads fantasy, I mean — that'd be great. But I'd better tell you about it first. It started out when I asked Mrs Barker if I could put up a poster in the library. I do this blog thing, where I review fantasy books. It's not huge, like some blogs are, but, I don't know, you might have seen it?'

'Um,' I said.

'It's called The Fantasy Reader.'

I shrugged, because I hadn't.

'That's okay, not many people have. I'm just starting out. I thought a poster in the library would be a great way of telling people about it. I asked Mrs Barker, and she said I could. Then she asked if I'd be interested in helping her do a display. She does these displays, to get people reading more, and to let them know about books they might like, things like that. She said it'd be great to have a display of fantasy books, and asked if I'd do one. That's why I'm doing the survey. Anyway, I'm putting it together after school today. And I thought, if you had some time, after school, to pop in, just give it a look, you know, that'd be great.'

'Um,' I said. Then I realised that wasn't an answer, so I said, 'Okay.' (Which, finally, broke the one syllable barrier.)

And Simon said, 'Great. Just pop in. After school. That'd be great.'

'Mm,' I said. (Back to that again.)

And he said, 'Great,' again.

Then he said, 'See you,' and went off to lunch, and I wondered what I'd just done.

The rest of the school day passed in something like a blur.

No, it wasn't like a blur. It *was* a blur. I'm amazed I didn't get called up by one of the teachers (Mrs Hambridge for Science, Mrs Morrit for Music) for not paying attention, but nobody seemed to notice me at all. It was like I'd retreated into this Region of Blur, where everything around me was a blur, and I was a blur to everything around me. And in the midst of my blurry world I kept thinking, 'I said, "Okay." To Simon Lawne. Why did I do that?'

It was so... so... what? Daring? Fantastical? Un-Carolous? All three. But hadn't I been complaining nothing had changed? And now here was something different.

Also scary.

Stupid isn't it, to find something like that scary?

But this is me. I find everything scary.

When the bell went for the end of school, I didn't know what to do.

Or, I did, but I didn't think I could do it. I might have

faced down Candice Cooper but wasn't that enough for one day? Shouldn't I go home and recover? Back to my old, safe life?

So I shouldered by schoolbag, and filed out into the rush and crush of pupils. Somewhere, deep in my depths, a little voice was saying, 'You have to go to the school library, now,' but I pretended not to hear. I made straight for the main gates — then walked through and headed home.

'Cowardy Carol, Cowardy Carol.' That wasn't Candice Cooper calling me names. It was me. And it was right. I am a coward. A coward going home when she'd agreed to be elsewhere.

'Oh well, nothing's changed,' I thought. 'I went on a fantasy adventure, came back, but nothing's changed. I'm still as useless as ever. I can handle it, though. I handled it before. And who cares? I'm a coward and I don't deserve a good life anyway.'

I crossed the London Road and walked down the no-cycling path at the end of Sanders Close to Willow Drive, and got to my front door, glum as a glumbleweed. I saw my hand reach into my pocket and take out my key and put it in the lock, saw it turn the key and open the front door, heard my shoes go shdum-shdum as I wiped them on the doormat, heard the ratch of my key as I pulled it out of the lock, saw myself close the door behind me with a click, thinking all the time, 'Coward, coward, coward...'

Then I realised I was in Hell. Or a war-zone or something. For a moment I actually thought burglars had broken into the house and were smashing things to pieces, or fighting among themselves for the few valuables we've got. Then I recognised the voices. Mum and Dad. They were in the kitchen, their favourite shouting place, doing their favourite thing, which was shouting. And occasionally bashing something for emphasis.

I walked down the little length of hall till I came to the

kitchen doorway. I stood there for a moment, looking at the two of them going at it hammer and tongs (or is it tongues?), and I remember thinking it was odd that Dad was home so early. After standing there for a moment, ignored as usual, I went upstairs.

I flopped onto my bed. (Being careful to neither floll nor flollop, as those are the domain of only the pink and fluffy.)

I lay there, not really listening to what was going on downstairs, but aware all the same of the dull shouting coming through the floor from the kitchen. It might have been the TV turned up too loud, but I knew it wasn't.

I wondered, if I went out on the landing, if the phantom stairs would be there. If they were, I could escape again. Surely it'd be safe to go back now that horrible Necromancer-shadow-thing had been dealt with? I could tell the Princess I'd given my world one more go, but had come to the conclusion there was no chance of things working out here, so would it be okay if I stayed with her?

And she'd say yes.

But she'd also give me that look. That look that goes right through you, that knows, in all truthfulness, that you haven't given it a go, not properly. That you haven't really tried at all.

I sat up.

'Wumpus, I'm going to do something different.'

Wumpus looked shocked.

'I'm going back to school. Right now.'

Wumpus, I realised, hadn't looked shocked at all. He'd merely used that as a ruse to get me to open up. He's very good at judging my moods, and knows precisely how to get me to talk about the things I most need to talk about. And, now he'd achieved his aim, he stopped pretending to look shocked and instead looked questioning.

So I said, 'I'm going to the school library. I've no idea why.'

Wumpus looked unconvinced.

'Alright, so I *do* have an idea why. I quite like Simon Lawne, and he asked me to go. That's why I'm going. It's silly, but... Actually, it's not silly at all, is it? It's the sort of thing normal people do all the time. So, for a while, I'm going to pretend to be a normal person, and see if anyone notices.'

Just then there was a loud clang from downstairs as someone, either Mum or Dad, threw a pot lid on the floor, no doubt to emphasise the subtleties of some important point they were trying to make.

I got out of my school clothes and put on something I hoped would pass, if not for trendy, at least for this-century.

'Wish me luck, Wumpus.'

'Good luck,' he said.

I was halfway out the door before I stopped and looked back. 'Excuse me, did you just say "good luck"?'

Wumpus looked totally innocent and said nothing.

I gave him a narrow-eyed look.

Still, he said nothing, and in fact did a remarkably good impression of a slightly tatty stuffed toy of precisely the sort that doesn't say anything, ever.

So I said, 'We'll have a talk about this when I get back.'

Then I went downstairs.

I was going to go straight out, but then I thought, considering the trouble I'd got into with the emergency money, I really ought to do things by the book. (Not that there *is* a book that tells you how to conduct daughter-parent relationships. I wish there was.)

So, I stood in the kitchen doorway. They weren't shouting as much now, but were still pretty intense. Mostly they were staring at each other, and when they spoke it was snarly and bitter. And sometimes they started speaking at exactly the same time, but when that happened they ignored the fact that the other person was speaking and just kept talking over them, as if to say, '*I'm* the one who's talking now, and I'm *not* going to stop for *you*.'

All very adult, in ways a fourteen-year-old could never hope to understand.

I waited for a gap, then said, 'I'm off out. See you.' And before they could ask where and why and how long for, I left.

Back up Willow Drive, back up the no-cycling path at the end of Sanders Close (passing an old bloke on his bike, but as he wasn't actually peddling, just freewheeling, I suppose that doesn't count as cycling, so I guess it's okay, and anyway, he gave me a friendly nod, so I'm not about to report him to the police or anything), then over the London Road and—

Dead halt.

Candice Cooper and her mates, perched on the school gates like vultures.

I had a horrible thought: this had been planned. Simon Lawne was working with Candice Cooper. They'd *lured* me here. They'd been chatting that time, hadn't they? This was what they'd been chatting about. They'd tricked me into coming back to school when nobody else was around, so Candice Cooper could get me.

But that was a silly idea. For a start, it's not like anybody has to go to such elaborate lengths to *get* me. I'm totally vulnerable to being *got* at all times. And secondly, if it *was* a nefarious plan, Miss Michalowski would have to have been in on it, and she, I know, would never do anything even remotely nefarious. I've never known anyone less nefarilike.

Still, I was going to have to get past Candice Cooper and her buddies or go home.

Going home was a serious option. But all I could think of was how disappointed Wumpus would look, so I told myself to remember the Manticore Pass and kept walking.

Canned Ice and her ice-cool buddies fell quiet as I passed, but said nothing. Once I was inside the school grounds there was a little burst of sniggering, but that was it.

I headed for the sixth form and library block, all the time ready for a teacher to pop out and ask what I was doing. Then I saw the warm light coming from the library windows, and felt safe again. Safe from Candice Cooper, and safe from random, questioning teachers. Books are things I know. I've always felt safe around books and bookish people. And thinking that made me realise Simon Lawne was a bookish person, too. That was a thought I liked.

I went into the library.

Mrs Barker was pushing a book trolley, shelving books. She glanced up, said, 'Hello Carol,' then disappeared down the Non-Fiction (History) aisle.

'Um, hello, Mrs Barker,' I said.

I didn't even know she knew my name.

(She's a *librarian*, Carol, she knows everything.)

Simon Lawne was over in the display corner. 'Carol, great!' he said (two words that aren't often in the same sentence). 'Went home to get changed?'

'Um,' I said, and shrugged, thinking, here I am, stuck with the um's again.

Simon stood back from his little corner of books and held up his hands, like he was basking in their warmth. 'So, what do you think?'

The display corner is basically a triangular table draped with a cloth, and some clear plastic book holders attached to the walls behind it. Simon had put a choice selection of fantasy books in the holders, but the real display was on the table. There, he'd arranged some books in a low pyramid, stacked so you could read their titles, and lying on top of them was a dragon.

I peered closer. It was a really real-looking dragon,

organic, wrinkled, warty and spiky.

I looked at Simon.

'It's like the books are his hoard of gold,' Simon said, then shrugged. 'It's an old tree root. I added to it a bit, and carved it a bit, and painted it, but it looked pretty dragonish to start with. What do you think?'

What did I think? All this time, I knew that question was going to come up. Simon Lawne had asked me here for my opinion, and I'd been spending a lot of time trying *not* to think about this moment. Why? You need to ask, diary of mine, after all these um's, uh's and oh's? Because I was going to have to speak to him in sentences of more than one syllable, that's why! Unless I just went 'Great!', gave him the thumbs up, and ran from the room.

But I didn't do that. Because, looking at that dragon close up reminded me of something. It reminded me of a conversation I'd had with my friend Philosophus, the Dolorous Lord. We'd been talking about dragons. 'Do they not exist in your world?' he'd said, and I'd had to admit they didn't. But now I could see I was wrong. They *did* exist. There was one right in front of me, as dragonish as anything you could hope for. (And let's face it, you don't often hope for dragonish things.) Which meant I lived in a world where fantastic things happened — where dragons sat on hordes of books, and Simon Lawne asked for my opinion. Both were equally fantastic, both were equally wonderful. I lived in as fantasy-ish a world as any of the books I'd read, only it had the added advantage of being real, and all around me, all the time.

I was thinking this, but couldn't say it all to Simon Lawne. Not in one syllable, anyway.

Or could I?

I looked him straight in the eye and said, 'It's totally, utterly voorish.'

And he grinned from ear to ear and said, 'Great!'

Then, for some reason, we both burst out laughing.

Si said he'd walk me home.

We said goodnight to Mrs Barker (who was very pleased with Simon's display, particularly the dragon), then we emerged into the playground and headed for the school gates.

Candice Cooper and her friends were *still* there.

'I don't believe it,' I said.

'What's that?' Si said.

'Um, nothing.'

But he knew it wasn't nothing. He said, 'She really bothers you, doesn't she?'

'Yeah,' I said, hanging my head.

'It's nothing to be ashamed of. She's a bully, we all know that. Don't let her get to you, though.'

'Yeah, but...' I looked at him. 'You were chatting with her that time, weren't you?'

'Only for my survey. And I didn't really need to bother. I could have guessed. Never uses the school library, and does *not* read fantasy. I heard you stood up to her this morning. Everyone was talking about it. I think you really shut her up.'

'Everyone?' I said.

'Yeah, they all thought it was great, funny as anything. There's not many can make her shut up, but you did.'

I'd never thought of anyone talking about me before, except perhaps to think how strange I am, and how I don't say anything, but I have to admit it felt nice to find they were. I thought, 'I don't have to worry about you anymore, Ms Ice. I really don't.'

As we walked past Candice Cooper and her creepy cooperative, they fell quiet again, but this time, I think for a different reason. Carol Tanner, with Simon Lawne? Yes, Carol Tanner with Simon Lawne. Don't go falling off the school gate or anything.

Si and I crossed the London Road, then went down Sanders Close and the no-cycling path to Willow Drive. We discussed fantasy books we'd read. A lot of them were the same, and we agreed to lend each other the good ones we hadn't both read.

We came to my house.

'Thanks for walking me home,' I said.

'That's okay.'

'I'd invite you in, but I think my mum and dad are murdering each other at the moment. They were when I left.'

'Really? They not getting on?'

'No.'

'Sorry to hear that. Well, if you ever want to get away, you know, you could come over to my place sometime. For dinner or something. Yeah, how about that? Why not this Friday?'

'Yeah, okay,' I said.

'Great,' he said. 'See you at school, then.' And he walked away with a wave.

I stood there for a while, thinking I couldn't believe any of this had happened. But it had, it really had. Maybe this is what most people's days are like. Maybe I can have others like it.

'I think I will,' I said to the world (and one bewildered magpie), then went inside.

The house was silent and dim.

I paused before closing the front door, waiting for the crash of a hurled plate or a shattering glass, but it didn't come. Instead, I heard something going tick-tick-tick... Had they started leaving bombs for each other about the house? No, it was only my watch. And if I could hear that, it really was silent in here.

I closed the door and wiped my feet.

Had they gone out? Had they knocked each other uncon-scious with simultaneously-flung frying pans? Had the neighbours phoned the police and had them locked up?

I started along the hall. The living room door opened, making me jump.

It was Dad.

'Carol,' he said. 'I'm so glad you're back. Can I — can I have a word?'

'Um, yeah,' I said, and followed him into the living room to sit on the sofa.

The TV was off. I guessed he'd been waiting for me to come back. Why? Something I'd done wrong, no doubt. Maybe neither of them had heard me saying I was going out, or they'd wanted a fuller explanation, and were mad at me for it. (And would they stop me going to Si's house on Friday? Of course they would.) Or maybe Mum had filled him in a bit more on that ten pounds I took and he agreed with her and was going to give me a fatherly talking to, and then discuss what I had to do, in addition to what Mum was making me do, to make up for it. (Including, of course, not being allowed go to Si's house on Friday.)

So I stared at my shoes, feeling there was nothing I could do to hold back the inevitable, but knowing I ought to say sorry, so I said, 'Sorry I went out, and sorry I, you know, took that money.'

'Carol,' he said, and sighed in a way that made me think sorry wasn't going to be enough, but then he said, 'It's me who should be apologising to you.'

I looked up, and looked at his face properly this time. He hadn't shaved today and looked haggard, like he hadn't slept in weeks. So he might have seemed even more scary than the last time I'd been in here with him, just before I ran off up the phantom stairs, only what made him not scary was that he was speaking to me, and not staring that dead-eyed stare. I remembered what I'd thought about him in the

Palace dungeons, that he was in a bad situation, like I'd been, and it made me calm down.

He looked at the carpet. 'I need to apologise because I've only just realised the effect Joy's and my situation must be having on you. It's easy to forget, when you're an adult, that you can't treat everyone in the same thoughtless way you treat yourself. Other adults might be able to take it, but not children.' He glanced up. 'You don't mind me calling you a child, still, do you?'

I shook my head.

He frowned. 'Recently, I've been so self-involved, thinking only about this situation with your mother, and my situation at work. I haven't stopped to think about the other things I should be thinking about. You, for instance.' He sighed. 'Carol, we all start out normally enough. We think, when we're young, we'll grow up to be a certain type of person, and live a certain type of life, like we're on a straight, well-marked path that's easy to follow. But things happen, and put you off that path. Little things at first. And that's okay, because you're only a little way off, and you tell yourself you'll get round to putting yourself back on as soon as you've dealt with this latest thing. But life keeps throwing things at you, and the further you go, the further you get from how you thought you were going to be, and getting back on that path becomes more and more difficult. Then suddenly you're miles from being who you thought you'd be. Instead, you're caught up in being who it all made you into. And sometimes you don't even notice that, till a real jolt comes along. You gave me that jolt, Carol.'

'I did?' I said, weakly. I'd almost been holding my breath all the time he'd been speaking.

'When Joy told me about you taking that money, I was just sarcastic. That's how I deal with things. But then on Sunday evening, when you came down here, I looked at you sitting there, and I remembered how I felt when you were a baby, how I wanted to protect you from everything bad in the world, but now here I was, not protecting you at all. In fact, I was part of what you needed protecting from. I realised I had to have a talk with you. Even if only to say sorry, and to ask how things were. But when I went up to your room, you'd gone. And you were nowhere in the house. I had this sudden image of you running away from home, living out on the streets, getting involved in all sorts of terrible things, and perhaps never seeing you again, or only in some awful photo in a newspaper or, I don't know, in a hospital somewhere. I realised I had no idea what might be going on with you. And that's part of the reason I took today off work. I knew something had to change. I think I took Joy by surprise, because she thought I'd gone out as usual. But I waited till you went to school — I can't tell you how relieved I was to hear you getting up and going out this morning — then I came downstairs to discuss things with Joy. So that's what we've been doing all day.'

Wow. My heart was pounding like I'd run a mile. When he said about going to my room on Sunday night, and me not being there — well, I guess that must have been when I was up those phantom stairs. (So I *hadn't* been lying there dreaming it all. Hey, I never doubted it!)

I couldn't think of anything to say, but perhaps I didn't need to.

Dad said, 'I'd wanted for us to come to a decision as to what we should do, Joy and I, so that when you came back from school we could discuss it with you. Unfortunately, by the time you came back, well, you saw how things were.' He gave a shrug and looked a bit foolish. 'The thing that did it was when I told Joy I'm going to quit my job. I've been hating it for years, but I put up with it by always telling myself I was doing it for my family, all the while having no time to spend with my family, which was falling apart anyway. But that's not the point. I want to do what I can, now. I know it's not much to start with, but this book you took the emergency money for. I don't believe you'd take that money for no reason. I guess it's a book you really want?'

'Yeah,' I said, embarrassed.

'Well listen, honey, I know it's not the right thing to do, and I know Joy will have my head on a plate for even suggesting it, so it's between you and me, okay, but I'd like to buy it for you. Not that it will in any way make things better, just because I want to do something for you. Is that okay?'

'Yeah,' I said. 'That'd be really nice.'

He sighed, and I realised he'd been a bit scared of how I'd react to all this, but now he was happier.

And then, just like with Miss Michalowski, I felt the need to say something to him, so I said, 'I've got this sort of date. On Friday.'

He looked up.

'Is that alright?' I said. 'I won't be out late or anything. I'm just going to this boy's house for dinner, then I'll be back.'

He smiled and nodded. 'Of course it's alright.'

We sat there in silence for a while, both feeling better about things. Then we heard some movement upstairs. Mum, leaving her room and going into the bathroom.

Dad frowned again. 'You know, what I said about me not being the person I wanted to be is true of your mother, too. The trouble with Joy is she's very self-critical, very harsh on herself. That was always true, but lately it's got out of hand, no doubt because of what's happening between us. The thing is, she not only turns it on herself, she turns it on other people, too. I bore the brunt of it for a long time. But when this whole situation between us started, I think she may have turned it on you, too.'

'Yeah,' I said.

'I'm not promising everything will turn out right, Carol. But if we can at least be more sensible about this, maybe things won't turn out as bad as they might.'

So then he got me to write down the details of *In Sleep a King*, because he said he could get it in his lunch hour tomorrow. He usually worked through lunch, he said, but he was going to hand in his notice first thing, so after that there wouldn't be much point in working so hard, and he'd need something to do with his lunch hour.

Then I asked if he wanted some tea, but he said he was fine, so I went into the kitchen and put the kettle on. I thought my brain would be whirling after all that's happened today, but I felt calm. Or perhaps dazed is a better word.

Anyway, I was standing by the kettle, practising throwing a tea bag into my mug to see if I could get it in from two then three then four paces away, when I heard Mum come out of the bathroom upstairs, and I realised I wanted to talk to her, because that was the one thing I hadn't done today. So, before she could get to her room and close the door, I rushed upstairs.

'Mum,' I said, 'I'm just making some tea, do you want some?'

'No thanks, Carol,' she said, and looked ready to close her bedroom door.

So I said, quickly, 'Mum—'

'What, Carol? I've got a headache and want to go to bed.'

'I just wanted to say, um, sorry. Sorry I took that money.'

'It's all very well saying sorry, Carol, but how am I ever going to be able to trust you again after what you did? How am I ever going to blah blah blah...' (No, don't give in to the blah-blah-blahs, Carol, keep listening.) '...I have enough on my plate at the moment as it is, without blah blah blah...' (This was really difficult. But I kept at it.) '...And I *do* worry what will become of you, Carol, if you do that sort of thing. I *do* worry.'

'Yes, Mum,' I said. 'Sorry. Goodnight.'

She closed her door and I went downstairs, but I thought at least I'd kept listening to the end, so I'd heard her say she was worried about me, which is, for her, actually quite close to saying she doesn't hate me, and maybe by blocking her out with blah-blah-blahs I've missed similar things she might have said, so maybe I ought to do my best to listen to her in the future.

Anyway, I'd said sorry, and even if she hadn't accepted it right then, it might sink in. Because I did mean it, I *was* sorry, even though I only took that money because I was so unhappy at the time.

I went downstairs and finished making my tea, then came up here to my room. And now I'm thinking perhaps I've done enough diary-writing for the while. It served its purpose (whatever strange purpose that may have been), but it takes an awful lot of time, and I'm thinking, maybe, I might need my time to be doing other things for a bit. Like reading *In Sleep a King* and, you know, going on a date with Simon Lawne!

I certainly don't need any strange, ghostly staircases taking me to fantasy worlds at the moment. I seem to be in one. This world, suddenly, is quite fantabulistic all on its own.

So this is me, Carol Tanner, signing off.

For the time being, anyway.

See you, whoever you are.

(And didn't I tell you not to read my diary? Oh, who cares. Too late now, isn't it?)

From the author

I hope you enjoyed *The Fantasy Reader*, my first published novel.

In case you want to know a bit about me, I was born in 1971 in the town of Reading in England. Perhaps because of this (though 'Reading' and 'reading' are pronounced differently), I've spent a lot of time since in the act of reading — often carolous (i.e., fantasy) reading. (Carol's experience in reading and re-reading *The Wizard of Eldara* — second book first, and so on — is pretty much mine, when I discovered David Eddings' *Belgariad* books at the age of 13.)

I'm pleased to find I've had the usual odd variety of jobs writers are supposed to have, including vitamin packer, porter at a mushroom farm, computer programmer, technical support, and postman.

That's enough rambling. For more rambling, even actual information, visit my website:

www.murrayewing.co.uk